Depths of Darkness

A Collection of More Than Thirteen Tales
From the Macabre to the Probable

By

Christina Estabrook

First Edition: January 2017

Book Cover Design: Digital Print Shoppe
www.digiprintshoppe.com

Printed in the United States of America

Table of Contents

Special Thanks

Special thanks to Angela Worden-Corey for all her help. Her advice, patience and suggestions were instrumental in the successful completion of this book.

Publisher's Note

Depths of Darkness is a collection of over 13 different tales stretching from the macabre to the probable, from the supernatural to the super creepy. A complete journey into the depths of the mind and your nightmares, each tale entices you to enter another realm where zombies can roam free until day light breaks, or where your own curiosity can leave you frozen forever in a petrified forest. Imagine entering a house where the walls show you every horror that took place — complete with stains and screams left behind. Or a world where the bugs you kill can turn you into one of them, laughing while you run for cover from their vengeance. Maybe you'll decide your parents' house isn't all that bad when you come across the doctor who will do anything to save his daughter — even when it means harvesting you. There's also some truth behind the rumors about that old man in your local shop. Be careful what you buy, you may get more than you bargained for — and the price is *your head*.

Open Wounds

"Anna. Honey, open your eyes for me."

His brown eyes were open wide staring for signs of movement from his daughter. Beads of sweat dripped from his brow and sticking strands of hair to his forehead. He reached a single gloved hand to the top of Anna's head. Gently he rubbed, pushing her long hair from her face. Anna opened her eyes just slightly and closed them again right away. The lights from the room were too bright to allow her to open them for long.

Jonathan walked over to the light switch on the far wall and flipped two of them down. The lights dimmed, but didn't mask a small streak of blood left smudged on the light switch and wall. He removed the first pair of yellow gloves and tossed them into the trashcan. The entire room smelled of ether and iron.

The old wood floors had been damaged and stained from all the blood they had caught over the years, but they were still solid beneath his footsteps. Jonathan walked over to the table behind Anna, carefully taking off his raincoat, which was soaked in blood, and tossed it into a bucket full of water.

He walked slowly toward the doorway, grabbed a stretcher, and pushed it toward the old dining table Anna was sleeping on. Jonathan had gotten older and his strength was waning, but he still managed to carry her when needed. His arms strained under her feeble body, though she hardly weighed more than a hundred pounds.

Jonathan placed his daughter on the stretcher, wheeled her out of the room, and down the narrow hallway. Family pictures of Anna and her mother adorned the walls. Pictures her mother painted had been dusted with age and filled the spaces in between. The wallpaper had started peeling at the edges and the once beautiful pine floors had deep gouges from years of wheels and large appliances being dragged across them.

The deep gouges make it difficult for Jonathan to control the stretcher, but he must. He pushed harder, wheeling Anna down the hallway through the doorway he'd made, and down the darker corridor to her room. He flipped the light switch on the wall and illuminated Anna's paradise that was also her prison. Anna stirred for just a moment as he picked her up off the stretcher and placed her in her four-poster bed. Tired as he was, he reached down to the foot of the bed, tugged the green comforter from under her feet, and pulled it up over her arms. He paused for just a second to grab a syringe from the foot of the stretcher and quickly gave Anna a dose of morphine before she had a chance to fully awaken in pain.

The old doctor watched his daughter sleeping heavily in her bed. For the time being she'd feel no pain and no tears would roll down her sunken pale cheeks. Her deep brown eyes would stay hidden behind their lids. *At least she will be comfortable for a few days*, he thought.

He looked around her room and leaned over to open her window just a crack. The fresh autumn air would do her some good. The light purple and green floral lace curtains swayed and twisted in the breeze. Her pink bathrobe, which hung on a hook near her closet doors, swung side to side and gently caressed the wall behind it. A few pages of her diary, left open on the white side table, fluttered in the wind. He pictured his daughter sitting at her desk writing about her hopes and dreams within the barren pages.

Fairies and forest scenes cluttered the walls meant to make this her paradise indoors. Jonathan turned around, barely looking up as he grabbed the stretcher and pushed it out of her room and a few feet down the hall. He pulled the heavy metal door shut behind him and continued on his way. He stopped to look at the pictures he hardly even noticed anymore. Sometimes he looked at his wife and remembered how she was; but now, thinking about how she died was too hard to bear.

2

"Clara, I miss you so much. I wish you were here. Every day I miss you more. Anna is so much like you. I promise I won't let it happen to her."

Jonathan reached up and touched the glass of the picture, clearing off years of dust and leaving a clean streak in its place. He walked a few more feet down the hall and pushed the stretcher into the room that was once his study. The dim lights were still on from his makeshift operation and the floor was still soaked with blood; not all of it Anna's. He left the stretcher up against the wall and proceeded to the dusty, old book shelf which once held books by authors such as Mark Twain and Edgar Allen Poe. There were encyclopedias, his physician's desk references, and even fairy tales he would read to Anna. But now it held surgical tools and items for sterilizing instruments.

It resembled Jack the Ripper's house more than a study. There was blood on the floor and the walls, paper towels and bloody instruments littered the room. The cleanup was a job all of its own, but necessary to keep Anna alive. He began picking up the instruments and placing them in buckets filled with alcohol. The paper towels he gathered were placed in a plastic bag that would get tossed into the fireplace in the living room.

Jonathan grabbed another roll of paper towels and a bottle of alcohol and began cleaning off the old table; once again placing all the used paper towels in the bag. He proceeded to the desk to repeat the process. Alcohol was everywhere, but even with so much of it wafting around in the air, filling his nose, it couldn't mask the smell of blood.

After the table and desk were cleaned up, he went about the floor sopping up as much of the blood as possible, but a good portion of it had started to coagulate. He poured alcohol over the blood, waiting for a few minutes for it to start loosening the dried spots.

The ageing doctor was completely exhausted already, but still

3

had more to do. He knew that the morphine and loss of blood would keep Anna asleep for hours to come, but that would give him just enough time to clean up and maybe take a shower and a quick nap. He grabbed the buckets that contained both the instruments and his raincoat and walked carefully out of the study and down the hall toward the bathroom.

He walked into the bathroom toward the shower and dumped the buckets carefully in. With a turn of a knob the hot water came on, filling the room with steam. He grabbed the showerhead moving it into position to clean out the buckets and rinse everything off. The huge mirror behind him illuminated his appearance, causing him to jump. Even with the raincoat on, he was covered in blood from his face to his feet. He always wore the same white painter's suit under his raincoat, but it was already stained with blood that had never washed out.

He held up his hands and looked at the blood caked in between the lines and fingerprints and caught in the cuticles. A tear welled up in the corner of his eye and cleaned a streak down his face. The deep lines of age filled up with blood and sweat; his smile marks seemed to be darker than all the rest. The grey and white strands of hair that had stuck to his forehead were tinged red and clumped together forming a strange widow's peak. He wanted to smile, but the blood on his hands had kept him from smiling for years.

Jonathan got undressed and hopped in the shower, quickly cleaning off before the hot water ran out. As he reached for the towel he stared at his reflection in the mirror. He was clean, there was no blood on him but his reflection told a different story. The wrinkled older man with grey hair staring back was still covered in bright red blood.

He grabbed the blue bathrobe and slippers that he'd left hanging the hook near the towel rack and hurriedly threw them on. He clutched onto the buckets and headed towards the bookshelf in his study. As he turned around to leave the room, a noise caught his attention. The slight muffled sound of groaning. He stopped and listened for a moment. *Is that Anna?* he wondered. He looked at the clock on the desk, but it was only 5 pm.

"Time flies when you're trying to keep your daughter alive," he whispered.

She should still be asleep for a few hours, he thought. He walked out of the room and down the hall taking the doorway on the left out into the living room. As he walked in, the noise got a little louder. It wasn't words but it was human just the same.

He knew, then, who it was. He walked slowly through the living room and into the dining room as quietly as he could. The night-lights he had plugged into the outlets were already on and gave just enough light to lead him to the kitchen. He couldn't remember the last time he had used the dining room to actually eat in.

Jonathan crept into the kitchen and tuned on the lights above the stove and the sink. These were pretty much the only lights he ever used in the kitchen. The stove was clean and the sink was clean, but the floors, other than getting swept, had suffered serious neglect over the years. The flooring was coming up from around the cabinets and the once white linoleum was now tanned with stains from food and dirt.

He ran his fingertips along the counter, feeling the dents and scratches in the faux granite top as he walked. The fridge was just as tanned as the floors from years without a proper scrubbing, but the inside he always kept clean. He grabbed the double handles on the fridge and held them tight as he peered around the corner and down the stairs to the finished basement his family once used as a den.

The smell of popcorn and the sound of Disney movies bounced around as memories of Clara and Anna sitting on beanbag chairs watching Shrek and Snow White. The old big screen television was still down there, but the TV hadn't been used since Clara died. He turned on the light switch at the top of the stairs and listened. The groaning was slightly louder than before and was beginning to sound more like crying now.

He started walking down the stairs slowly, holding the rails that he'd handmade. The couches had once been centered in front of the television, but were now stacked up against the walls, and the carpets had been rolled up, leaving the bare concrete floor exposed. His slippers scuffed along making swishing sounds as he went. The groaning suddenly stopped as he approached the first of three appliances that resembled deep freezers. They were lined up in a row along the back wall of the den. Each one had a tank feeding oxygen into it and a bulletproof glass window fixed into the top.

He peered into the window of the first one, what peered back was the face of a homeless girl he'd convinced to stay in his home. With a promise of a hot meal and a warm bed, his soft-spoken voice and kind-looking face had been able to coax her into his car and into his home. Tears rolled down her cheeks as her blue eyes stared back at him. The tube in her mouth that fed her oxygen prevented her from speaking, but not from making sounds.

In order to keep his donors alive and out of the eyes of the public, he kept them in groups of three, each with their own unit. They were drugged, once in his house, so he could outfit them with the breathing apparatus and feeding tubes that went directly into their stomachs. He looked down at the machine attached to her feeding tube and pushed the button on top. The machine made a suctioning noise and squeezed a syringe full of food through the tube.

On the underneath side of the unit, there was a bedpan situated on top of puppy training pads. When the donors did their business, it would be collected below where he could easily remove it. Now, the smell let him know that he needed to change the pads and clean the pans.

He turned the handles on the unit and pulled open the lid. The young lady was in her early twenties and very thin, not just from having one of her kidneys and a lung harvested, but from being on the street. *She has lasted over two months in this unit; by far one of the longest,* he thought. He checked the straps holding her arms and legs in place and reached toward her chest, pulling the blanket down enough to see the incision.

"No signs of infection," he told her. "That's good. I'm just going to clean you up a little."

He reached over and grabbed a small bottle of alcohol and some paper towels.

"This may sting a bit. Unfortunately, I don't have any peroxide or iodine, and I don't want you to get an infection."

He tipped the alcohol bottle onto the paper until it was dripping wet. Her eyes welled up and tears rolled again. She tried to struggle against the straps knowing she couldn't escape or move, but still, she tried. The alcohol dripped off the paper, slipped through his fingers, and splattered the floor. He put the bottle down and squeezed the paper over her chest and stomach. She winced and groaned, clutching her fists and crying.

"Shhhh, I know. I know. I will try to remember to pick up some peroxide the next time I go out. I don't want you to be in pain. I don't like hurting you, or anyone else for that matter."

After he cleaned her incisions, he grabbed a fresh paper towel and the water bottle he kept handy to help make the food easier to push through the tubes, and he washed her face.

"No reason why you shouldn't look presentable, right? You should really try to stop crying, you're just going to make yourself have a stuffy nose and make it hard to breathe, even with the machine. It would be hard for you to clear your throat if you get phlegm in it. I wouldn't want you to die of suffocation."

He turned around and checked her IV and then walked over toward the mini bar. He fumbled around until he found his syringes and morphine. He filled three needles and walked back over to her.

"Sandra, I am going to give you a shot of morphine, this will keep the pain down and allow you to sleep. I think I will turn the stereo on for you for a little while. You would like that, wouldn't you?"

She didn't make a sound or move her head, only squeezed her fists as he administered the shot. The morphine burned going in, but soon enough the ceiling began to spin. Her eyes began to close and before she knew it, she was no longer sure if she was in a bad dream or reality. The doctor watched her drifting in and out consciousness and closed the lid softly.

The room was now quiet, no more groaning or crying. He walked a few steps over toward the next unit. It was now empty, but he still needed to get rid of the sheets and the pads beneath them. He reached into the open unit, gathering the white sheets stained with blood, urine, and medications, and stuffed them into the bag. The unit was otherwise clean. He turned off the oxygen machine, grabbed the alcohol and paper towels, and cleaned the tubes before closing the unit and moving on to the third unit.

Jonathan looked into the window at the teenage boy he'd lured in to clean his yard. The young man was awake and stared back at the face of his captor. He struggled to get free, but just as with Sandra, he was tethered to the unit with leather straps. A breathing tube was duct taped into his mouth, so he couldn't speak or yell. His eyes begged to be let go.

Jonathan had already placed the feeding tube and covered the young man with sheets, but none of his organs had been taken yet. This young man wouldn't be needed until Sandra was either dead or could no longer offer organs needed for Anna. This young man was the back up. For now, Jonathan kept him as comfortable as he

8

could. The boy would be fed through the tube; he would have no need for morphine, would be given a bath daily, and turned to avoid sores.

Jonathan looked down at the boy and smiled slightly. He rubbed his head for just a second and pulled the sheets up a little higher. He grabbed the plunger from the feeding tube and pushed it in, making sure the boy had food.

"I know you don't know what's going on and why I have you in here, but you're my daughter's chance of survival. I will promise you that I will not harm you unless I have to, and I will try to keep you comfortable, but for now, I cannot let you go."

Jonathan repeated the same cleaning process he had done with Sandra's unit and closed the door. As promised, he walked over to the stereo system and turned it on. He spent a moment looking for some music he thought they could tolerate. Locating an oldies station of 70's music, he settled on it and turned it up just a little. He turned around and looked at the units one more time, then walked up the stairs and back into the kitchen.

He thought for a moment and realized that he had not eaten anything since the previous night. The operations took hours to do and then there was the cleanup. *Some days I am lucky if I can grab an apple with all the chaos,* he thought. *But it's worth it to keep Anna with me.* He opened the fridge and grabbed a package of chicken salad and walked over to the counter.

The house was relatively quiet except for the hum of the small stereo he'd put on in the den and the oxygen machines. There were no bugs in the house, considering it was fall. Most houses in New Hampshire have an invasion of ladybugs, but this house had not been infested for years. *Even the bugs won't come near here*, he thought.

"I just don't understand why I am not affected, but my wife suffered greatly, and now my daughter," he whispered.

He peered out the window over the kitchen sink, watching the leaves fill in the cleaned spaces in the yard that the young man in the den had raked. The yard was large and had been severely neglected over the years. He had two acres of land in the front alone, fenced off from the world by an 8-foot sandstone wall with a black gate. The memories he had of a younger Anna, playing in the gardens and picking roses from the many bushes that surrounded the wall, made his heart fill with sorrow. He pictured the swing set and heard the sound of his daughter's laughter, which continued even after her mother died.

Anna loved that swing set, but she loved the old wooden swing I made even better. He tossed the empty container in the sink and leaned over just a bit so he could see the remnants of the coy pond he and Clara made. The wooden swing was dangling from a branch on the oak tree above the pond, which is now dried and nearly completely filled in with dirt and leaves.

He hated the fact that the very science he had loved, that he had worked so hard to create, was what killed his wife. He hated that he could not cure what he'd created, and didn't know why. He hated that every day he had to look at his once happy healthy daughter, only to watch her deteriorate slowly; wasting away. He didn't mind so much killing the people he lured to the house.

"It's for a good cause," he told himself.

He walked away from the sink and watched his feet as he made his way toward the dining room. The landscape was getting darker by the second and soon he would be ready to take care of the body in the back yard. Jonathan went into the living room and opened the front door. The smell of the cool autumn air swirled around him. The leaves circled the step of the concrete porch and filled-in the spaces in between the flag stone path.

He walked off the steps and around the back side of the plantation style home. The investment of aluminum siding had paid off years ago. The house still looked new, and he had not even sprayed the siding down. The pillars around the porch were the only parts showing some wear, since he could not put siding on them. The stone pillars showed some growth of green algae, but he felt it only added to the character of the house.

He tiptoed past Anna's open window and carefully listened to see if there were any signs of her stirring or waking up. She was snoring; a clear indication the morphine was still going strong. He continued on toward the back of the house and the black yard bag waiting for him. He left the shovel in the back yard all the time, to save himself a trip to the garden shed. The handle was worn smooth and the paint had come off years ago. The metal shovelhead had dirt and mud forever caked on it, and was beginning to rust.

Jonathan reached out and picked up the shovel. His hand fit around the handle and he felt surprisingly relaxed, as if shaking hands with an old friend. His shoulders no longer hurt as he dug holes in the earth. His back didn't cause him days of pain after his job was done. He had grown so used to doing this part of the job that it was second nature and he had it down to an exact science.

He dragged the black garbage bag towards the hole and pushed it in. He was safe and secure in his yard, no neighbors to see what he was doing, surrounded by trees. He was sure to listen for Anna, but he heard nothing. He began throwing loads of dirt over the black bag and around the body, watching the shallow grave fill up. A few minutes later, he was scraping leaves over the dirt just to blend the patch in with the rest of the yard as much as he could. It was dark now, but he could see with the lights coming from the house. He walked back toward the house and leaned the shovel against the side before walking back to the front.

He turned again, staring back at where he came from; making sure it wasn't too obvious that there had been some digging there. Satisfied with his work, he proceeded back up the steps, and wiped his slippers off on the welcome mat before going in for the night.

As he shut the door, he heard Anna's voice. Being far down the hall behind her closed door, it was soft and muffled. She would be slightly hungry, but he could not allow her to eat until morning, to be sure she didn't throw up. He also needed to give her anti-rejection medication, which was starting to run dangerously low.

He no longer had his medical license and no access to the hospital medical storage areas, but he had been squirrelling away medications for years, as some doctors do. With all the treatments, he had to give Anna, and with all of the surgeries, he'd begun running low on basics like antibiotics, peroxide, gauze, sponges, and anti-rejection medication.

"Daddy!" he heard Anna cry.

"I'm coming, honey. Daddy's on the way," he replied.

Jonathan opened Anna's door and flipped on her light. He walked over to his daughter, who was clutching her stomach and whimpering. He placed his hand on her head and rubbed her bangs out of her face.

"Daddy, my stomach hurts and I'm hungry. Where were you? I called for you, but you didn't answer."

"I was taking a walk in the yard. The weather was nice and the temperature was cool and I wanted to see how many trees still had leaves on them."

"Okay, Daddy, but I'm hungry."

"I know you are, honey, but you know the rules, no food twelve hours before the transplant and at least six hours after you wake up. I do need to give you a shot, though."

He reached over to her nightstand, grabbed a syringe and the small vial of medication, and proceeded to give her a shot in the arm. Anna, having gotten used to the shots over the years, flinched, but only a small bit.

"Okay, Anna, I'm going to turn on your television and let you watch it. Stay in bed and rest. Try to get some sleep. I am going to go to bed, too. I will check on you in the morning and you can call for me if you need me. Tomorrow, I will need to make a trip to the store in town. I need some peroxide and a few things. I will look in on you before I go."

Jonathan grabbed the remote and turned on the wall-mounted television. He put it on Nickelodeon and handed her the remote. She was half in and half out, but the sound of the cartoons in the background seemed to comfort her.

He made his way past the study and past the living room doorway to his room. Clara's robe still hung next to the closet door. Her hairbrushes and jewelry still lay out on her dresser. He had not cleared out any of her belongings and had even left the book she was reading sitting with her reading glasses on the nightstand. Her dresser was still full of her clothing and though he washed the sheets and blankets, he left her pillowcase on her pillow and had never washed it.

His body was exhausted and his mind ran wild with the events of the day. Tomorrow would prove to be no shorter, since he needed to run to town for supplies and to start laying the trail to collect another person. Though Sandra has lasted two months, this generally was not the case. The last heart he gave Anna had held up quite well, but if it started to reject or he ran out of rejection medication, he would need a new heart right away. The same could be said if her lungs or liver started to give.

He leaned over and set his alarm clock for 7:00 am. He needed to get the medications and bandages from the store and lay out a few help wanted for yard work flyers under the bridge and at the laundry mat in town. It was imperative he be back before Anna woke up. He rolled over and shortly began dosing off. He fell asleep fast and slept like a log. The alarm went off and he darted up quickly to be sure he didn't disturb Anna.

Leaving the windows open the night before had made the house very chilly. He rushed to close his windows and grabbed a pair of grey slacks and a black and grey sweatshirt from his dresser. He slipped his loafers on and quickly proceeded to the kitchen. He grabbed a water bottle from the fridge, a package of strawberry Pop Tarts, and walked quickly toward Anna's room. He tapped on the door softly. If she were awake she would hear him, but if she were asleep she would not answer him.

There was no answer, so he walked silently in. She was sleeping soundly. Her room was cool, but not as chilly as the rest of the house had been. Jonathan reached over, closed her window, and placed the water bottle and Pop Tart on the nightstand. She would surely wake up starving and thirsty. He felt her head and cheek; there was no sign of fever, her color looked good, too. Satisfied that she seemed okay, he left the television on and walked out of her room, closing the door behind him.

He went down the cool, dark hallway into the living room and grabbed his wallet and keys from the bowl on the table. The sun was bright when he opened the door and with all the wind last night, the entire yard was once again covered by leaves. Jonathan put his hands in his pockets and walked down the flag stone path toward the long driveway and made his way to the gate. He opened the gate and walked to the very end, staring at the road left and right. The road was picturesque, with gold and red leaves littering the ground from the canopy of maples and oaks that lined the street. Only the occasional sporadic mailbox was in view.

He turned back to walk to his old blue Malibu and let a grin sweep over his face. He loved the fall, the colors, the crisp, clean feel and smell in the air. The fact was, the fall and winter made his task easier. Homeless people were ready and all too willing to accompany a stranger back to an unknown house, with no force needed, on the promise of warmth and a meal.

He cranked the engine and waited for the defroster to start working before closing the door and backing out of the driveway.

The drive to the main road was not overly long, but the New England fall provided a beautiful journey from almost anywhere; from Connecticut all the way up to Maine, no matter how short. Grafton was just another small town like any other in New England. It had its good parts and its not so perfect parts; he'd drive through both sections today.

The leaves swirled in the air and hit the windshield. It sounded like light rain on the car as he drove with the radio off. The first stop in town was the laundromat. It was open, but no one was in there this early to see him place flyers in the bathroom and over the change machine. As he rounded the corner, he noticed a few people huddled up under the bridge. He slowed down and placed a Snickers bar on a flyer, rolled it up, wrapped a rubber band on it to keep it together, and tossed it out the window.

"This might help!" he yelled.

He drove off as quickly as he could, to try not to bring attention to himself. As he got to the intersection and came to a stop, he noticed the small beach area next to the Warner River where a few tents had been set up. *That's new*, he thought. He turned slightly to the right and pulled over. He repeated the process with the flyers and the Snickers bars, tossing them at the tents before driving away.

The rest of the drive to the drug store went smoothly. The traffic in town was always light, but this early almost no one was on the roads, and the ones who were, were on their way out of town. Since the water treatment plant closed down last year the townsfolk had to go outside of town for work. He looked at the clock on the dashboard; it was 7:35. He had made pretty good time and had gotten enough flyers out for the day.

"People will call. They always do," he said. "Besides, if they don't, I will hand out a few more flyers in the other areas, but for now I still have two people. Well, one and a half."

He pulled into the local drug store where there were already a few people in the parking lot. Mostly it was older people and employees, nothing to be alarmed about. He parked close to the entrance and went inside.

***

"Daddy! Daddy!" Anna yelled.

But there was no answer. She carefully and slowly sat up. She was starving, but a Pop Tart was not going to cut it. She grabbed the water bottle and drank it down. She was so thirsty. The operations took so much out of her and sometimes she wasn't sure that it was worth it. She struggled to get up, managing to get to her feet. She had not been strong enough to walk by herself in weeks and it felt good to stand on her own.

She wanted to stretch, but the incisions in her stomach wouldn't let her. She staggered a few steps trying to get her balance and peered out the window. No sign of her father, but the yard, all covered in leaves, was beautiful. The trees were gold and red, she was happy she had not missed all of the fall colors. She couldn't help but smile at the sight of them. She put the bottle back on the nightstand and walked slowly over toward the door.

"Daddy! Where are you?"

There was still no answer. She turned the doorknob and pulled the heavy metal door open. The walk up the ramp her father had made to connect her room to the rest of the house was small but steep, and she leaned forward to give herself enough power to make it. It was almost 8 am and the hall was still dark. She kept one hand wrapped around her stomach, while the other hand felt the wall as she walked. She reached the study and peered in from the doorway, but no one was in there. She stared for a moment, thinking about how different the study looked when it was set up for surgery, but also how sad it looked when it was not filled with books anymore. She turned around and continued down the hall, past the doorway to the living room, and into her father's room.

"Daddy? Are you in here?"

She flipped on the light switch, but he was not there either. The bed was left unmade and his robe was still on the hope chest. His slippers were still in the middle of the rug and he was gone. She turned the lights off and went back into the hallway and into the living room. She walked past the burgundy couch and looked down to see if he had fallen asleep on it, but it didn't look like any one had sat on it in years. The seat of the couch was covered in a layer of dust, as were the coffee tables.

It had been so long since she had come back into this part of the house that a chill ran up her spine. The house smelled musty and old, and the carpet needed to be cleaned. Each step she took flung a cloud of dust into the air and she fought off the urge to sneeze and pull her stitches. The windowsills had been covered in dust and pollen, which had settled into the screens. She dragged her feet a little as she made her way toward the dining room door and on to the fireplace. Her mother's portrait still hung over the mantle, her beautiful smile staring back at Anna, and her eyes seeming to follow her every step.

There was still a log in the fireplace, but it was covered in dust and dirt, also. Cobwebs clung to the sides of the fireplace and the poker, too. As she made her way into the dining room looking around, the feeling of sadness and slight fear came over her. How bare the room was with the table now in the study. It was a dark, lonely little room now, with the blinds drawn shut. She held her stomach a little tighter to keep herself from shaking and headed into the kitchen.

Her father was still nowhere to be found. She looked around the narrow kitchen at so many things that had changed. The floors looked so dull and dirty, the counters that her mother loved so much were covered in deep scratches and gouges. The vases and ceramic fruits her mother once had hanging were strewn about the counter and a few were missing. There was dust and cobwebs over the pantry doors and in the corners. She flipped the light switch, but the light never came on.

Anna took a few more steps, now a bit more labored, and turned on the light above the stove and sink. She walked over to the fridge and opened the door. There was a two-liter bottle of Coke, which she reached for. She hadn't been able to have Coke in a long time, but today she would. She saw eggs and made up her mind that she was going to make herself a few. She grabbed them and walked over to the stove. *Three scrambled eggs ought to do it*, she thought.

She cracked the eggs one by one, grabbed a plastic cooking spoon from the hook on the wall, and began whipping them together. She turned the stove on and smiled as they started to cook right away. The burners smelled, she could tell that her father had not used the stove in quite a while. The eggs finished cooking quickly. She didn't even bother to look for a plate or a fork before she began eating them right from the pan. Eggs were pretty much the only thing she knew how to cook, but she cooked them well and was happy to wolf them down.

The carbonation from the first sip of Coke made her throat tingle, but it was so good. She smiled from ear-to-ear and slowly walked to the other side of the fridge towards the den. If her father would have been home, surely, he would have smelled the eggs cooking and came to find her.

Anna turned on the lights at the top of the stairs and looked down. The radio was on and the television was off. She started to take a step, when a pain in her chest caught her off guard. It was hard to breathe. She could feel pain in her neck and her arms, and her legs felt weak under her. She leaned against the wall for a minute and the pain started to subside. She was still having trouble breathing and felt a bit light-headed, but for the moment the pain was going away.

Jonathan walked in, grabbed a handcart, and headed toward the first aid aisle. He grabbed several packages of gauze and sponges and continued looking for the peroxide. Along the way, he decided to grab antibiotic ointment and Ibuprofen to control the swelling. The peroxide was the last thing he grabbed, and he decided to get six bottles. He headed back toward the checkout line and noticed the clock. It was 8:15; he needed to get back soon.

He rushed toward the checkout, where there was no line and no cashier, either. He rang the bell frantically and started pulling items out of the cart and placing them on the small counter. A small old lady came to the counter and looked at Jonathan.

"Good morning," she said, smiling at him.

Jonathan smiled back and through gritted teeth replied, "Good morning to you as well."

He waited patiently as she bagged his items and allowed him to pay the bill. He grabbed his two bags, hurried out of the store, and back to his car. The parking lots of the pharmacy and strip mall were starting to get a little fuller and the traffic had started to pick up, but it was still headed out of town while he was headed back in, so the drive home would be fine.

Anna took a few more deep breaths and started to feel a little better. She slowly headed down the stairs. The couches were stacked up on the other side of the room, which was no comfort to her. She would love to sit down to rest on the old couches and watch a little television on the big screen. She bounded down the last step and noticed the freezer-looking machines on the opposite wall.

"I don't remember having a deep freezer, much less three of them," she said.

Curiosity got the better of her; she walked closer to the machines, and saw one of the windows. She leaned over the window and Sandra stared back at her.

"Oh, my God!" Anna said.

She grabbed the handles and pulled the lid open. It took all her strength to get it up as sharp pains from her stomach shot through her like a bolt of lightning. She pulled the sheets down and saw the incision and noticed the oxygen machine feeding Sandra. The wound was left partially open in her chest, since her father had no reason to close the rib cage after taking one of Sandra's lungs. Eventually, he would be back for the other one or maybe the heart. Anna was no doctor, but she knew she couldn't save Sandra. She would not live if the machines were disconnected.

She felt her chest and the incision and looked down at Sandra again.

"I am so sorry," Anna whispered.

Tears filled her eyes as she realized what had been happening and thought about how many people over the past few years her father must have done this to in order to keep her alive. She thought about all the late-night trips to town and all the times she thought she'd heard voices or smelled perfume. The image of Sandra was forever burned into her mind. Now she couldn't help wondering how many others there were. She was now pretty scared of her father, too.

Keeping me alive or not, he is still killing people, she thought. She closed the lid and walked carefully over toward the middle machine, but no one was in it. She walked over to the third one and peered in. There was the young man her father had hired to do yard work the other day. Anna opened the lid and peered down at him. She removed the sheet, his chest was intact. She lifted the sheet a little more and saw that other than the cut for the feeding tube, he was intact.

"My name is Anna. I am Jonathan's daughter. I have an illness that causes me to need constant transplants to stay alive. I think that's why you are here. I just found out this is how my father has been keeping me alive. I am not going to let him use you for my sake. I am going to set you free, but I can't do it until my dad gets home. I cannot remove the tube because I don't know if you would bleed, and I wouldn't be able to fix it. I will be back, but I am going to wait for my father," she told him.

The young man's eyes filled with tears as she shut the lid and walked away. Anna's chest hurt once again from the incision and from heartache. She knew what her father was doing and why, but it was wrong and he had to be stopped. Anna looked over at the mini bar and saw the syringes and morphine. She filled the syringe completely with morphine and sat at the bottom of the stairs to wait for her father to get home.

Jonathan drove as quickly as he could through town and down his long back road. The leaves fell and spread out away from the drag of the car. He left the radio off and stared straight ahead. When he got to the start of the sandstone wall he slowed down to make the turn into the driveway. He grabbed the bags and quickly went to close the gate. He made large strides trying to get to the door and into the house, hoping he was able to get home before Anna woke up.

He opened the door and smelled the eggs right away.

"Anna, honey, are you still awake?" he called out.

He walked in, shut the door, and went toward the kitchen.

"Daddy, I'm down here!" she called back.

"Anna, what are you doing out of your bed and way out here?" he asked.

He was hoping she was still in the kitchen and had not gone into the den. His heart sunk as he flew into the kitchen and she was nowhere in sight.

"Anna?" he called.

"I'm here, Daddy," she replied.

Jonathan set the bags on the counter and made his way toward the den, where he found his daughter waiting at the bottom of the stairs.

"Daddy, I know what you have been doing. I know where all my donors were coming from. You can't do that, Daddy. It's not right."

Her voice was small and sad as she looked at her father with love and fear at the same time. He started down the stairs slowly, headed right for her.

"Anna, baby, you're my daughter, my little girl. I had to save you. I did what any daddy would do to keep their little girl alive and well. I did it for you. I will keep doing whatever it takes to keep you alive until I find the cure. Now come on, baby, let's get you back to your room. You need your rest."

He reached down to pick Anna up off the stairs, but she moved away and stood up. She was weak and struggled to stay on her feet.

"No Daddy, I told that boy over there I would get you to set him free. Now go get the tubes out and let him go. You said you would do anything to save me because I am your little girl. Well Daddy, that boy is someone's little boy. That woman is someone's daughter. You can't kill people for me. I am not going to let you anymore."

Anna looked at her father, her eyes filling up with tears. "Mama would not have wanted this either," she told him.

Anna held up the syringe. It was completely full. "I love you Daddy, I always have, I always will, but I can't live knowing how many people died because of me. They didn't die from accidents. They died because you opened them up and took their organs, you left open wounds, and you took their lives. And while I'm sick and you know what's happening to me, their parents don't know where their child is." She plunged the syringe into her heart and pushed in the plunger, but dropped to the ground before the plunger was all the way down.

"My Anna, no! Oh, God, no!" Jonathan yelled.

He ran to her, scooping her up in his arms. He pulled the needle out of her chest, but there was nothing he could do. An overdose of morphine straight to the heart would kill a full-grown adult in the best of health. He held Anna in his arms watching her eyes slowly close and heard her whisper. "I love you, Daddy, and Mommy says hi."

He gave her a kiss on the forehead and she stopped breathing.

Jonathan picked Anna up and placed her in the middle machine and covered her with a sheet. Picturing his little girl running and playing in the yard, in the leaves, and hearing her laughter echo through his ears, he took the syringe and plunged it into his heart. When he did not immediately die, he filled the syringe with air and plunged it into his jugular. He fell to floor at the bottom of Anna's machine.

Alone

"Rocco! Here, Rocco. Come on boy, wait for me!" Gavin shouted.

He trailed behind his best friend in the small wooded section between his house and the dried creek bed. There hadn't been rain in this area all year and the creek bed was as hard as a rock. He had made a fort using the walls of the creek and dried, fallen branches for the top. He liked to play in there while waiting for his school buddies to show up. This was their place. No parents, no chores, no rules; just a few friends and a cooler full of soda. Rocco always came with him, but this time it was different. Rocco seemed to be in a hurry, running fast toward the creek.

Gavin followed the trail pressed into the underbrush, making it past the old crepe myrtle tree that was barely clinging to life in the current drought. A horrible smell nearly stopped Gavin in his tracks. He pulled his hands to his face, looking around for the source of the odor.

He and his friends had come across many dead animals in the woods in the past few weeks. The water was gone from all the creeks and swimming holes and they were dying left and right, but this was not the smell of some poor animal. Gavin heard creaking and cracking all around him as branches fell from the trees. He peered upward through the canopy and noticed how they all seemed to be bent down as if weeping and sad.

"Rocco!"

He could hear Rocco, not too far off in the creek bed, barking at something. He thought maybe he'd found a squirrel or a copperhead. Gavin walked slowly past the tree that served as a landmark for the fort. He went to the left and down the small hill looking down the creek bed at Rocco. Rocco's tail was sticking up and his fur was on end. He snarled and growled and dug at the bottom of the creek. The smell was stronger and made Gavin's eyes water.

Gavin stepped in front of Rocco and saw a small puddle at his feet. It was green like algae and only as big as a Frisbee, but the smell coming from it filled the air for a good distance. Gavin bent down, while pinching his nose closed, to get a closer look. Rocco kept digging with his front paws, turning his golden yellow fur green and muddy.

"Rocco. Leave that alone. Mom will skin you if you get that all over you. She's not going to let you in the house with that smell on you, either," Gavin said.

He reached over and took hold of the red collar on Rocco's neck and tried to pull him away from the strange puddle. The roots of the trees around the creek seemed to stretch out for the green wetness, but the roots that were touching the puddle were shriveled and black. Rocco snarled more and tried to pull himself closer to the puddle, but Gavin lost his grip on the collar and Rocco was sent face first into it.

"Oh, that's great. There's no way you're coming inside now. Mom won't even let you sleep on the porch tonight," he said.

Gavin started climbing back up the bank. The fort was still a few feet down, but he couldn't get inside from this part of the creek. They had camouflaged it by using natural fallen wood, branches, and leaves spread across the top so that it's roof blended into the surrounding ground making it nearly invisible.

He went to the opening of the fort and headed inside. He sat on the old black bench that he and his friends had dragged down. There was also a green and white cooler that they kept soda and water bottles in and a few packages of chips. They had their flashlights, a few packs of matches, and even a few candles. *It wasn't the best fort,* he thought, *but it was theirs.* Rocco was still barking, but he seemed to be calming down a bit.

"Gavin, you here, man?"

Over the sound of Rocco's barking and the rustle of the dead leaves in the wind, Gavin heard Cory's voice.

"Yeah, I'm in the fort."

Cory slid down inside the fort; as usual he was smiling and happy. "Look what I got. My dad brought it home for me today. It's a Swiss army knife, a real one, and it has nail clippers, and a can opener, and of course, a knife."

"Wow. That's cool," Gavin said.

"Yeah, but I have to hide it from my mom. She says knives are dangerous and hates when my dad brings me stuff like this. She'll take it if she sees it."

"Well, you can leave it in here. She won't find it for sure." Gavin told him.

"Hey man, what's wrong with Rocco? He's really barking it up out there. I didn't see anything when I looked down at him."

"There's a weird green puddle over there. I don't know what it is, but that's where this nasty smell is coming from. He won't get away from it. I tried to pull him away, but he's obsessed with it, and covered in it, too."

"Cory, did you ask your mom about camping out with me?"

"Yes. She said it was okay. So, I'll come over tomorrow after I get my sleeping bag and my iPod. Is that puddle where the smell is coming from?"

"I think so," he replied.

They began making their way out of the fort, walking back to their houses. The sun was setting, there were strange shadows on the ground, and the smell was still pungent in the air. It seemed to follow them.

They could no longer hear Rocco; no scratching and digging, no barking. He must have gotten sick of the puddle and gone home. Gavin could still hear Cory's feet softly in the distance. The light on his back porch was visible through the sparse tree trunks. It illuminated his yard, which was far from any grassy place where you'd want to play. The drought had made the grass nearly disappear, there was more dust than dirt, and it covered everything. With every step, he took, clouds of dust covered his feet, and he left footprints that would remain until the next breeze swept through.

The brown picnic table was coated in a layer of powdery dust and pine needles, and his pool was almost completely evaporated. They weren't allowed to refill it, since his father was afraid the well would run dry. He walked around to the front of the house to see if his father was home yet. The black Honda passport was sitting in the driveway. Dust covered most of it, making it appear grey under the motion light.

When he approached the porch, he could see Rocco lying down on his bed in the laundry room. He was panting and appeared to be sleeping. The smell from the green puddle he'd played in was still strong and made Gavin grimace, but Rocco seemed to like it. Gavin bent down to make sure Rocco had water in his bowl before entering the house.

His father was watching the news and his mother was dashing back and forth from the stove to the table with plates of spaghetti.

"Hey, Gavin. How was school today?" his dad asked.

"Same as usual, I guess. Just boring."

He walked into the kitchen and washed his hands in the sink.

"Wow, what's that smell? Gavin, what did you get into?" his mother asked curiously.

"That's not me. It's coming from Rocco. He rolled around in something he found in the woods. The smell just followed me into the house when I opened the door," he replied.

"Well whatever that is, you're going to have to give him a bath tomorrow," his mother told him.

Gavin sat down at the table waiting for his father and mother to join him. The smell seemed to linger in the house, making it hard to enjoy their food. After he was finished, he waited for his parents to be done before taking the table scraps out to Rocco. He cleared the table and walked out the front door. Rocco didn't move.

"Hmm, that's strange, Rocco normally comes running for dinner." He walked into the laundry room and found Rocco sitting up looking at him. He still had the green stain around his face and on his feet, and he smelled worse than before. Rocco growled and snarled at him. He raised his fur and flashed his fangs, showing teeth that were red and covered in blood that dripped down his chin

Gavin placed the plate on the floor in front of Rocco, and slowly reached out to pat him on the head. At this, Rocco lunged at Gavin and nearly bit him. Gavin jumped up, pulled his hand away, and stumbled out of the laundry room. Rocco staggered, trying to get up. With every step he took toward the plate of food Gavin offered, he left bloody footprints behind. Gavin looked over to the blanket Rocco used as a bed. It was covered in the green stuff and in Rocco's blood. Rocco noticed Gavin still standing there and took a few steps closer, growling and whimpering at the same time. His eyes seemed black and coated.

"Rocco, what's wrong? It's me, Gavin."

Rocco stepped out onto the porch. Gavin could see that his fur was matted and falling off in a few places. He turned slowly and opened the door to the house, shaking from head to toe.

"Dad. There's something really wrong with Rocco. I think we need to take him to the vet. He is bleeding from his mouth and having trouble standing up. He was growling at me and even acted like he was going to bite me when I tried to pet him."

"Okay. Well that's a bit odd, but maybe he got bit by another copperhead and he is having a reaction to the bite. It sounds like he got bit on the face. That would sort of explain the bleeding from the mouth, the reaction to the venom could cause the trouble walking. He's been bit before, and it's late, so there aren't any vets open right now, but if he is not better by tomorrow, I'll take him to see Dr. Folley," he said.

"Dad, this isn't like last time. Rocco's been hurt before and it has never looked like that. He's also never tried to bite me before. I really think something is wrong."

Gavin turned to see his mother standing behind him. She put a hand on his shoulder before he walked away to his room.

"Maybe we should go have a look at Rocco, Drew. I mean Gavin seems really worried," she said.

Drew got up and walked to the door. He knew it was best to do as his wife suggested or there would be no sleep that night. He opened the front door and flipped on the porch light. There were bloody paw prints all over the porch and a puddle of blood in the laundry room.

"Shelly, bring me a towel and another bowl of water, please."

He shut the door behind him and slowly walked into the laundry room. The plate Gavin had brought out was empty, except for the bloodstains left over from Rocco's bleeding gums. There were patches of fur scattered all over the porch and laundry room that were being blown around in the breeze. Rocco was lying down on the blood-soaked blanket growling and panting. Drew slowly made his way closer to the dog, softly calling his name.

Rocco's ears perked up and moved toward the sound of his voice. He growled and raised the side of his lips bearing his bloody teeth and gums. There were holes, as if he'd gotten into acid. Drew leaned in a little closer just as Shelly opened the door.

"Stay back, Shelly. Gavin wasn't exaggerating. Rocco isn't

doing so well, he's acting like he is rabid, but without the foaming mouth."

Shelly handed him the bowl of water and the towel, then stepped back and watched from what she thought would be a safe distance. She also wanted to make sure she could shield Gavin from whatever was going on, if he came out of his room.

Drew reached out slowly with the towel in his hand, to try to wipe the blood off of Rocco's face. He was checking for injuries that he couldn't see. He was already getting nauseous from the smell and his knees were covered in the green water from the sodden blanket. It was heating up on his skin like Icy Hot. Drew bent over farther and touched the front of Rocco's nose.

Rocco sat up quickly and growled. He bit at the towel, nipping Drew's hand and first finger. Drew dropped the towel, stood up, clutching his bleeding, throbbing hand, and walked out of the room. Rocco followed him out, snarling and growling. Shelly opened the door and pulled him inside.

Drew ran to the sink and started washing his hand, while Shelly stood by the window and watched as Rocco limped off the porch and away from the house, dripping a trail of blood as he went.

"Are you alright?" she asked.

"I think so. I can't believe he bit me. I've known that dog since the day he was born. He barely got me, but it's bleeding a lot," he said.

He grabbed a dishtowel off the oven and wrapped his hand up.

"I have never seen him like that before. It was scary. That was not the sweet dog I know."

"Drew. Listen to me. Rocco took off. To be honest, I don't think, judging by the way he looked, that he'll be back. I also don't think we should tell Gavin if he doesn't come back. I think that he ran off to die and if we tell him that: one, he'll go looking for him to the ends of the earth, and two, he'll be devastated."

"Yeah, I think you're probably right," he replied.

Shelly walked down the hall and knocked on Gavin's door. He was already fast asleep with his ear buds in. She closed the door and went back down the hall, finding Drew sitting in his chair again. He was still holding the dishtowel on his hand, the small bite was still bleeding, and the towel was already soaked through with blood.

"Baby, that's still bleeding? That's pretty bad for such a small wound. But if you can't get that to stop bleeding soon, then maybe you should go to the hospital," Shelly said.

"I'll be fine. I am not going to the hospital with this. They would laugh me right out of the place."

He squeezed the towel a little harder. A few drops of blood dripped off, landing in his lap. He looked up at Shelly, who shook her head before walking to the couch and grabbing the remote.

"Shelly, this stuff is starting to burn," he said.

"What stuff?"

"There was some sort of green stuff on the blanket that Rocco was lying on. It was also on his face and on his feet. I knelt down on it when I was trying to wipe his face off. It was warm, like when you put Icy Hot on a sore muscle, but now it's really starting to burn."

"Okay. Well, let's get your pants off since that's where the stuff is. Maybe we just need to wash you off."

She walked over and started to undo his pants, helping him to shimmy them down. She had gotten used to the smell by now and didn't notice it getting stronger as she helped him undress. The green stain was on his legs and there was a sore starting up. It was red and inflamed, with deep, thin wounds that had begun to trickle blood. It looked like he had been stabbed.

Shelly went to the bathroom, collected the peroxide and a washcloth, and headed quickly back to Drew. He was starting to fall asleep in the chair. His head bobbed up and down, and where he let his hand drop over the arm of the chair, dripping blood had formed a puddle on the tile floor.

Shelly poured the peroxide on the washcloth and started rubbing the wounds on his leg, hoping this would stop the burning. As soon as she applied the washcloth Drew opened his eyes. They were red and blood shot, and he glared at her and watched as she slowly rubbed the green stain off of his leg. Her hand was already feeling the warmth from the substance on the cloth, so she added a little more peroxide. The wounds were getting bigger, however, and blood was starting to flow down Drew's leg. She grabbed his pants and tied them around his wound.

"Drew. Your wounds are bleeding pretty good. Whatever that stuff is, it has some sort of anticoagulant properties. We need to get you to the hospital. I can't fix this here," she said.

"No. I'm not going anywhere, except to bed," he said.

He stood up and started limping down the hall toward their bedroom.

"I'll be fine once I get some sleep," he told her.

Shelly went to the kitchen and tried to wash her hands. She hoped that if she washed them quickly there wouldn't be time for the substance to have the effect on her that it had on Rocco and Drew.

She scrubbed with hot water and dish soap until her hands were red, then took a Benadryl and rubbed alcohol on her hands.

If this doesn't stop a reaction, nothing will, she thought. She put the towel back on the counter and walked into the living room to turn off the television and the light. She glanced out the window to see Rocco sitting in the driveway under the motion detector light, his fur glowing red, staring at her in silence.

Shelly turned off the light, made sure the front door was locked, and headed down the hall. Drew was already in bed, with his leg and arm sticking out from the covers, and there was oozing blood visible in the moonlight. She could smell the odor coming from him now that she was all clean. The smell was getting stronger and closely resembled decomposition. She turned on her nightstand fan, hoping the smell would stay on his side of the bed. She pulled the covers back and slid into bed. Off in the distance she could hear screaming. *Corey's parents must be fighting again,* she thought. *Poor kid, he never seems to get a good night's sleep. They must have taken the argument outside for me to hear it this much.*

Shelly pulled the pillow over her ears and tried to block out the voices. *Maybe his mother is drinking again,* she thought, *They were really having it out this time.* She pressed the pillow against her face harder and slowly drifted off to sleep.

Gavin woke up while it was still dark out. Screams, he wasn't sure if they were dreams or real, pierced the silence. He waited another minute to try to figure out what they were. He heard nothing. He got out of bed, quietly putting on his slippers; he walked slowly toward the door and placed his ear on it. Still nothing. He thought it must have been a dream.

He cracked the door open, the hallway was dark. His parent's room was right across the hall from his, but it was too dark to see in. He opened the door all the way and stepped out into the hall. He could hear something, but it was faint, and he could hear slurping-like noises. Just then, the air conditioner tripped on and made him jump. He reached back into his room, flipping on his light switch. The light flooded through the doorway and illuminated the hall.

His mother's side of the bed was showered in yellow light. Gavin was able to peer inside his parent's room. Blood covered the sheets and dripped from his mother limp hand and onto the floor. Gavin looked to the left to see his father's face, which was pale in the light, but covered in bright red blood that dripped from his chin.

"Mom!" Gavin yelled.

His father turned and looked at him, then growled and returned his attention to his wife, who was barely breathing and bleeding from her face and neck. Gavin shut the door to his parents' room and ran toward the living room. He was hoping to buy a little time to get away. He rounded the corner and went to open the front door, but when he peered out the window he saw Rocco running from the driveway toward the porch. He was covered in blood from head to toe and had green water dripping from what was left of the fur around his mouth.

Rocco jumped on the door, scratching and growling and snarling. He was throwing himself against the door, trying to get at Gavin. In all the commotion, Gavin could hear screaming coming from all around his house. It was faint, not in his yard, but he recognized the scream…it was Cory.

I have to get out of here, he thought, *but Rocco will get me if I go outside.* Terror swept over his body as he realized he could either be killed by his father, or by his dog. His friend was out there somewhere. Gavin walked to the back door and quietly opened it. He propped the screen door open and made sure the metal storm door was open just enough for him to squeeze through. He walked over to the living room window and opened it. The screen would not make much of a deterrent for Rocco and that was just what he wanted. He made his way out the back door, pulling it closed, just as Rocco jumped through the window and slid into the back door. He could hear Rocco growling and snarling. He hoped Rocco would not figure out how to go back through the window to get back outside.

Gavin ran through the dusty yard, leaving a trail of clouds in his wake. The moonlight gave him just enough light to find the small trail into the woods, which led to his secret fort. He hoped that since they never told their parents where it was, that his dad would not discover him there. He also hoped that Cory had made it to the fort. Two teenagers weren't much protection, but it was better than being alone. Right now, that's exactly what he was…alone. He was scared and cold in the night air, and he was alone.

He rounded the tree and slid down the opening into the fort. Cory was there, with his knife pulled, and he nearly stabbed Gavin as he slid inside.

"Cory! It's me," Gavin said.

Cory's face was pale and he was dripping in sweat. He was shaking and tears streaked his face. Gavin didn't bother to try to take the knife at this point; he was kind of relieved that it was there. This wasn't much of a shelter, but he hoped they were hidden. He also knew that his dog could still find them, and they really had no place to go if he did.

"Cory, what happened?" he asked.

Cory looked out the doorway and through their little spy cracks. Satisfied that no one was there for the moment, he began talking.

"Gavin, my dad was working in the backyard chopping wood. He came inside with a gash from a piece of wood that ricocheted back and slit his arm. He had some of that green stuff on his clothes and in the cut. He just went crazy. He went after my sister and killed her. He was eating her!" he screamed.

"I tried to pull him off, but his eyes were dark, and they looked like black olives."

He continued, "I managed to get his mouth off of Madison, but he had chunks of her in his teeth. She was bleeding and gasping. There was nothing I could do. He turned to grab me and I ran. I went to see my mom and she was on the couch. There was green stuff on her as well and she was growling. There were huge holes and chunks of her skin missing. She wasn't getting up, but I could tell she was going to end up like my dad. I just ran out of the house and tried to find my way here. There are people screaming in their houses on my street and there are puddles of that green stuff popping up everywhere."

"I'm so sorry man," said Gavin. "My dad went the same way and my mom, too. I saw him doing that to my mom. I think it started with Rocco. He was acting rabid and he was trying to tear me up. I managed to get my parents door shut and I got Rocco in the house, but he can get out from the window. I'm afraid that Rocco will find us here or lead my parents to us."

"Where are we going to go? People are eating each other and killing each other and there are no houses we can go to where we can trust anyone," Cory whispered.

He peered over Gavin's shoulders and through the cracks between branches, holding up his finger signaling for Gavin to stay quiet. He could hear movement in the underbrush. Leaves crunching and twigs snapping. Someone or something with some weight to them was moving through the woods.

Gavin sat as still as he possibly could, his back pressed against the side of the creek bank, under the small overhang of earth. Gavin hoped he wouldn't be seen by anything passing by the opening to their fort, but also that no one would be able to look through the cracks in the moonlight and see them from above. The more he thought about their little secret hiding place, the more he realized that they were sort of trapped inside if anything came for them.

Cory didn't move. He tried to peer through the spaces in the branch-covered roof. He could see shadows moving, but with the breeze and the moonlight, there was no way to tell what it was. He crawled slowly, a tiny bit at a time, toward the opening—not wanting to make any large movements and draw attention to himself. The shadow got longer; he could see the shape was human. They could hear the footsteps getting closer, shuffling the leaves and creating a cloud of dust that drifted past the opening of the fort.

Cory pushed himself back into the shadows at the bottom of the creek. He again put his finger to his lips, watching as a pair of feet staggered by. The shoes were his father's, he was looking for them. He was heading toward Gavin's house. They stayed still, listening to the footsteps get fainter and farther away. Cory threw himself down next to Gavin.

"We have to get out of here. That was my dad, I could tell by the shoes. We have to go somewhere. He's headed to your house. If he opens the door, your dog and your parents will get out. We can't stay here."

"I think I know where we can go, that abandoned house on North Country. The last resident moved out two weeks ago, the landlord lives in Ohio and isn't supposed to be coming back again 'til February. Since I was helping to repaint the house, I know where the key is hidden. Inside, there's still an old couch to sit on and a mattress upstairs. The windows are all good and there is a closed-in attic. If we had to, we could hide in the attic and no one could get up there. There are a lot of boards and stuff in the back yard, too. We can use them to board up the windows and door," Gavin said.

"That sounds good to me. It's definitely safer than where we are. We still have no supplies though, and we have no water or food."

"Well, the water is still on there and so is the power. The food is still a problem, but we need to get there first, then we can worry about food later. We can take our cooler, or at least the ice chips in it. That's a start," he replied.

Gavin opened the cooler and dumped out the water. It was much lighter with no ice or water in it. Cory peered out of the opening in the fort and crawled out just a bit. He stared out into the woods, looking for movement, and listening for sounds of footsteps human or otherwise.

The hair on his arms and neck were standing on end. He was sick to his stomach. The abandoned house was only down North Country, but that walk could be the last walk they would take. If they stayed off the streets, it meant cutting through yards, and who knew what was in the yards or who would be coming out of houses. If they took to the streets, it would be faster, but they were more exposed.

"Gavin, come on. We should probably stay out of sight, so let's stick to the woods and go through my side-yard along the border until we get to the corner. Mr. Mayes hasn't cut the field yet and we can sneak to the house through the tall grass. We may have to crawl through, but at least we can try to stay hidden," Cory said.

"Okay. I'm right behind you."

Cory started walking with Gavin fast on his heels, looking back and forth and over their shoulders. They couldn't decide if it was better to walk on the leaves and take their chances with the shuffling noises or to walk in the dust, creating clouds, and watching their footprints show up. As they approached Cory's house, they could hear banging coming from inside. Groans and gurgled yells filled their ears. Cory's face was pale and tears were streaming down his cheeks. He looked to the window and could see his mother walking back and forth in front of it. The moonlight illuminating her body showed it covered in blood. She noticed Cory and slammed her hands against the window pane.

"Come on man, we've got to go! That glass won't hold forever and she may try to get to the door," Gavin whispered.

They ran through the corner of the woods bordering the field at Mr. Mayes property line. They could hear dogs barking and growling from all directions and groans and shrieks filled the air. The rancid smell of the green water enveloped them now, running down the gutters in the streets. They heard a door slam shut and turned to see Angel, Corey's young neighbor, running down her driveway. The small girl was covered in blood and crying.

"Cory…" Gavin started.

"No, leave her. We have to keep moving," Cory replied.

Gavin looked back again to see her mother staggering down the driveway after her. She reached the little girl and pulled her to the ground. They were at the end of the street almost to the longer grass when they heard Mr. Mayes scream. His gurgled voice lasted only for a few moments before a gunshot rang through their ears. More dogs started barking. Cory looked back down his street seeing more people emerging from their houses, making their way to the streetlights. He threw himself into the grass, crawling quickly, and making sure Gavin was close behind.

"Gavin, where's the key at?"

"It's on the back porch, under the welcome mat."

They made their way through the grassy field, keeping their heads low to the ground, stopping every few minutes to listen and see if they could hear anyone coming in the grass. The moon shown down from above, making the tops of the yellow grass seem to glow, while the inside remained pitch-black.

As they got to the edge of the grass, Cory held his hand back for Gavin to stop. He peered out from the blades looking to see if there was anyone in the yard or on the street. He saw nothing from his vantage point. He stayed at the edge and signaled for Gavin to follow him. They made their way around the side of the little blue house to the small screened-in back porch.

They opened the screen door and flipped the welcome mat over, retrieving the key. Cory unlocked the deadbolt as Gavin pushed the small wooden bench in front of the screen. It wasn't much protection, but he thought maybe they would hear if someone was trying to get in.

They closed the back door and locked it behind them as they made their way through the dark house, feeling safer than they had in hours. The moonlight flooded into the house, but they tried to stay out of it. They went through the kitchen where Gavin placed the cooler on the counter. They found the living room, with a large picture window covered in old heavy curtains. Cory tiptoed quietly on the tile floor and pulled the curtain open just a crack.

Black eyes stared back at him, belonging to his father and Gavin's parents. They had bloody faces and pale skin, stained green in the dim light. Cory looked past them and into the street where he could see people staggering as they made their way toward their safe house. He let the curtain go and stepped back toward Gavin.

"They know we're here. I'm betting that little girl may have seen us come here. Either way, our parents are here and there's more on the way. We need to get to the attic now."

"The doors are locked, we should be okay, but maybe we can push the couch against the window and find some boards or the mattress to cover it so they can't get in," Gavin said.

"No, we have to hide. Maybe they'll go away if they think we got out, but they can get in the windows. Glass won't hold them back. If they didn't know we were here, I would say we would have had time to board them up, but now we need to stay out of sight, and away from the windows."

They began hearing growls and yells as they started heading up the stairs and into the hallway. More people were surrounding the house now and were banging on the windows. They could hear them at the back door trying to move the bench and push it open.

"Where's the attic, Gavin?"

"It's over here. We just have to pull the cord to get the ladder down."

He reached up and pulled the cord, the ladder dropped down

40

slowly. The spring creaked loudly and the bottom of the ladder made a slight thud on the carpet.

"Cory, you go first. I'm going to try to pull the bottom of the ladder and keep the cord with us so we can close the door without them being able to get in."

Cory headed up the old ladder and waited for Gavin. Gavin stepped up, grabbing the bottom and folding it up onto itself. He leaned over, grabbing the cord, and pulled hard, but it wouldn't close.

"Cory, hold onto me and help me to pull this closed."

Cory grabbed onto Gavin's waist and pulled, while Gavin tugged the rope again. The trap door closed slowly. They crawled toward the attic window and peered down. The sun was starting to rise over the house tops and trees and there were hues of orange and purple flooding their line of sight. They peered down below them, watching their parents try to open the front door. Mr. Mayes, covered in blood, was trying to break the window.

As they sat alone in the attic, the sun was getting higher, and light flooded in from the window. They watched as the sunlight hit the little girl still walking down the road. She seemed to melt before their eyes, leaving a green puddle where she stood. They could see green puddles popping up everywhere.

The green puddles seemed to seek each other out, forming larger puddles that slowly inched down the driveway toward the gutter. The yells stopped and their parents were gone before their eyes. They watched Mr. Mayes hit the window one more time before the light shone down on him. Then he was gone just as the window cracked and glass fell to the floor.

Gavin and Cory sat still in the dimly lit attic. They stared at each other, wondering if it was all over. They crawled to the other window and looked down into the long grassy field that they had navigated through to get to the house. There was movement in the long grass, but they couldn't see what it was.

"Gavin, are you sure no one can open the attic?"

"We have the cord up here, and unless they are really tall, they can't reach the door. Why?" Gavin asked.

A moment later they heard glass shattering and growling and snarling in the house below them.

"Rocco?" Gavin whispered.

Velvet Choker

Mona lived in a quaint village, with only 1200 residents, just outside of Boston, Massachusetts. Not much happened in the sleepy little village. Everyone knew everyone and they pretty much stuck to themselves. Mona worked in the small flower shop on the corner of Park and Lotus. She had never travelled more than 30 miles in either direction in her whole life. Her sweet smile always looked so happy to the people she passed on the street, but her smile hid the truth, that just beneath the surface was a woman screaming to be let out.

She walked to work on days that it didn't rain, taking in the familiar faces of the old stone buildings, and enjoying what little scenery there was. Only a few little shops lined the cobblestone roads in town. There was a small grocery store, adjacent to an equally small wooden building just off the main road on a dirt path. The building housed a new-age shop dealing in incense, herbs, and knickknacks. Mona laughed a little at the thought of going in there, but had heard many of the local folks speak of the man who owned the place. He was a short, older gentleman with white hair, cataracts, and a thick Irish brogue, who was always there alone. The very idea of being seen there was laughable to her, but for weeks now there had been something…a little part of her that wanted to go check it out. Something tempted her to go see what was behind the wooden walls and the dark curtained display window.

The wind blew a chilly gale that made Mona instinctively pull her jacket a little tighter. Fall in New England was beautiful, but the wind could be a bit blustery. She automatically stopped and looked both ways before crossing, although the barren streets made her wonder why. As she unlocked the door to the flower shop, an eerie feeling swept over her. Once more, she turned and stared at the little wooden shop for moment before she entered her flower store. She pushed hard against the door, forcing it closed as the wind fought back. The sweet smell of flowers and plants of all varieties filled the air. The lights came on at the flip of a switch and the sound of automatic sprayers echoed off the walls.

Mona had always been a pretty woman, but she was very plain and shy. She desperately wanted to find love and be taken away from this little town, but there weren't many men to choose from and most of her friends from high school were lucky enough to have left and made their lives elsewhere. She felt trapped inside of herself in this town. The days went by slowly and not a single person came to the store. Lately, the only time people came in was to plan funeral flowers. The sad situations only added to her feeling alone and separated.

By the time four o'clock came, it was already dark outside and still not one customer had come in. Mona had cleaned the windows and the floors. She had fed and watered the plants and flowers and was cleaning the keys on the cash register when the old man from the new-age shop came in. He walked slowly, hunched over slightly, with a cane made from a banyan tree. He seemed to almost float, rather than walk, as he made his way up to the counter. He smiled and looked directly in her eyes.

"Hello there, my name is Ronan Vesport. I own the little shop down path," he told her.

"Yes, Mr. Vesport. I know who you are, how can I help you?"

The sides of his mouth curled upward in an awkward smile and his cataract-covered eyes seemed to stare through her, rather than at her.

"It is I who may be able to help you," he replied.

"Excuse me?" Mona asked, with a look of surprise that swept the smile from her face. She wanted to escort him out of her store. Feeling a bit edgy, she walked around the counter.

"Mr. Vesport, I was just about to close shop for the day, so if there is nothing here that you need, I would like to close up," she said.

Mr. Vesport smiled even wider, giving him a more sinister appearance. He placed his hand in the pocket of his old, wool coat and pulled out a red velvet choker. He held it up, and in the light shone a single, large, white pearl. It was beautiful, without as much as a scratch or chip on it.

"I found this on the ground in front of your store. I think it belongs to you," he told her.

"No, I do not own a necklace like that," she replied.

"This necklace is a very special necklace. This necklace makes things happen to the women who wear it," he explained.

Mona stood quietly and listened to his every word. She wasn't sure why, but something deep inside her needed to know about this necklace.

"Great things indeed," he continued, "but one must understand that when you don this necklace you are bound to it forever. The things you most need or want in order to be happy will come to you when you wear this necklace. You can never take it off, the necklace itself becomes part of you, you bathe with it, you wear it constantly, and it keeps you alive and well. If you remove it, so too, do you remove your life," he explained.

Mona didn't know what to believe. *This is absurd,* she thought, *just the rambling of an old, lonely man.* On the other hand, something in her wanted that necklace; something wanted to have it around her throat.

Mona stared at the necklace as it dangled from his hand and it seemed to breathe and pulse as she watched. She was unexplainably drawn to the choker. She started reaching out toward it slowly. She felt unable to stop herself, but then again, she didn't really want to.

"Mona, I must make sure you understand you can never take

this off and you must never tell anyone why or where you got this or what it does," he snapped.

"Yes, yes I understand."

A smile swept across her face as Mr. Vesport placed the choker in her hand and closed her fingers gently on it.

"Mr. Vesport, what happens if I tell someone why I am wearing it, or what happened once I put it on?" she asked.

"My dear, to be honest with you, the choker, as I said, becomes part of you, if you talk about the powers it possesses, it will become tighter and tighter around your neck until, well…you understand. You cannot tell your parents, your friends, or even the person you decide to spend your life with. There will be great temptation and it can become too difficult to resist. The choker has won a few of these battles," he explained.

"I get it."

Mr. Vesport turned to leave, his cane in hand, his coat on tight as he stepped toward the door. The streetlights had all come on, but the town was still very dark. Mr. Vesport was about to walk outside and begin his journey home when Mona called his name.

"Wait, what can I give you in return for this?"

"Ah, I would like a single white rose, which I have already taken," he answered.

Mr. Vesport smiled and reached his wrinkled hand into his coat pocket retrieving a single long stem white rose.

Mona's lips parted slightly as she turned her head toward the only vat of long stem white roses in the shop. They were all the way on the other side and Mr. Vesport had never left her counter area. Mona looked down at her fist clutching the still pulsing choker and back to the door, but Mr. Vesport was gone. She took a quick glance around the store to make sure he was not in there somewhere, before she turned out the lights and walked out the

46

door.

The streets were relatively safe in her small town and now, at only a little after 4:30, they were vacant. There was no one walking on the sidewalks other than her. She looked up at the full, glowing, yellow-orange moon and felt the breeze on her face, crisp and cold, making her eyes water, but she didn't care. The beautifully colored leaves on the ground which lined the streets and piled up in orange bags seemed to give her child-like energy as she clung to her choker.

The short walk back to her small one bedroom apartment on top of the hill was even shorter than usual. Mona skipped half the way. The choker bounced and bobbed up and down left and right, as she climbed up the stairs to her door. The kitten welcome mat and matching door hanger told the story of a lonely single woman. She opened her door and placed her purse and coat on a small glass table.

She still clutched the choker as she made her way to the small living room. It was a room cramped with pastel yellow curtains, floral print over-stuffed sofas, and a wooden coffee table. She kicked off her shoes, slid on a pair of old, comfy white slippers, and walked to the kitchen. As she walked behind the couch, she caught sight of the mirror on the wall and stopped in front of it. She pulled her hair over to one side before holding the choker up at her neck to see how it looked.

The luxurious red-colored velvet and beautiful pearl enticed her even more to put it on. A smile stretched slowly across her face as she fumbled with the small hooks on the back of her necklace. The velvet felt so soft against her skin; she couldn't help but rub it with her fingers from one side to the other. She carefully traced the smooth round pearl with her index finger.

Mona grabbed the remote from the coffee table and turned her television on. She watched the news alone every evening during dinner. The same people telling the same stories, but somehow it always made her feel just a little better about her life.

What I wouldn't give for a day of excitement, she thought.

She watched the leaves fall off the tree outside and swirl around in the air before making contact with the ground. The gentle scraping noises of small branches on the concrete and the creaking as the tree swayed with the wind always made her feel comforted. She sat quietly listening to the sound and felt something touch her; a little bit of movement from the choker.

She walked to the mirror and stared just for a moment as it happened again. The choker seemed to be breathing. As Mona's jugular pulsed, so did the choker; when she took a deep breath, it seemed to breathe along with her.

"The choker will become part of you," she whispered.

The words of Mr. Vesport came through in stereo as she watched her choker and felt it move. Now a bit frightened, she could not help but wonder if she'd made a mistake.

Mona walked slowly away from the mirror and back into the kitchen. She placed her bowl in the sink and filled it with water. She had begun to get a little nervous as she thought about never removing the necklace.

"Too late now," she whispered.

Finishing in the kitchen, she was surprised to realize how tired she was. She decided to watch TV in bed.

At every mirror Mona passed on her way to bed, she couldn't help but look at her reflection. She fought the urge to touch the choker or remove it each time it seemed to move. She walked into the small bedroom and turned on her side table light before undressing and climbing into bed. She propped her pillow up and prepared for what she believed would be a sleepless night. She figured she would sit up all night a bit freaked out about the choker every time it moved.

At eight o'clock, the alarm went off as always and Mona got out of bed. She had slept soundly and seemed to have not noticed the choker in the night. She went to the closet, pulled out a tan skirt and maroon long-sleeved shirt, and proceeded to the bathroom. The big mirror left nothing to the imagination and somehow, in Mona's eyes, it reflected something different. She felt pretty, even excited for once. She rushed to brush her hair into a ponytail. She brushed her teeth in a hurry and walked quickly to the front door.

Mona walked even more briskly than usual to her lonely flower shop. She smiled and waved to every person she saw, even though she didn't really know them. As she passed the little dirt path of the tiny old shop, Mona noticed something that took her by surprise. The little shop was being boarded up. Mr. Vesport turned and waved, a somber look on his face. Mona waved and began walking again. Somehow, even knowing the little shop would be no more, she still felt as though nothing could go wrong.

Mona opened her little shop and took her usual place behind the counter. A few tourists poked their heads up against the glass taking in the small-town feel, but no real customers entered. Suddenly, a handsome dark haired man walked into the shop. He said nothing at first, just walked around slowly looking at the many flowers and plants before he came full circle at the counter. Mona smiled softly, waiting to see if he would speak. When he didn't, Mona did.

"Can I help you find something?" Mona asked.

The man smiled back and Mona couldn't help but notice how white his teeth were and how beautiful his green eyes were.

"Yes, I think you can. My name is Alex and I would love it if you could tell me where I could take you out for dinner tonight," he told her.

His face flushed with red and he was clearly a bit shy about what he had just done. Mona was as red faced as her choker, with the biggest smile she had ever had. Mona had only had a few dates in the past year and had never been asked out by a man quite this handsome. She even wondered why she had never seen him in town before.

"My name is Mona and there is a little place just around the corner. We could meet there, say around six, for dinner."

"Great, six it is then," Alex replied.

Mona watched his every move as he left her store. She could hardly contain herself. The choker too seemed excited. It pulsed and throbbed against her neck, reminding her all the while that it was there.

The rest of the day passed quickly, as Mona could think of only her date.

All the things you want or need in life to be happy will come to you, she thought.

A huge smile overtook her face once more. As it began to get dark, Mona prepared to close the flower shop for the day and get ready for her date. She quickly cleaned the windows and the floors, watered the plants, and turned off the lights. Butterflies filled her stomach as she locked the flower shop and began her walk to the Half Moon Restaurant.

The date went off without a hitch. They both stared at each other, hardly touching their food at all. They took turns speaking about their childhoods, what they liked to do for fun, even what they wanted for the future. They spent more time together and before the fall of the following year, they were married. Mona closed up the flower shop and together they bought a home just inside the Boston city limits. It was a large three story Victorian style home, Mona's dream home. All this time Mona had not removed the choker, and Alex had begun asking about it.

"Mona, that is a beautiful choker, but why is it that you only wear it and no other? I bought you a diamond necklace and even other chokers, but you don't ever wear them," he said.

"I love everything you have ever gotten for me, but this necklace is very special. It's very old and I will never take it off," she told him.

Alex looked a little saddened by Mona's reply, but accepted her answer for the time being. Mona got up, noticing her husband's agitated mood about the necklace, and walked into the hallway. There her mirror stood and she looked at the choker on her neck.

It pulsed and tightened slightly around her throat and then sat still again. Mona touched the pearl in the middle and rubbed the velvet. The velvet had not aged or frayed, even though it was slept in, bathed in, and touched over the past year. She smiled and continued down the hall to her front door. Large stained glass French doors opened up to a beautifully landscaped front porch, complete with a porch swing. She stepped out and took a deep breath of the cool fall air. She sat on the swing and took in the beautiful flowers in her yard. Just sitting there, she thought about everything she had gained in the past year. She thought of what may have happened to Mr. Vesport after the closing of his shop. She still wondered why he closed it to begin with.

The choker was still on Alex's mind; the thought of all the money he had spent on necklaces for her and the thought that she didn't even take it off for their wedding. She just made sure her dress had enough neckline to cover it. For some reason, the choker had started to make him quite angry, almost jealous.

What is she hiding from me? What is it about that choker that makes it so important to her, and why is it that she will not talk to me about it? he wondered.

Eventually, he occupied himself with things around the house, but the choker remained in the back of his mind. Mona came back in from her relaxing time on the porch and began to make dinner.

The kitchen, with granite countertops, golden oak cabinets, and a matching island, was her favorite room in the house. While turning on the oven and taking out stuffed mushrooms and pork chops to bake, she realized that Alex was becoming increasingly annoyed about the choker.

Why can't he just let it go? It's just a necklace, or at least as far as he is concerned, she thought.

Mona stood quietly in her kitchen admiring the new stove, matching fridge and dishwasher, and the hardwood floors which she adored, while the heavenly aromas of dinner filled the air. She could hear Alex upstairs somewhere moving furniture around.

He is probably setting up his office, she thought. She shook her head in amusement and looked at the clock timer on the oven. The mushrooms and chops only needed about twenty minutes to cook.

She turned around and opened the cabinets and took out two plates and two glasses. As she turned to walk over to the table, she was surprised to see Alex standing behind her.

"Oh, you scared me."

"I'm sorry. I just came down to see if you knew where the scissors were."

"If they are not on my sewing table, then they may not have been unpacked yet. Dinner is just about ready, I am setting the table now," she replied.

"Okay, I'll be right there."

He left the kitchen and proceeded through the living room to a small sunroom surrounded by windows and white silk curtains. This was the room where the most natural light came in and was perfect for sewing. He looked around the built-in shelves and on the sewing table, but there were no scissors. He even looked on the floor under the sewing table, but to his disappointment, there were no scissors to be found. Alex walked back out of the small sewing room and made his way to the kitchen table where Mona had dinner set out for them.

Alex would occasionally glance away from his plate to look at Mona. Each time he did, the choker caught his attention and he was once again agitated. Mona noticed his glances a few times, but tried to ignore them. She had hoped to keep a conversation about the necklace out of the topics they might discuss over dinner. Somehow, Alex's face seemed to change with his glances. Where there was once a smile, there was now a frown. He seemed to be getting angrier as the minutes passed. His mind was becoming consumed by the unanswered questions.

To Mona's surprise, Alex never said a word, not one comment or question. She wasn't sure if this was a good thing or a bad thing, since this had not happened before. Mona felt a little worried about that, but didn't want to ask him about it for fear she would be dragged into a conversation with a bunch of questions she couldn't answer. After Alex finished his plate he took it to the counter and left it there. He looked in the drawers in the kitchen and even on top of the refrigerator before he left the room. Mona watched him, wondering what he was looking for now.

She finished her food and took her plate to the counter. She was able to see out the window above the sink and watched a few birds fly past as she rinsed the dishes and wet a cloth down to wash the table. The sun was starting to set behind the apple trees in her yard and the colors of the sky against the red and orange leaves was breathtaking.

It was true, she thought, *everything I needed or wanted did come to me, but at what cost?*

Mr. Vesport was right, there was so much temptation to tell her husband, and she could see he was getting very annoyed. It was so hard to not tell him and coming up with excuses was nearly impossible. Mona walked back to the large round table and began wiping it down. She placed the salt and peppershakers back in the middle of the table and pushed the chairs in before she tossed the cloth back on the counter.

Once again, she felt the pulsing of the choker ever so lightly on her neck and she reached a hand to touch it. A part of her was still so happy just to have the choker, while there was sadness in her heart. This was more like a feeling of guilt, knowing how she must always keep the secret from her husband no matter how much it hurt her or how angry he got.

She turned off the light to the kitchen and proceeded around the corner to the sewing room. She opened a few boxes and placed her patterns and sewing books on the shelf, then returned to set up her sewing machine. The desk was left by the previous owner and was a perfect fit for her needs. She opened another box and pulled out all of her needles, bobbins, and sewing thread. There, in the bottom of the box, were two pairs of scissors. One was a small thread pair, long and slender, curved for cutting close to fabric. The other pair had a short, stubby, straight edge with plastic handles for cutting whatever else.

She pulled out a small blue cup and placed the scissors and a few pens in it.

"Alex, I found the scissors if you still need them," she called out. "I put them in a blue cup on my sewing desk."

"Okay," he said.

Mona walked back into the living room. There were still a few boxes lining the floor. These were mostly little knick-knacks and a few pictures. She was too tired to try putting them away today. She walked through the living room and into the hall to the staircase. The office was on the second floor next to the main bedroom. Mona could hear the boxes being broken down and continued on as Alex unpacked. As she made her way up the stairs, she could feel the choker once again tighten and release, a gentle pulsing around her neck. She kept her hand on the rail as she walked up the stairs.

Mona made her way to the right and could see Alex placing pictures on his desk. Their wedding photo was the first one Mona noticed. Then there were pictures of his parents on the other side. Mona stood quietly in the doorway watching him bend down to pick up his desktop planner. When he realized, he was being watched, he stopped and asked, "Mona can you turn on the light for me? It's getting dark up here."

She did as she was asked before proceeding into the room. As she walked up behind him, she softly placed her arms around him, holding him close. She could feel his warm back against her and he gently rubbed her arms in return. As she felt happy so did the choker, pulsing, but only so that she could feel it.

"Come downstairs with me and watch a movie or let's go for a short walk," Mona suggested.

"I would love to, hon, but I really need to get the office up and running."

Mona released her grip around him and backed up.

"Oh, okay," she said.

As she made her way back toward the door, she turned and looked at her husband who was already back to unpacking. Mona walked down the hall, but the choker started getting tighter as she went. She reached for the choker, but could do nothing to stop the squeeze. Her neck was starting to hurt and she was even having a little trouble breathing. Mona sat down on the stairs, unable to catch her breath or call for help. She didn't understand what was going on. A few seconds later, the choker released its grip and returned to normal.

Mona sat there trying to catch her breath, tears in her eyes as she rubbed her neck and the choker. Her husband, still in the other room, had no clue what had happened or how scared his wife was. She knew she couldn't even tell him what happened, even if he had seen it. She slowly got to her feet, clutching the banister, making her way down the hall to her room. She wished she no longer had the choker on.

I haven't told him or anyone anything, she thought. *I haven't tried to remove it either.*

She walked in and sat down on her bed to look into the mirror. The choker was still. Her heart was pumping fast and her entire body was shaking. For once, the choker did nothing. Mona kicked off her shoes, backed herself further up on the bed, and laid down. She tried to relax, to push what had happened out of her mind. She grabbed the remote for the small TV they kept on her dresser and turned it on. The news was on and Mona turned the volume up just enough to hear it.

Still tired from the move, Mona dozed off rather quickly. Alex, now satisfied with his office, turned out the light and headed downstairs to look for Mona. He didn't see her in the living room. He walked through to the sewing room, but there was no Mona. Alex noticed the plastic handled scissors and placed them in his pocket. *These should be in my office,* he thought.

He made his way back through the living room and turned off the light. He walked down the dimly lit hall to the bedroom to find Mona asleep. The choker was sitting quietly on her neck almost taunting him. Alex tiptoed over to her side of the bed and watched her sleep for a moment.

"That's it," he whispered, "the choker has to go."

He pulled out the scissors and carefully and quietly leaned over the bed.

She'll just think it finally wore out, he said to himself, *and if not, oh well, it has to go.*

He slid one slender smooth blade under the choker and closed the scissors. As soon as he made the cut, Alex watched in horror as his wife's head rolled off to the left and settled on his pillow.

There was only the smallest trickle of blood that came from the choker, rather than his wife's head or neck. He watched as the choker slowly floated to the floor, seeming to mend itself.

***

The choker lay in perfect condition on the floor at his feet; no cut, no tear. He bent down sobbing and picked it up, staring at it in disbelief. He returned his gaze to his wife and was surprised to find, on the pillow next to her head, a single long-stemmed white rose. He bent down to touch her, just as the news ended. Her face was white and milky and she looked like a porcelain doll. Next to her, the white rose began to wilt, and the choker disappeared in a cloud of smoke. Alex sat down on the bed next to Mona, crying as she too began to wilt…and in a cloud of smoke she was gone as well.

Some Houses Have Secrets

It is said that at the bottom of Druid Street it gets cold and stays cold all year round. There is only one house there; it's the only house that will ever be built on that road. The old plantation home had seen better days; the wood, rotten from age and neglect, and the shutters hanging only by their hinges. There are stories passed down from generation to generation about the former owners and what happened in the house and around the property. Tales that only people from town and maybe the towns in either direction from us would know. To anybody else, it was just an urban legend or ghost story and nothing to think twice about.

The old magnolias, the great big oaks, and weeping willows that covered the sprawling land have secrets to tell, but their stories will go unspoken. The vast emptiness and rage of deaths long ago have not forgotten themselves within the walls. They stand by waiting for the day this old house will come to life. They sit waiting for the next set of owners to wake them from their long slumber.

My grandma would wait until my mom was gone and tell me my scary story for the day; stories of what happened in that place. I would come downstairs and sit on the floor at her feet as she spoke. The story always ended the same way, no matter how it started or who was in it, they all died. My favorite tale was always the one about the first owners and their daughter, the only ones who would never leave the house.

In the summer of 1925, the house was built for the Andrews family. They looked like a normal family of the time, yet they were anything but. The small girl they had with them was named Angelica. Her blonde hair, sweet smile, and green eyes were as deceiving as they could be. Behind her eyes was a devil, grandma would say. She bent her parents, and anyone else who came into the house, to her will, and everyone was afraid of her, especially if she got mad. Something changed when she got mad.

Grandma told me the wind would howl and blow nearly bending the trees in half, the sky around that house was always dark, and it looked like it was constantly raining just over that place. The town folk got so they wouldn't farm around the property and the maids would not work for that family or step foot in the house. As the years passed, they saw less and less of the family. It seemed the girl never attended school. No one knew what, if anything, the father did for work. And the mom, well after the first day they moved in, no one ever saw her again.

As Grandma told it, one day the town folk heard horrible screams. These weren't just screams of people, but screams like you couldn't imagine. They carried on the wind she would say. They were screams of unimaginable pain and anguish; and there was something else that seemed to follow them. They were so loud that they were heard all the way into town, over a mile down the road. "I remember it like it was yesterday," Grandma would say.

"The whole town seemed to stop dead in their tracks; we all knew it was coming from that house. Something terrible was happening to that family. The sheriff, Sheriff Waller, was the only one who would respond. He got into his car and headed for the house. We all knew something was wrong and we begged him to leave it be, but he wouldn't. The sky was as dark as night above that house and there was a smell like fireworks all around. The screams continued for over an hour and then there was silence. When Sheriff Waller returned, he was covered in blood, holding a handful of blonde hair, and all he would say was, 'There's no one there.' He just kept repeating it over and over. We stood there in the town square just looking at him covered in blood, there were tears in his eyes, and he stood there for what was the longest few minutes I have ever felt.

"When he did speak again, it was between sobs, as he clutched the handful of hair for dear life.

"When I got there, the screams were louder than ever....dreadful sounds were coming from that house. I called out for them to open the door; I even tried to knock it down," he sobbed.

"His face was twisted and he looked as though he wouldn't be able to stand much longer. He leaned against his car, his eyes blank as a slate. 'The girl,' he said. He was now holding up the clump of matted hair. 'She wasn't a girl. I don't know what she was, a demon, the devil himself, but she was no little girl,' he told us.

"I remember I stood there, just a child myself, but I couldn't take my eyes off of him. I had to hear more, I had to know more, this was something that had never happened before. I had never seen so much blood on a person in my life, and the smell; I can still remember he smelled like iron or the way a penny smelled. My dad, who was there with me, was trying to place his hands over my ears, he even pushed me behind him, but I twisted myself around. No way was I going to miss his story. The next thing I knew, Sherriff Waller was mumbling something about the trees.

"'They're the trees,' he mumbled. That was the last thing he said about that house, according to grandma.

"No one in town ever wanted to go see that house. Maybe a few kids or teens over the years had tried to do the old truth or dare thing, but every time someone thought about buying that old house, things always started to happen. The noises would start up again, even though no one supposedly lived there. The sky, a permanent shade of grey, would get darker and the sulfur smell in the air would carry through the entire town. The old saying, 'If these walls could talk...' comes to mind. Old houses have secrets. Grandma said she always wondered what he meant by, 'They're the trees.' I know he was in shock or something, but I always wanted to know what that meant.

"One day, I found out for myself," she said. "I will tell you

60

about that when you're older." I waited for years, begging her over and over again to tell me.

"I'm bigger today," I would say.

"Yes, you are and you will get bigger every day, but I will know when the right time is," Grandma would reply. Her big blue eyes shined brightly from behind her glasses as she sat in her favorite easy chair, the story-telling chair, brushing her long white hair. She would sit and brush for hours as she spoke. She always had a dish full of mints and butterscotch and would hand me a piece of candy to suck on while she told me the stories.

She would always ask, "Are you comfortable, have you gone potty, gotten your drink?" I would always answer yes, so she would get right to the story. But this time it was different, Grandma didn't ask her usual pre-story questions, she didn't sit brushing her hair as she told me this story, and her face looked frightened as she spoke. I knew when I heard her voice so shaky that there was something wrong, something she had been holding in all these years, something very scary.

Grandma began, "The summer that year had been a particularly hot one, everywhere except for that house, of course. It was so hot that we had been going down to the end of Druid Street just to be in a semi-cool spot. None of us dared go down the street any further than the end because of all the stories that had been passed around, but that's not to say we didn't stand around betting each other to go just a little further up that road."

I saw a little smile come across her face as she remembered that part, but after that her face was once again straight as an arrow.

"The three of us: my friend Stacey, her sister Angie, and I, would sit there for hours talking as girls do and staring at that house. That summer the clouds seem to move in, all focusing on that house. Then we heard it. Howls and screams from nowhere. To this day, I don't know whatever got into us, but we ran up that street to the bottom of the drive and stopped. The screams were horrible. We opened the cattle gate slowly and started to walk down the dirt drive. The wind picked up almost immediately. The sounds seem to encircle us…it seemed to know we were there."

"The closer we got to the house, the wilder the wind got, slamming the gate shut behind us. We walked through the yard, slightly away from the drive, trying to see in the windows. The trees, all of them, seemed to be crying. The screams were literally coming from the trees."

I looked at grandma, I almost wanted to laugh, but the look on her face told me I better not.

"Stacey and I walked a little closer to the first tree, a weeping willow. It was bent over and the branches were nearly touching the ground. The noises stopped as soon as Stacey touched a root that was sticking up. There wasn't as much as a bird near that property, not even a crow.

"There were no curtains on the windows and we could see handprints on the windows in blood. They were small handprints, that of a child just tall enough to see over the window ledge. We walked slowly up to the front steps, looking behind us, to the sides of us, and pretty much everywhere we could. We were terrified. We could not stop ourselves from going now that we were there. The steps creaked and moaned under us. As we held hands, each little noise made us jump and we were covered in goose bumps, not just from the chill, but from fear.

"The paint on the porch had completely faded away over time, but the blood stains and foot prints were still there and still as bright as could be. The sulfur smell mixed with the coppery smell of all the dried blood was sickening, but we crept closer to the door. It was open just a crack, but it was enough to get a small glimpse inside. The blood trail was all over the living room. We pushed open the door and saw that blood covered the walls and that the ceiling fan was still spinning after all that time. The door closed as soon as we were all inside. As we turned back to the door, we saw that the blood was gone. There were no stains, not on the window, not on the floor. The blood was gone. You could still smell it, though. The trees were all bending and swaying and the wind was once again howling. We walked further into the house, taking in all that we could. The old wallpaper was still clinging in a few spots and the ceiling had started to peel from blood that was still there, but was somehow hiding. We walked over to the old staircase and looked up, the little girl's handprints and finger marks were still on the banister all the way up, and bits of hair clung to the rails.

"We looked at one another, each of us thinking the same thing, but no one wanting to say it aloud. We walked one behind the other up the stairs, listening for any sounds. The faintest sound of footsteps running across the upstairs floors filled our ears and we could almost see her clear as I see you. Her blond hair was in two braids and she wore a blood-covered dress with little blue flowers all over it. Blood streaked her arms and legs, yet she still smiled and giggled as if nothing were wrong. As fast as she appeared, she vanished when we got to the second floor.

"As we slowly walked down the hall, it was as if we were stepping into another world. The second floor, though covered in dried blood, was seemingly untouched. There were pictures of the family still on the walls and the mirrors and candleholders sat in place on tables. The pale yellow wallpaper still hung on the walls as nice as the day it was put on. We continued down the hall to the first door, the bathroom. We saw bloody handprints on the white porcelain sink and tiny footprints on the tile floor. The freestanding tub was full of red-stained water. In the middle of the floor lay a pair of scissors; the blades open just slightly, blood covering every inch of them.

"We didn't want to touch anything, but we had to keep looking around. We left the bathroom and continued to the left. As soon as we reached the hallway, the bathroom door slammed shut and the water began to run. We tried to open the door, but it was locked from the inside and we could hear the little girl laughing from behind the door. As she held the handle to the door, blood started to run from the keyhole, causing us to jump back and nearly fall over the edge of the banister.

"Blood flowed in a small stream down the door, hitting the floor and making a path. It flowed freely down the hall as if beckoning us to follow it. We did. The blood stopped in front of a room, which had clearly been the parent's room. On the large four poster bed lay a blue and yellow blanket, matted and twisted, and sagging to the floor. Family pictures hung above the bed and in the open closet hung long dresses and suits. As we walked further into the room, the ceiling fan turned on. Out of the corner of my eye, I saw her once again. I turned just a little bit to check if what I was seeing was true and there she was. She was smiling and pointing at the bedroom door. I asked my friends if they saw her, they said they only saw our reflections in the mirror, nothing else was there. I knew what I saw. I saw that child.

"For some reason, I knew I just had to follow where she was pointing. I was not really as scared as I was when I first got there, but knew I was there to see what she wanted me to see. I led all of us out of the room and down the hall, following the blood to a closet door with a lock on it. I reached out my hand to open the door and before I could touch it, it swung open. What I saw made me want to cry. There on the shelves were scalpels, knives, needles of different sizes, and containers for collecting blood.Some were still full; sealed and marked with dates in black ink. Hanging from the ceiling was a single light bulb and from the walls hung tubes like IVs and ropes. There was a mattress on the floor, stained with blood and clumps of hair, all colors.

"We all clutched hands and the door slammed shut by itself. The blood stream started to move again and the girl appeared in front of me. She still smiled, but she looked sad somehow. I followed her down the hall to the next room. It could have been a guest room or torture chamber, take your pick. There was a bed still made and hanging from the posts were straps or cloth, white and yellow from age. On the floor, at the foot of the bed, was a large copper pot starting to tarnish and turn green. I remember looking into the pot and finding it was empty. I remember actually thinking thank you for it being empty.

"The walls were blood free, but you could see scratch marks in the paper and small hand prints, just dirty ones. Over on the far wall by the window, which was boarded up, was a crib. There were old stuffed animals and toys in the crib, but no room was left for a child or baby. I didn't think it had been used in a while. The closet in that room was crammed full of the same kinds of stuff we had found in the hallway closet. I was beginning to see this house was used for terrible things, what happened inside those walls must have been horrible.

"We walked out of that room, more curious to find out what had happened to these people than before. As we reached the doorway and started to make our way to the little girl's room, screams came out of thin air. We could hear hundreds of voices screaming all at once. There were howls of what sounded like animals, too. These were horrible sounds, the same as we heard that day in town, only now we were right there. The walls seemed to move and we could hear pounding as if someone was trying to get out, trying to get away. We stood there hoping the noises would stop, but they just kept going.

"The longer we stood there, the louder the screams seemed to get. The girl had appeared to us again and we began to follow her once more. The girl pointed to another hall with a downward staircase and what looked to be a dead end. The wall had been put up years ago, to hide the fact that there was a room there at all. You could push on the wall and it would swing open sort of like a rotating door at the mall. There were shelves with toys and doll houses, beautiful dresses hung in the open wardrobe, and a large mirror with painted flowers bordering the wood frame set the scene for what looked like a loved child.

"There were chains on the real door, which was still there, and locks…large ones. As we walked into the room, we could really get a look. There were huge gouges, like claw marks, raking down the walls and onto the floor. There was a small window that looked out onto the trees in the front yard, which seemed to be bending toward that very room, as if trying to get in. The branches scraped and scratched at the side of the house and the windowpane. All three of us walked into the room a little further, concentrating on the gouge marks, and whispering to one another, trying to think of what could have made them. The image of the girl appeared again, this time all of us could see her standing on a small box looking out at the trees, terrified.

"Her pale skin was almost glowing in the dim light as the noises started up once more. The little girl turned around, nearly falling off her little box, as she ran over and jumped on her bed. We could hear her sobbing, weeping from under her floral covers. The ceiling above her room seemed to shake and rumble and the pounding on the walls was louder than before. Tiny pieces of the ceiling fell on the floor, but landed without making a sound and disappeared as quickly as they had fallen. The room began to get dark. As we looked over to the window, the ground seemed to move, covering the window and then settling back down like waves in the ocean.

"We heard stomping on the floors and the blood stream that had led us to this room began receding out and back up the stairs. We stood there watching in complete disbelief. As we turned around to walk out of the room, the little girl on the bed let out a roar, a scream like no other. Blood flew in every direction and she began pulling out handfuls of hair, scalp still attached to a few pieces.

There seemed to be no one else in there with her as she destroyed herself.

"We ran out of the room trying to follow the blood as it retreated faster and faster. The entire house was dark as night and it seemed the grey clouds had once again turned black, as the windows were looking out into darkness. As we ran past the bedroom toward the bathroom, the door was now open and we could hear the tub draining. The blood receded to the bathroom where it first came from and back into the tub. We stopped at the doorway and watched without entering.

"We stood there for what felt like an eternity, just watching from the door as everything changed back to the way it was when we first saw the bathroom. We turned around and began walking back toward the staircase that led to the living room. The bloody banisters were still there and the living room was once again covered in blood, just as it was when we first walked in the house. We headed downstairs and I remember feeling chills go up and down my back. The temperature in the house seemed to have dropped drastically.

"As we got to the bottom of the stairs, the kitchen caught our eye and we made our way past the windows, where some light still came in. Large pools of blood shone in what little light there was. This was darkness like no other, where normally there would be stars in the sky or the moon, there were none of these when you looked out the window. There was nothing but darker outlines of the trees.

"We crept along slowly with our hands on the wall, feeling our way around the room. The windows were starting to lighten up a little as we got to the kitchen doorway. The old stove still sat there with food left in the pans from the last meal that was cooked in them. The wood floors had a noticeable pathway worn down from walking and the plates were broken and littered the ground and counter tops.

"The fridge still had pictures, colored by that little girl, hanging from it and an apron lay dangling from the counter. The table was still set as if they were going to walk in and have dinner that night. We walked around looking at the kitchen that, with the exception of the broken dishes, was seemingly untouched. Stopping in the middle of the kitchen we could see out the windows into the back yard. A swing hung from a branch on the largest magnolia tree, moving back and forth. The tree was perfectly still, except for that one branch that swayed on its own. A small pond sat nearly dried up in the middle of the yard and what would have been a set of rose bushes stood dead and black.

"We walked closer to the window and peered out, leaning to see the other side of the yard. After all these years, clothes and a sheet still hung on the lines, rusted with age, and a basket, still full, lay on the ground in front of it. There was a sand box that looked as though it had been over grown with weeds and grass a long time ago. I thought that none of this made any sense at all. I took a step back, while my companions continued to look out the window. There was something about the trees that demanded their attention. I looked over at the fridge and noticed, next to the picture of the tree and swing, a note that I hadn't seen before.

"I walked up to the fridge and took the note down. It was written in crayon and barely legible. It said, 'I know you are still here, but it's not the same. You can't come in and I have to die to get out.'

"I placed the note back on the fridge as my friends walked up. I looked at them and told them what the little note said. I turned around, looked out the window one more time, and I just knew I needed to get out of there, I needed to be in the yard.

"My friends pretty much just followed me wherever I went that day. I think it was because they knew how much I wanted to know about what had happened all those years ago. They never really asked questions while in the house and stayed by my side. To tell you the truth, by the time I had decided to go out back, I couldn't have cared less if they were there or not. That was the only house I had ever been in that didn't have a back door. I never thought about that until just now.

"I started heading back toward the living room to the front door. It was so quiet in there I could hear the floor creaking. The pools of blood were now dried to just stains on the floors and walls. Her handprints were there on the glass. Only this time I knew in my head why they were there, why only two handprints were on those windows. Her short note on the fridge explained that part. She was there looking out. As I got to the door and grabbed the handle, I realized the door was locked. I tried to turn the knob, but it would not move. I tried to twist the lock, but nothing would happen.

"Then she was there again, standing by the window crying, her sobs growing louder and turning into howls. The trees were once again bending and swaying, but there was no wind. I pulled on the door harder and tried turning the knob again, but it wouldn't budge. I was starting to get scared and I know Stacy and Angie were too. We huddled close together for a minute, just watching her stand at the window staring and sobbing. Then I saw it, just for a second as she placed her small hands on the window, she was holding a huge clump of her hair.

"It took me a second to think back, but I remembered the pair of scissors we saw on the bathroom floor upstairs when we first went up there. She was just standing there for the longest time with a lock of hair, the trees were really going crazy by now, and the weeping willow was dropping leaves and white puffs of seeds making it almost look like it was snowing. She turned toward us and we all jumped. It was as if she was staring right at us. She reached up and took another handful of hair and then I saw the gashes on her arms.

"It wasn't just her hair she had cut in that bathroom. I also knew why the tub was full of bloody water and why her arms and legs were covered in blood as well. The words from her note kept replaying in my mind over and over again. Her tiny handprints had been made on the window after she cut herself. She turned her gaze back out the window and I heard the door unlock. I ran over to it, opened it as quickly as I could, and ushered my friends onto the porch. I left the door open as I went to join them.

"We looked at the window, but other than the bloody handprints, dried up and rust-colored, we could not see the girl. We could hear her; I am sure the entire town could hear her. I started to walk down the steps to the yard and out toward the back of the house where I had seen the swing. I could hear the willow tree once again, softly moaning and even more noise was coming from the large magnolia holding that swing. Stacey and Angie followed me closely. As we rounded the corner, we could see the swing careening madly back and forth. The branch was creaking and groaning and petals and leaves were falling to the ground.

"The rose bushes we saw from the window were not dead after all. Like everything else here, they were locked between then and now. There were roses on the bushes; they were black, but not dead. I walked closer to the magnolia tree and grabbed the swing. It felt heavy, as if someone was sitting on it, even though I didn't see anyone. I stared at the tree closely, knowing there was something special about the trees ever since Sheriff Waller came back that day.

"'Stacey, come hold the swing for a second,' I told her. She did as she was asked, while Angie stayed back a few steps. I had seen a glimpse of a face, just a glimpse, and then it was gone in a flash. I saw the man who was in the family portrait in the house. I saw her dad. I jumped back, asking Stacey and Angie if they had seen what I saw. To be honest, I was relieved to find that they too, had seen it. Stacey let go of the swing. I turned, and together, we started walking back toward the driveway in the front of the house.

"We had all of our questions answered. We knew no one would

believe us, so we said we wouldn't share our experience with anyone else. We never did go back to that house or to the end of Druid Street again. As we got to the front yard, I looked at the weeping willow and saw a face in that tree, just for a second. It was then that I knew why no one had seen the mom since right after they moved in. I don't know why, but I had the urge to look back. As I did, I saw the little girl sitting on the swing while it rocked back and forth."

"But Grandma, how did her parents get turned into trees?" I asked.

She replied, "I don't know. I guess some houses just have secrets."

Bugs

"Oh, my God, Jane! Where are you? I can't see you. Jane! Answer me!"

"Adam, I'm in the bedroom doorway. What's happening? There aren't no earthquakes in Oklahoma!" she screamed.

"I don't know. Hold on. Stay where you are. I'm coming."

The small, two-bedroom ranch house shook violently. The windows cracked and showered glass into the house. The lights flashed on and off for a moment, then total darkness flooded in, replacing the noon light. Adam scrambled to find Jane in the darkness. He stumbled over furniture and crawled to find the doorways that he knew were somewhere in dark rooms before him. He could hear Jane sniffling from the bedroom down the hallway and tried to use the sound of her cries to find her.

"Jane, are you alright?"

"I think so. I just wish I knew what was going on. Why is it so dark? Is it a twister?" she asked.

"I've been in many twisters living here, but this was no twister. I don't know what it was, or what's going on. But I know we need to get out of the house and find a safe place to go," he told her.

Adam reached the doorway, feeling Jane sitting just inside it. Her outstretched hands were braced across the doorway. He felt her hands; she was trembling so hard he could feel it in his spine.

"I got you, Jane. Do you still have the flashlight in the top drawer of the dresser?"

"Yes. I haven't used it since the last time the breaker blew in the basement. The batteries should be okay."

"Okay. Stay here. I'm going to go get it and see if we can get out of here."

Jane removed her arms from the doorway and pulled her knees to her chest. She was still scared, but somehow knowing Adam was right there made her feel better. She wasn't alone in the darkness. She listened hard, hearing Adam push things out of his way as he crawled to where he thought the dresser should have been.

"Alright, I found the dresser. It's still standing, but the drawers are all out of it."

He began fumbling around, tossing clothes and items from the top of the dresser aside.

"I think I found it."

He flipped the button on the flashlight and illuminated a small part of the ceiling and his face. Jane turned around to find the ceiling was full of cracks. The ceiling fan was dangling dangerously above them by the wires. Adam crawled back over to her and shone the light down the hallway. There was broken glass from their pictures scattered and poking up from the carpet.

"Come on, Jane. We have to get going."

He stood up and held out a hand for Jane. He pulled her to her feet and led the way down the hall.

"Adam, shhh, do you hear that?"

"Hear what?"

"Listen, it's like scratching sounds all over the place."

Adam stood still for a moment, shining the flashlight on the walls and ceiling and back down to the glass covered floor. The ceiling seemed to be raining down in little flakes and the cracks on the walls were slowly spreading like a spider's web.

"Maybe the ceiling and walls starting to come down around us is what you're hearing. We have to move quickly," he told her.

He grabbed her hand and began to pull her quickly down the

hall to the living room. The furniture lay tipped over in the middle of the room. The windows were gone, yet it was completely dark. He pushed the end table out of the way and led Jane into the room. He shone the flashlight at the windows and realized that they were looking at earth. There was no yard, no trees, and no sky. They were looking at dirt, as if a wall of earth had been built around their home.

"Oh, my God, what is that?" Jane whispered.

Jane pointed to the floor under the broken window. There was movement. The entire wall under the window seemed to be moving like a wave, getting closer to the floor. The noise was growing from a soft scratching sound to a rumble and humming noise as the wave grew.

Adam shone the light on the wave and tried to see what it was. The walls cracked more and chunks began hitting the floor around them. The door was just beyond the couch, but there was something scraping against it from the other side. Adam grabbed Jane and pushed her behind him. He walked slowly, a few steps at a time, closer to the couch, trying to peer over it to the floor.

As he rounded the side of the couch the ceiling, by the picture window, collapsed in the corner. The corner of the room began filling up as the humming got louder and louder. There was some light piercing the darkness from the corner and the eerie red hue called to them.

Jane's scream startled him as he shined his light down on her feet. Thousands of worms and centipedes were trying to make their way up her legs, covering her feet. She jumped up and down trying to shake them off of her, brushing the ones off that made it to her waist and stomach. Adam held the flashlight tight, trying to help her brush them off, but for every one they dislodged, there were hundreds more climbing on. The room was filling quickly and bugs began pouring in from the cracks in the walls and ceiling.

"We have to move, the ceiling is caving in. The attic must be full of them," he said.

"Okay, get me out of here!" Jane yelled.

Jane cried and tried to keep them from crawling over her chest, arms, and face. She could feel them dropping from the ceiling onto her hair. She brushed her shoulders and flipped her hair around, but that only tangled them in more. Adam walked through the swarm of bugs and worms that were filling the room. He grabbed the doorknob and pulled the front door open. A wall of centipedes flooded in, covering him like a wave in the ocean.

Adam was thrown back to the ground and covered in bugs. Jane screamed and rushed to help him stand up. The living room was slightly brighter, with the small red hue flowing in from the open door and holes in the ceiling. They waded through the sea of creepy crawlers, feeling pinchers and stingers penetrate their clothes, and spiny legs cling to their skin.

They made it out the door to find themselves in a world of bugs and worms. Their house was all but swallowed by them. The sky was red and orange; the sun was shadowed by a swarm of locusts and large dragonflies filling the air around them. They staggered out, slipping on the ground, and peered out into nothingness.

"Adam, where's the other houses? Where are the streets and cars? Where's anything?" Jane asked.

"I don't know. Come on, let's keep moving. We need to find some shelter or see if we can find other people."

Adam took her hand and they started to slowly make their way away from the house. They brushed centipedes off of each other every couple of steps, trying to keep from getting bit on the face and neck. The buzzing in their ears from the locusts was almost deafening. The wind from the dragonflies overhead only seemed to aggravate the centipedes trying to ascend their bodies. There was a rancid smell making Jane nauseous, but she knew she had to keep going.

She looked back at their little ranch house just as it started collapsing in on itself, disappearing under a sea of bugs.

"Jane, look. Isn't that the mimosa tree from the middle of the front rock garden?"

"I think it is. There are still flowers on it and it's in the right place, but where are the rocks? For that matter, where's the neighbor's house?"

The closer they moved toward the tree, the deeper the bugs around them got. They were covering every landmark and suffocating everything around them. Adam leaned forward, trying to help propel himself through the slimy mass of legs and pinchers, making a small path for Jane to follow closely behind. He reached the tree and grabbed for the slim trunk. Jane reached out and grabbed the trunk next to his hand and proceeded to climb up just a few feet. She hoped to see something, some sign of humanity, some sign that they were not alone, and that they were not crazy. As she looked, heartbreak ran through her like electricity.

Just beyond the little tree they were on was a cave. Bugs and worms were emerging in droves from it, but there was nothing else. There were no houses, no streets, and no people. It was as if the world got rid of everything except the two of them and the bugs.

"Adam, there's nothing except a cave. Maybe we should try to go through it. Maybe we can get away from here."

Jane jumped back down into the pool of bugs, now waist deep, that were trying to follow the warmth of her skin. She placed her hand on Adam's shoulder and started pushing him around the front of the tree and down the hill. Covered in slime from worms and bug parts, they slipped and slid down toward the cave.

The walk to the cave felt like miles, when it was only a few yards. They were sticky and drenched in goo. Jane and Adam made it to the opening of the cave and tried to peer in. Squeaks and scratches along the sides and bottom of the cave, along with a foul odor, made Jane stop and think twice about going in, *but what choice do we have*, she wondered.

Adam shone the flashlight into the mouth of the cave, but all he could see were more and more bugs. He pushed his way in and started to slowly walk through the mass of critters scurrying to get out and invade the open landscape, which he and Jane were desperate to get away from. Jane held her hands to her face, peeking through her fingers as she walked.

"There are just so many of them. Where are they all coming from?" Jane asked.

"I don't know. Jane, look, I didn't want to get into this with you, but I think I have to now. Centipedes are venomous. They may not do much to a person with just a few bites, but a lot of bites are deadly. I can't say how many stings we have gotten, but if it's anything like bees, they can smell when some have bitten us and send more to fight. I haven't been feeling well, and to be honest, I feel sort of numb on my skin. I think that's a symptom of their venom. We need to find a place to go. There has to be something. I mean the entire world couldn't just go away. There has to be people or a town or something. I wonder if our house fell into a sinkhole or something. It makes as much sense as any other possibility," he said.

"Well I guess, like you said, anything is possible, including that. I mean we did feel the house shaking and we are going into a cave that was supposed to be on our property that we never saw before. We are wading through bugs and worms and let me say, my phobia of bugs; well, I think we are way past that now," she replied.

"I bet," Adam continued. "I forgot your fear of bugs. You definitely faced that fear head-on."

They walked a little further, their legs started to feel heavy under the weight of their soaked, bug-laden clothes. Their arms were starting to feel a bit numb and were getting hard to lift. Even the flashlight was getting heavy in Adam's hand.

"Jane, look, there's light up ahead, it looks like daylight."

They pushed through faster, not bothering to try to brush away the bugs. The closer they got to the light, the more bugs began to drop from the ceiling of the cave. Adams lips were starting to go numb and his eyesight was getting blurry. Jane followed behind as quickly as she could, but she was having trouble with her eyesight, too.

Adam reached the end of the cave and looked out into the light, the heat was intense. He stumbled out of the cave and landed on the green grass below. Jane rushed out after him. She was so happy to be out of the cave and see real sun that she hadn't thought about the heat. She lay next to Adam on the ground, hoping to rest for a moment, so maybe the venom would start to wear off.

She began to fall asleep. Adam rolled over and grabbed Jane's hand. He was sweating profusely; his eyes could no longer see anything except the light. He was breathing, but his chest felt heavy, as if someone was sitting on him. He tried to take his shirt off, but the shirt was stiff. It would not bend or move and his pants were becoming solid. He blinked his eyes and tried to squint. He managed to roll over onto his belly; he could just make out the outline of Jane next to him.

"Jane," he said.

He knew what he wanted to say, what he was hearing himself say, but that's not what was coming out of his mouth. He reached over and touched Jane's shirt. Her chest felt stiff and cold. His eyes cleared and he was able to see. The grass was green, but it was steaming and turning yellow in the distance.

"Jane, we have to move, something isn't right here," he said

He touched her face, but she didn't move. He pulled her face over toward him. There were two antennae protruding from her scalp. The yellow patch was getting larger and a new wave of bugs was rushing toward them. He covered Jane's body with his and placed his hands over her face. Centipedes and cockroaches came swarming over them now. He could hear their screams, as if they were in pain, as if they were saying run.

He could feel them all over his body, pushing against him as they swept over them. He felt a bump and placed his hand over his ears. The sound of all the bugs was like a tornado. Their prickly legs were tearing into his face and arms as they scratched their way past him to reach the cave. As quickly as the wave started, it was over. Adam looked up to see the yellow path almost directly in front of him. All that remained was the foul odor and a mist almost like fog rolling closer.

For a moment, he had almost forgotten about Jane. He looked down and she was gone. He tried to stand, but his legs were stiff. He pushed himself back and saw a cockroach beneath him. The cockroach was lying on its back. He wanted to get up. He wanted to get away, stand up, and stomp on it. He could hear something, his name. It was Jane's voice, so faint, calling for him. He looked around trying to make her out in the distance. *Did she get swept under me?* he thought. *Was she dragged back in the cave?*

"Jane! Where are you?"

He waited, listening as hard as he could. He held his breath, hoping she would call out for him again.

"Adam! I'm right here."

He heard her again, he knew he had, but it was so faint. She was so far away. He wondered how she could be so far away.

"Adam, here I am."

He tried to push himself to his feet. His arms were stiff and turning brown. He looked down at his hands and they were turning brown and scaly. His fingers were stiff and hairy and were starting to stick together, becoming one appendage. He heard her voice again, he looked down at the cockroach that still had not made an attempt to run off. *Something about this roach was weird,* he thought. He looked at it closer and saw Jane's face.

"Jane?" he said.

The cockroach smiled, rolled over, and scurried off toward the cave. Adam looked down at his hands and arms once more. He waited there, unable to go anyplace else, unable to follow or find his wife. The fog rolled over him and the unmistakable smell of bug spray drifted into his nose. The oily feel of the mist made his body heat up and he was hardly able to breathe. He looked up through the mist and saw the shadow of a large hand holding a huge can of spray.

He screamed out, "No, please, wait! I'm human. I'm alive. Please stop, you're killing us! Please, what did we do?"

There was no answer, only more spray. He tried one more time to get up one more time. His shirt was gone and so were his pants. He tried to turn around and head for the cave, but a large foot came down and trampled it, just as he had done before to many anthills.

He ran toward the yellow grass as fast as a he could, but the spray came raining down on him again. Adam choked and gasped for air, his eyes and chest burning. He wanted to die. He rolled over on his back and stared up at the shadowy figure holding the can of spray. The figure leaned closer and he could see her face.

"Jane?" he gasped.

"Adam, wake up."

He opened his eyes to see Jane leaning over him, her face as white and soft as ever. Her long dark hair was dangling over his face and tickling his nose.

"Whatever you were dreaming about must have been pretty

bad. You were screaming my name and coughing. Are you okay?" she asked.

"I'm fine. It was a strange dream. Do we still have that exterminator coming out to tent the house next week?"

"Yes, on Monday," she replied

"Okay. Well on second thought, it was only one cockroach we saw and a few centipedes in the yard. I think we can cancel the exterminator. You know we just don't need to spend the money on that for a whole three bugs," he said.

"Sure, if that's what you want. I will call them tomorrow."

Adam rolled over and noticed a large cockroach sitting on the windowsill. The moonlight flooded in, allowing him to see the cockroach clearly. It wiggled its antenna and scurried away. Adam smiled and rolled over, draping his arm over Jane.

Broken Silence

Laurel stared blankly at a picture hanging on her mirror. A young, beautiful brunette stared off into the distance. The sun in the background illuminated the trees behind her and her smile shone like the sun itself. She flipped the mirror over to the magnifying side and pulled out her pancake base cover-up. She began dabbing it heavily under her eyes and around her cheeks, blending it as carefully as she could.

Next was the mineral veil foundation and then eyeliner. The deep black line around her piercing blue eyes, with the added shimmer from the foundation, made her look tired. But she was as ready as she would-be. She grabbed her blush, brushing a quick streak of pink across her upper cheekbones, hoping she could fake a slightly sun-kissed look. *I just had to get through this night and it will all be over,* she thought.

Her performance tonight was everything. She couldn't let on that anything was wrong or unusual. She must not let on the surprise ending or it would all be ruined, and she would never have this chance again. Every bone in her body was shaking and fear was washing over her. She blotted cover-up around her lips and slathered on a heavy layer of bright red lip stain to last the night.

Laurel got up from her black vanity and walked silently to the bed. Her husband was already downstairs welcoming the guests and awaiting her perfectly timed entrance. She was to be the last to arrive, with a graceful glide down the master staircase. All eyes would be on Laurel and, once again, she had to play the beautiful adored wife of Mr. Challender, the mayor of Harlow, Texas.

More like the leader of a small cult, she thought.

She donned her cherry-red sleeveless, backless dress and slipped into her red heels. Laurel walked back to her vanity and pulled the hot rollers out of her hair. A few grays appeared, but nothing a bit of Clairol wouldn't fix, and certainly not enough for the fifty or so guests to notice. Laurel ran a brush through her hair and fluffed up her large waves. She was a stunning woman, but at only thirty-five, she looked much too old for her age.

The years have begun to take a toll on her and she was feeling weak. Not weak from her age, but for her life as it was. She looked in the mirror, listening as the chatter picked up downstairs as more guests arrived. The caterers dropped off the food just over an hour ago, and the wine was calmly sitting at room temperature. Surely, Marko would indulge in his glass of wine as soon as the time was ready and then use his flask to hide the fire whiskey he would spike his own drink with the rest of the night.

This night would mark fifteen years of these parties that Laurel has attended. Each one she hated more than the year before. Each party where she was an outsider, forced to look inside a world she desperately didn't want to be a part of anymore. She didn't belong here. She had no friends here. These were Marko's people, after all. These were police officers, doctors, and politicians, all people on his side, to do his bidding. Laurel was just a trophy to sit and talk about. Marko would point to her while holding a lukewarm glass of wine, she always thought tasted like alligator piss, and toast her. But all the while, it was just Marko's way to make sure she spoke to no one unless spoken to, and that she played the perfect little wife. He would slip her a drug that would make her walk and smile, but pretty much do nothing else without his guidance.

She knew this was being done every year. But not this time. This time, Laurel needed a clear head to pull this off. She needed to be able to speak and understand and have her own range of movements. This year she had to be ready. When Marko made his usual announcement that she was tired and retreating for the night, she had to make her move.

She looked down at her shoulders and arms, they needed something. There were too many spots to try to cover up. *There was no way I can get it all,* she thought. She quickly went over to the closet and walked in, flipping on the light switch on the wall. She peered over at the gloves in the glass cabinet, pulled out her black velvet long-sleeved gloves, and wriggled them on. They fit snuggly and went up to the middle of her upper arm. They covered everything she needed covered.

Laurel turned off the light and walked out of the closet, shutting the door behind her. The full-length mirror allowed her to admire her appearance from all angles and make sure her every hair was in place. She practiced her smiles and head nods. Her approach and her manner of speaking had to be perfect. Everything was contingent on her performance tonight. She had to be on the ball, fooling the guests and her own husband also.

She was as satisfied as she was going to be with her appearance and walked past the bed, tiptoeing the entire way, so as to not let Marko know she was finished yet. She looked down at her chocolate brown comforter and shams, feeling the silky ruffle of the edge. Leaving everything behind was going to be hard.

She pulled the chain on her bedside lamp and peered out the Egyptian blinds at the courtyard below. The lights along the cobblestone-walking path to the house looked inviting and peaceful. They led up to and around a stone fountain encompassing a statue with the likeness of the beauty she once was. Anger welled up inside her. Years of being alone and lonely within a home she never felt was hers, but with no privacy, had made her all but a shell of her former self. A husband who seemed to adore her beauty, yet appeared to be hell-bent on making sure it dwindled with her, as her whole sense of self vanished. *Anything had to be better than this,* she thought.

Laurel watched a few more guests walk slowly up the path arm in arm. They smiled and laughed and seemed so happy. She wondered if they had a few drinks in the limo before they pulled up. *Speaking of,* she thought, *I could use a shot just to calm my*

84

nerves. She bent down and opened the drawer to her nightstand. She pushed her diaphragm and her reading glasses aside and grabbed a small bottle of vodka she saved from their last business trip to Japan. The mayor wanted to gain cheap computer recycling deals with an overseas market. He failed miserably. The very thought of his embarrassment made her smile. He would not remove his shoes, refused to bow, and when he finally did bow, it was too deep and was looked at as insulting. The small smile turned into a full grin as she quietly twisted the tiny silver lid off the square bottle. She hated the taste of vodka, any brand, but over the years she had developed a taste for pretty much anything that got her through. She didn't dare touch her husband's prized scotch or his whisky. The wine was only allowed at dinner and special occasions and she was only allowed one glass.

Marko wanted control over nearly every aspect of his life and hers. The routine was strict and in place all the time. He decided when they ate dinner, if they ate out or in, and even when she took showers. Most women would love it if their husbands ran baths for them, poured wonderful smelling bubble bath in the tub, or even sat on the commode to talk while they bathed. But not when this was done purely to maintain control and a sense of fear, too.

It was nice years ago, the relationship seemed picture perfect, and in fact it was. That's the only time it was perfect, inside pictures. Behind closed doors it was as prisoner and warden as it could be. She went shopping only when he was by her side. She was not allowed access to a computer and correspondence with her family had to be in writing and on the phone, where she was forced to lie and say it was for security measures. In a way it was, basically for her security. Her every word was listened to and she was allowed cell phone calls from numbers he would program into her phone, that were also tracked by GPS.

Any letters that came in she was allowed to read, but anything she wrote back had to be read first before it was mailed. She was never to open any mail or notes addressed to him. He tried to tell her it was to keep her safe, if she didn't know secret information no one could ever come after her expecting her to know it. *This could be true to some extent,* she thought, *but not to the extent that he played at it.* Being the mayor of a small Texas town was not at all dangerous, like being a secret spy or government agent.

Laurel had become quite knowledgeable over the years about her husband's practices and routines; who he spoke to daily, who he made plans with, when he was to leave or come back, and what drugs came into the house and when. His salary as a mayor was nowhere near enough to keep them living the lavish lifestyle in the mansion with all his precious cars and marble statues. He had been part of a major drug cartel for years that included child slavery and many other underground atrocities she didn't even want to think about, and she wasn't supposed to know about.

The cobblestone walkway was a cover for a tunnel he had dug many years ago. The tunnel led out into the woods beyond the property line and out through an old mine shaft. He used the tunnel to cart drugs in and out of the wine cellar, but also to traffic people. She was never allowed to go in there and Marko made it very clear what would happen if she did. This tunnel could be her only chance to escape. If she could get to it, a friend from her childhood days had hidden money she had been mailing as Christmas gifts, every year since the year after she got married.

This was the only one of her friends who was allowed to visit anytime and was trusted by Marko. Cally had been Laurel's friend since she was in kindergarten. She was the only friend who knew anything about what her life was like when the curtains were closed and the doors were locked. Cally had been trying to convince Laurel to leave since the second year of the marriage. She came to visit unannounced and noticed Laurel trying to cover up a face and chest full of bruises. Laurel told her friend she had walked down into the cellar and seen Marko with the chief of police and a few other people, they were bringing people who were bound and gagged into the cellar, and milk crates filled with bricks of cocaine. When she gasped, Marko pointed to the stairs, excused himself for a moment, and forced her up to their room where he roughed her up for meddling in his affairs and embarrassing him.

Cally begged her to walk out, to leave with her right then and there, but she couldn't. Like most women caught in that situation, she was hoping it would be a onetime thing. She was also insured that he had to make an example, to show he was in charge and not weak, or they would turn on him and it would mean trouble for her as well. So, with that in her mind, she stayed. But that was also when the rules and the control all started. That day her life changed and she was a prisoner from then on.

Fear kept her at his side, control kept her smiling, and a constant watchful eye kept her from escaping. Over the years, she had known this one night of the year to be so busy for her husband, that he resorted to drugging her with Valium, so she would go to bed and he could attend to business in the den after the party was over. The cellar was open and she just had to get past him. She would be free. If he discovered what she was doing, or if she was wrong and he had people guarding or bringing inventory in, she was probably not going to make it out alive.

Cally had hidden nearly 25,000 dollars in an envelope under some rocks, near the path that lead to the entrance of the mine. She couldn't wait for Laurel at the entrance or she would be caught, and surely the plan discovered, or Cally would be looked at as knowing too much. Laurel hated putting her friend in danger like that. She shuddered to think what could happen to Cally if she was caught. Knowing how many people, even children, her husband and the others had brought in and out, she knew she could disappear easily, if he wanted her to. Her nerves were still buzzing as she waited for the vodka to kick in just a little.

Am I crazy to try this? she wondered. *Can I really make it?* she thought. She knew the first person Marko would go to was Cally, once he discovered she was gone. Then her family. The very thought of what he could be willing to do, or have done to them, was terrifying and consuming. But she had to leave or she was going to die anyway. *There's always plan B,* she thought to herself. She glanced over to the nightstand and grabbed a pack of matches she used for her candles and placed them inside the toe of her shoe. She had no way of knowing if there was any light in the tunnel, or if there wasn't, she probably shouldn't use the matches or risk getting noticed.

A few more guests clip-clopped their way up the cobblestone walk, dressed in their black ties and/or black dresses. The fountain seemed to glow in the darkened sky, taunting her from behind silent eyes.

Well it's almost time, she thought.

She took a quick look around. There was really nothing she could bring down with her now that wouldn't get noticed and questioned. She looked over at her purse.

I should grab my social security card, my birth certificate, and my identification. I can put them inside my panty hose or in my shoes, but at least I will have them.

She walked over and quietly rifled through her small purse, grabbing the important papers, and putting the rest back in. She made sure to hang the purse back up in the usual spot, so it didn't get noticed. Then she tossed the empty vodka bottle in the waste paper basket beside her vanity and went into the restroom to brush her teeth.

She flipped the lights on and looked in the mirror, she looked calm, but inside she was a complete wreck. She grabbed her purple toothbrush from the porcelain angel holder and applied a little toothpaste. She looked at her brush for a second.

Man, I can't even take my tooth or hairbrush with me. I am really leaving with nothing, she thought.

She quickly brushed her teeth, rinsed the sink, and made her way out of the bathroom and toward the bedroom door. *Well, here I go,* she thought. She turned the lights off and headed down the hall to the top of the stairs. She glanced at the grandfather clock just as it chimed, 8:00 on the dot.

The room below was packed full of people, but they all stopped talking and looked to the top of the grand staircase. Laurel raised her head up just a little as a sign of pride and tossed a forced grin to her husband who was waiting at the bottom of the stairs with his hand out, showcasing her descent. She slowly took her walk down the stairs, not a person spoke. The room was so quiet you could hear her breathing and, for a moment, she thought they could hear her thoughts.

Laurel took her husband's hand at the bottom of the stairs. He kissed her cheek and spun her in a circle.

"You look lovely," he told her.

"Thank you," she replied and tossed him another grin.

At that moment, the people knew it was okay to begin talking and parading around as they were before. Marko took Laurel by the hand and walked around the room, saying their normal hellos and good evenings They made their way around, speaking to each person at least once before making it over to the table where the food was. Laurel let go of Marko's hand, grabbed a small plate, placed a few pieces of shrimp and lobster rolls on it, and proceeded to the salad area. No one else was paying much attention to her, but Marko was staring daggers through her. The hair on the back of her neck stood on end and shivers went up her spine.

Does he know something? she wondered.

Laurel ate slowly, trying to pretend that she was happy at the turn out. Marko walked over and handed her a glass of wine.

Laurel looked over at the clock, it was 9:15, he had waited an extra fifteen minutes this year. *Must be slipping,* she thought. She put her plate in the basket on the back of the table and wrapped her hands around her glass of wine.

"Marko, I am feeling a bit under the weather today. I don't really want to drink anything. I think I may be coming down with a little stomach bug. I think I would rather get a little milk, may be some Pepto, and head upstairs. If, of course, you don't need me down here," she whispered.

"Well, you do look a little more pale than usual and I think I can handle it down here. I will try to keep everyone quiet, if you want to head upstairs," he replied. "Look, the party is wrapping up already anyways, so you won't be missing much."

Marko pointed out into the room, the ladies were already being escorted out of the house, laughing and half drunk, and the men were grabbing the usual cigars and starting to retreat to the den.

"Okay, hon, I am going to go get my slippers, some sweat pants on, and then come get my warm milk and Pepto. Oh, the caterer you got this year did a great job with the lobster roll," she added.

Marko took the glass of wine, poured the wine into the bucket, and placed the goblet upside down in the basket. White powder clumps, small but noticeable, stuck to the sides and bottom of the glass. *I can't believe that worked,* she thought as she looked back at Marko, waiting for his good night kiss. She leaned in and gave him a kiss and a warm hug, with a moment of cuddle so he would not be suspicious and she waited for him to release her. She walked away toward the stairs, Marko watched her every move.

All the guests had cleared the living room and the remaining men were in the den. A thick cloud of smoke was pluming out into the hallway. *The staircase is just ahead,* she thought, *this might actually work.*

"Laurel, I noticed you weren't wearing any perfume tonight, not even the new one I bought for you."

"Yeah, I know, it's my stomach. I love Vanilla Fields, you know that, but I was afraid that if I put it on it would be too strong and overpower me."

She flashed him a sheepish grin and saddened eyes for good measure.

"I remembered the last time you had the flu, you couldn't wear anything for two weeks, baby. I hope you're not getting that, you were so sick."

"Me, too, I think maybe the chicken salad I had yesterday was a little off. I hope I will be feeling better after a good night's sleep, some Pepto, and maybe a scary movie, if I can find one to watch."

She started back up the stairs again as Marko turned to go through the kitchen and down the hall to the den where the rest of his partners were waiting for him. They would be busy for at least a few hours. *This is just too easy,* she thought. She kept going back up the stairs and down to the bedroom. Laurel flipped on the lights and shut the door, making sure to lock it behind her. She took her shoes off first, placing the papers she had taken just under the bed, in case Marko came to check on her. That was a possibility she had not thought of until now, the caring, nurturing side of him. *The winter nights in Texas were not always cold and it rarely snowed, but to try to leave in a sleeveless dress and high heels in the woods is crazy,* she thought.

Laurel left her panty hose on, pulled off the dress, and proceeded to hang it up in the closet. She took off the gloves and placed them in the cabinet. She grabbed her sneakers and her old book bag and left the closet open. She wanted to try to at least take some underwear, and socks, and maybe her travel makeup and hair kit. *If I only take a few pairs of each, he won't notice right away,* she thought. *I will leave the rest of my makeup right where it is, he probably won't think to search the luggage for my travel kit, if I leave the luggage behind,* she hoped.

She took three pairs of undergarments and socks, a t-shirt, and an extra pair of light workout pants. It wasn't much, but if she was in the woods, or if she got out and her friend was not waiting, she had a dry pair if she needed them. It was miles away from the rest of the town, but it was farther away to get help. No one in this town would lend her a hand. They are all under her husband. Laurel grabbed her travel kit and shoved it in the bag. It wasn't nearly full, but that was a plus. That meant it was light and was easier to hide. She pulled out her black sweat suit and put it on, along with a pair of socks and her shoes. Then she reached up to the vanity and took a hair tie and pulled her hair back in a makeshift bun.

She returned to the foot of the bed and pulled out the papers she had stashed there and put them down the leg of the panty hose. They wouldn't fall out and they were out of the way. If she had to get rid of the book bag, she would still have the papers, and since she had no pockets, this was the best she could do. She stopped for a moment and listened as hard as she could, but she couldn't hear anything. She looked at the bed and ruffled the covers to make it look like she had lay on the bed and reached for the remote.

She turned on the flat screen mounted to the wall and flipped through the channels. When she came across the weather channel, she went ahead and watched for a moment. The weather in her area called for cool, foggy conditions, with showers all day the next day. She continued on through the stations and settled on 'Children of the Corn'. She put the remote on her nightstand and proceeded toward the bedroom door.

Laurel put her ear against the door and listened, but she could hear nothing. No one on the stairs, no one walking on the hardwood floors in the living room. *This is good,* she thought. *Here I go.* She quietly unlocked the door and waited a second; turning to look one more time at the bedroom she had spent the last fifteen years as a prisoner in.

Satisfied with hearing nothing, she slowly opened the door, at first only a crack, and peered out into the hallway. No one was there, so she pushed the door open a little more and scooted out, looking both ways, like a child before crossing the street. She pulled the door shut behind her and proceeded down to the edge of the staircase. She stopped at the top and looked down, no one was in the living room. The front door was right there, every part of her wanted to go out that door, and just take off running, but the house was surrounded by surveillance cameras and more were located on the gate at the end of the driveway.

All the cameras were fed to an internal feed, monitored on the computer in the den. He would surely be watching, since his parties were not small time news. People all over town and everywhere know about his parties, and people he was enemies with knew this night was a busy time for him. *He will be on his toes,* she thought. She headed down the stairs, tiptoeing and stopping on each stair to listen for any voices or footsteps. Laurel reached the bottom of the stairs and was surprised to see that the catering people were not cleaning up yet.

Perhaps Marko had told them to leave it until tomorrow, since she wasn't feeling well. Maybe he had told them to come back tomorrow so they would not overhear or see anything they shouldn't. Either way, this was out of the ordinary for him. Normally, the living room would already be cleaned and there would be no sign a party ever took place. She carefully walked past the table, still filled with food and empty plates, and peered into the kitchen. The kitchen was empty. The counters were filled with empty wine glasses and wine bottles. Plates were stacked in rows with napkins and silverware strewn across it.

The lights flickered over the bar area and the cellar door beckoned to her. Laurel turned and looked down the hall. The door to the den was still closed, she could hear the men talking, and the cigar smoke was still heavy in the air; they were still in there. She tiptoed into the kitchen and turned to the left. The white ceramic tiles threatened to squeak under her feet and give away her plan. She tried to step lightly, passing the sink and the fridge. The cellar door was in reach and she adjusted her book bag behind her and slowly turned the doorknob. The stairs to the cellar were deep, that she remembered from her brief encounter years ago.

She grabbed the matches she had in her panty hose and shakily struck one, pinching it hard between her thumb and forefinger. She started on her way down and closed the door behind her. She was really going to do it. The stone stairs made no noise as she walked, but the match burnt out quickly. She felt her way down to the bottom of the stairs and stopped. She listened for any sound of footsteps or movement above, but none were heard. The laughter of the men carried and echoed down the stairs, bouncing off the walls into her ears.

She fumbled around and struck another match, now able to see the masses of crates stacked up, which surely held more drugs than she could ever imagine. She walked faster, past the boxes, and around the tables, looking for the end of the cellar and the beginning of the tunnel she knew was there, but had never seen.

The cellar is damp and humid, even now in the winter, and the air is surprisingly pungent, she thought. The match burnt out and she quickly struck another one. She rounded another batch of stacked crates and noticed a strange shadow bouncing off the one to her right. Startled, she stopped and peered over them. A woman sat tied at the ankles and bound with duct tape. She shackled with her hands above her head to a rod sticking through the cellar wall. She moved her head side-to-side and stared at Laurel. Laurel took a few steps toward the woman and saw that she was young, maybe early thirties at the most, and quite fragile looking, bruised and beaten.

She was covered in dirt and shivering. The woman started

crying and moving her arms as much as she could, begging for Laurel to help her, but Laurel couldn't. She had no keys for the shackles and no time to search for them. She had to find the exit and she needed to move quickly. Laurel looked around for something she could light that would last more than a match, but everything else would produce smoke and a smell that would surely alert her husband if he didn't know already that she was gone or where she was.

"I'm sorry, I can't help you," Laurel told the girl. "But I promise, if you don't tell anyone you saw me, once I get out of here I will tell the police or the FBI or someone, and I will get you out of here," she whispered.

Laurel touched the girl on the head before striking yet more matches and turning around to find the door. The door was heavy black metal and was latched with a large metal post. *Beyond this door is freedom,* she thought. As Laurel took a few more steps toward the door, a foul odor caught her nose. She looked around and could see nothing that would cause the smell. It was an unmistakable smell and she hoped it would be an animal from the woods around the property that had been hurt or gotten lost. With this hope in her mind, she turned, took one more look at the woman chained to the wall cold and scared, and every part of her knew she was probably wrong.

The woman nodded her head and tried to keep Laurel's attention, crying a little louder and banging her head on the wall. Laurel looked at her and held her finger to her lips. The girl had duct tape from the bottom of her chin up to just over her nose, leaving her nostrils exposed, but just barely.

"Shhh, please, I have no keys and I have to escape or I can't send help. Please, be quiet," Laurel begged.

The girl shook her head no and tears streaked her face. Laurel lit another match and grabbed the post across the door, it was heavy and cold, but Laurel had to lift it. The sound from the woman sniffing with her runny nose was annoying and she couldn't help but think the girl looked familiar, but she couldn't place why or how she thought that. Finally, the metal pole lifted and sent Laurel stumbling back a few steps. She caught herself, but not without sending the left side of the pole crashing just slightly into a stack of wooden crates. A loud scraping sound and a clank echoed on the walls, she hoped that no one upstairs heard it.

Laurel looked back one more time and the girl had her head down, still crying, but with such a great sorrow about her she could no longer look up.

"I will send help somehow, I promise," Laurel told her.

She quickly turned around, placing the rod against the wall, and grabbed the handle; she carefully tugged on the heavy door and pulled it open just a little. The cool air rushed in from around the sides and she could smell the odor so heavily now that it made it hard to breathe. She stopped for a moment to light another match and grabbed a piece of paper from the crate next to her. Once she was in the tunnel with the door shut, she supposed it wouldn't matter if she burnt something small that would give her some more light.

She pulled the door open a little more and peered into the tunnel. There didn't seem to be any one in the tunnel. She stepped inside, carefully pulling the door shut behind her. It made a slight clicking sound as she closed it, *but not anything that would raise eyebrows,* she thought. She struck another match, rolled the paper into a tight tube, and proceeded to light the paper. The orange and blue flame caught quickly and she began walking quickly down the dark corridor. She could no longer hear any voices from the house. There was no more laughter and she could not hear the girl she left behind crying, cold and alone in the dark room.

Her whole body shook with chills and adrenaline. *The makeshift little torch is working much better than stopping every twenty seconds to light a new match,* she thought. The farther down the tunnel she got, the colder it seemed to get, and the smell was constantly getting stronger. She now held her forearm to her nose as she went. The torch was burning faster and was nearly three quarters the way burnt when she caught a glimpse of a face out of the corner of her eye.

Laurel stopped, dropped the torch, and listened, she heard nothing, but the face protruding from the clay cement wall staring back at her was enough to make her lose her composure. She recognized the partially decayed face of the rookie policewoman who had gone missing a few weeks ago. She was supposed to patrol the border of the city, watching for unauthorized entry from Mexico. There was a single bullet wound to the front of her head, and deep inside Laurel hoped that was all it had taken.

Laurel grabbed her book of matches, ready to light another one as the little rolled up paper neared the end of its time. She turned around in a small circle and didn't see any other faces in the wall, *but one is more than enough,* she thought. She lit the match and left the paper to burn itself out as she pushed forward.

What kind of monster was the man I married? Surely, he knew about this, maybe he did it, she thought. *How many others are buried down here?* she wondered. *How many missing girls, women, and refugees, have met their end at the hands of the man I once loved?*

She couldn't help thinking back to the woman she left in the cellar. *How long had she been down there?* she wondered. *Did she see anyone get killed? What horrible things have already happened to her?* Laurel's mind spun with all the terrible thoughts streaming in her head. If her husband could hurt her and keep her prisoner in their own home, what unspeakable things has he done to total strangers? The fear she had for her husband churned inside her. She wanted to throw up, she wanted to cry, and she wanted to help that woman. She was running out of matches already and there was no light in the tunnel. The floor beneath her was getting harder to walk on, becoming more sand than clay, and she was thankful she put sneakers on before leaving.

She lit another match, noticing she only had 4 left after that, and not knowing how much tunnel she had left. Her backpack, though light, was getting heavy and she was out of breath. She listened hard in the upcoming darkness for voices, crying, anything. But she couldn't hear anything above her own breathing. She walked faster, feeling the fire get closer to her fingertips, and burn just enough for her to drop the match and strike another one. *I have to be getting close, the tunnel feels like it is going on forever,* she thought.

She stopped just a moment to light another match and felt a breeze gently kiss her face in the darkness. *Fresh air, oh God, I'm going to make it,* she thought. She tried to strike a match, but the breeze was a little too strong and circled her. She turned around and put her back to the wind, but still could not light the match. Laurel kept the book in her hand and put her hands out in front of her, taking small slow steps, and pushing on in the direction of the breeze. Slowly, the sounds of the woods came alive. It had been so long since she had been in the woods anywhere, but the sounds of crickets were unmistakable.

Her excitement was hardly containable, but she had to keep going. The sand was thick beneath her feet and the moonlight was just starting to peek in from the opening of the fake mineshaft. She walked a bit faster, gasping for her breath, hoping she would see the rocks her friend spoke of and the envelope of money waiting for her. The moonlight poured in now and the entire shaft was illuminated. The logs that held the opening strong were visible and leaves covered the ground. She could see the tree branches, bare from the winter fall, but they were trees just the same.

The sky was a deep blue, not black and the moon looked light grey in the shadows. The crickets seemed to not notice her coming to the entrance of the cave, but she was nearly there. She kicked sand and it showered back to the earth, covering the dried leaves with a thin crunchy layer. A smile crossed her face as she reached the entrance and stopped to peer out to both sides. The trees were scattered and formed shadows on the boulders and fallen logs in the night. The clouds seemed to move across the sky at a fast speed, as if trying to get away from there on their own.

Laurel stepped quietly out of the shaft and turned to look at where she came from. The light from outside seemed to go in only a few feet and then peter out into solemn darkness; she knew where that darkness ended. She readjusted her book bag and started walking up the narrow path into the treeline, looking for the pile of rocks her friend said would contain the envelope and a small note as to where she would be waiting for her. Laurel scanned the ground and the leaves for a pile of rocks that would stick out to her, but still fit in with the background. She climbed up a small embankment and was now surrounded by the woods. She took a deep breath, amazed she had gotten this far, and wondering if her husband had noticed she was gone yet.

There were several small animal trails littering the ground and she decided to stick to the one she was on and follow it down a bit. She stared into the trees ahead of her, but couldn't help glancing back in the direction of the shaft. She felt bad about leaving that woman behind, and knew that woman would not have to tell them she had seen her. The fact that she could not re-latch the door would be a dead giveaway, as would the trail of burnt matches and the small pile of ash from the paper. She only hoped she would be far away from there by the time they noticed how she had gotten out.

As she got further into the woods and farther away from the shaft, the trees got thicker and the forest got a little darker. She could still see and did not want to risk any fire or light for fear of being seen. She walked carefully, trying to avoid making any more noise than necessary on the leaves, or falling over a root. She passed by a willow tree, barely hanging on to dear life, leaning up against another tree. *It must have been knocked over during Hurricane Katrina,* she thought. She looked at the tree, thinking how appropriate the name weeping willow was for that tree. She walked a few more feet, and at the base of a dark moss-covered log, was a small pile of rocks. A few white rocks caught her eye in the moonlight, but the rest seemed to be pieces of fossilized wood, very common in these parts.

This has to be it, she thought, *it's the only pile I have seen so far. She* bent down and carefully, quietly began moving one rock at a time. She came across a small white envelope wrapped in a clear sandwich bag. She tugged the envelope out and pulled the baggie off. There was the money and a note, as promised. She pulled the note out, but it wasn't Cally's writing. Her heart began to beat a hole in her chest, her mouth watered, her hand shook so violently she could hardly read the note.

"Yes, my dear, I knew of your little plan months ago. I knew you wanted to leave me and I knew you had told Cally about everything. Well, everything you knew about. Oh, Laurel, how I loved you and still do. Why couldn't you just settle in and accept things this way and be happy? I gave you a nice home, nice clothes, vacations, the best foods, and fine jewelry. But you had to meddle in everything. You tried to make me look like a monster, and maybe I am, but that's just business and the nature of the beast. Oh, your friend Cally, she was more than willing to tell me everything I wanted to know with a little persuasion.

"No, I haven't killed her yet. No doubt you saw her on your way out. Some friend you are, leaving your friend behind. How can you say she is your best friend, when you didn't recognize her, and left her behind? You think I am a monster, my dear, you have yet to see anything. You know I can't let you leave now. Unless you are completely monstrous, you won't want to leave, knowing Cally is in the cellar. She has been kept company by the rest of the visitors and has also seen way too much for her to be let go. I will always love you and you will always be mine."

Laurel backed up slowly, sitting down on the ground, crying. The wind picked up and a small chill swept up her spine. The money was still in her hand, and for the moment, no one was near her. She could still leave.

No, I can't leave Cally, she thought. *If I go back, he will never let me go, and Cally will either die there and be buried in the wall or sold like the rest. I have to get away, I have to send help,* she told herself.

Her mind raced back and forth, so scared, angry, and confused. Her tears ran like faucets and her makeup dripped from her face. The darkened purples and greens she worked so hard to cover up, now exposed.

She staggered to her feet and began walking down the trail, money in her hand, hair swaying in the wind. The leaves crunched under her feet and she clenched her fist. She wanted to fly away like a bat in the sky. She wished for wings, she wished to be a crow flying over her husband's dead body, carrying his soul to hell. She wished to be anybody, but who she was, and anywhere, but there.

She starting sprinting, the woodlands around her starting to get a bit sparser, and the view of street lights ahead made her feel a bit safer. She ran down the small hill and toward the street, if she could reach the edge of the road, she could just stay in the tree line and follow the road into town and call for a cab. She could go to Houston Intercontinental Airport and get a ticket anywhere. *I'll make a call anonymously and save Cally and maybe others, too,* she thought.

She had to keep going, her husband would expect her to come back. *But, I'm not going to,* she thought. *Let him search for me, he won't find me.* She looked to the left and the road seemed clear.

She stared off to the right and saw no cars, no people. *Maybe I should cross the street, not be tied on his property,* she thought. She took another quick look and felt a sharp pain to the side of her head.

***

Laurel opened her eyes and the sky was passing over her. She gazed dazedly at the moon and felt the ground under her heels. She tried to move, but her legs were duct taped and she was gagged. Her arms felt as though they were being wrenched from the sockets as she was being dragged past the same trees she had just gotten away from. The trail went up the embankment, she let her head fall backwards to try to get a look at who had her.

Her head throbbed and blood trickled down the side of her face and neck. She recognized the baldhead of the police chief, who was her husband's best friend and ally, and smelled his Axe deodorant. The stale smell of cigar smoke funneled off of him and swarmed her nose. Tears streamed from her face as she saw the sides of the shaft close in on them both. He dragged her down farther into the shaft. This time the tunnel was completely lit, a bright row of hanging lamps lit the way. The tunnel walls were pockmarked with hammer marks, shovel marks, and sporadic slabs of cement littering the wall in strategic places. This was not just a tunnel for trafficking drugs and people, this was also a tomb for the people he killed.

Laurel tried to struggle against the massive man dragging her down the corridor. She could hear voices, her husband's and others that had attended the party. *Do they all know what I have planned? They must,* she thought, *they all know who Cally is and that she is down there.*

She got close to where the cellar door was and heard it slide open against the floor.

"I got her Marko, right where you said she would be."

"Good, glad to hear it. Let's get this over with, we have a busy day tomorrow, after all we have a missing person to report. Well, two, actually, to file," Marko replied.

They both laughed a bit, Cally was brought out and laid right next to Laurel. Laurel reached out for Cally. Her face was clearly visible in the bright lights. Her nose had been broken and her eyes, though open, were still very swollen and bruises covered her face, neck, and body. She had finger marks on her neck; clearly, they had tortured her friend or tried to kill her. Laurel cried after seeing the pain her friend was in and knowing she was going to leave her behind. Her friend would have been fine, safe at her house, but she was trying to help her.

Cally didn't move, only looked at Laurel with tears running clean streaks down her once beautiful olive skin. She was thin and her lips were chapped. She had been down there for a while.

"You wanted to help your friend so much, huh? Wanted to save her from the monster, did you? You wanted to see her anywhere, but here and with anyone, but me, right? Well, here is your chance, Cally, you two won't see anyone but each other from now on!" He snapped at them.

"Do it!"

The chief grabbed Cally and hoisted her up into a hole carved out of the wall and shoved her in. Cally tried to struggle to get out of the hole. He picked up his gun and fired a single shot into Cally's head. Laurel could do nothing to help her friend. She watched, bound and helpless, as a small trickle of blood inched its way down her forehead, her eyes open, staring blankly off into the abyss as death whisked her friend away. Laurel cried and tried to get on her hands and knees, she wanted to hop, to crawl, to try to get away.

Her husband got in front of her and ripped the tape from her mouth.

"You are a fucking monster! You're crazy and evil! I hope you rot in hell, you son of a bitch!" Laurel screamed.

"Oh Laurel, you'll be there way before me."

"I've been there for the past fifteen years, at least this will be a break from you!" she yelled back.

He grabbed her by the hair, forced her head back, and kissed her long and hard, while she cried. He pushed her back to the ground and stared down at her, crumpled up on the ground. Bloody, bruised, and filthy, she gasped for breath.

"You'll never get away with this!" she yelled.

"I already have, dear, you have been writing letters about your plans to leave me for months now, you took the money from the hiding spot, and you made it down to the street where your friend was supposed to meet you. So, when they start looking for you, you're an estranged wife who left a spouse. I'm golden, since I will be filing with the local police here. Well, we all know how this is going to end."

Marko looked up at the chief and nodded. The chief bent down, shoving a sock into her mouth, and duct taping it in place. Marko bent down and pulled Laurel's hands down and they tapped her hands to her knees.

"We both know how much you like to be on your knees and we want you to be as comfortable as possible."

They hoisted her up and shoved her in front of Cally. Marko grabbed a small wood and plaster wall and shoved it in front of Laurel, wedging it in place. They began heaping loads of quick dry cement in place, just leaving a small window where they could look in and see Laurel.

"Don't forget these, it's going to be very dark," Marko said, as he tossed her last three matches in her face and closed the window.

The Shallows

"My Lord, we have more news about Bellows. They have succumbed to the illness and fallen. The ships that fled from Greece have also been stricken and Greece was lost. The oceans are not a barrier against it and the underground tunnels could not save the people of Bellows. What are we to tell our people?"

"We can tell them nothing that would give them anything better to look forward to than what they see now. So, I think we tell them nothing. We are on our own island here. Maybe if we prevent travel and do not allow port on our shores, we can stave this off. Send the order, Marvin. No one shall be permitted to leave the island. No one is allowed to port. Also, have Arious send a few of our fleet just out past the drop off to make sure no ships come near. We will turn away any ships with force, if necessary."

King Draven sat back in his throne and stroked his beard. He stared out the window and felt the breeze that came off the ocean, while the salty air filled his nose. The king listened to the clapping of Marvin's feet as he made his way down the stone corridors toward the royal guards. So far, they had managed to stay free of disease, but that very fact might be what brought them down as word spread.

Draven got to his feet and slowly walked closer to the window. He peered down into the courtyard, watching the village children play in the grass. *They seem so care free and happy,* he thought. *How could I take this away from them without illness here to show a reason for it?* Bellows, Greece, and the others must have done something to bring this on them.

"My Lord! My Lord! We have received a message from Ireland. Nepetus has been infected. There is more, Sir. Jasmine has taken ill, too."

King Draven clutched the open window and staggered a few steps before steadying himself. He looked out at the calm sea just as three of his largest and best-equipped ships left dock and headed to the horizon.

"My little girl. My sweet daughter. Why God, have you forsaken us? We have prayed. We have been righteous in our quests and in our lives. Why, when you have my wife, must you take my daughter, too?"

"Sire, the word is getting around the villages and the people are starting to panic. They are saying it's God's wrath, that it's the end of the world. They are starting to line up at the front gates looking for answers. We have to tell them something. It has been a long time now since you have been to see the priests or the sorceress. Maybe you should go see them."

"Marvin, my old friend, when my father was dying, the sorceress told me he was too old and sick for her to help, and the priests said that God was calling him home. When my wife died during childbirth, the priests said God wanted her to care for my daughter from heaven. And now, with all the countries and people dying, including my daughter, my faith has gone well past shaken. I have long ago given up on prayers alone; though I know the rest of the kingdom has not. "

"I can't put my faith and trust in someone or something that seems only to work in ways that cause hurt and misguided thoughts. I have caused no harm. I have done no wrong, and yet, I continue to suffer. I have been a merciful king. I have been a fair and tolerant ruler, but and yet your God mocks my every attempt, by taking away anything that makes me happy."

"Yes, my Lord. I understand. Yet here we are, still alive and well on this island, our home. Here we sit able to see children running and playing. We see men from the village fishing and women washing clothes. There must be something still worth praise, Sire?"

"No, Marvin. There isn't. What you see is only blissful

ignorance, people who don't travel, see or go to war. Villagers who only know this island, and not what exists beyond our borders. They hear only what is spoken in chapel or told by travelers who stop to port and barter. They await the news that the princess will soon be gone and that Greece has fallen, as well as Bellows."

"They await answers I can't give and a solution I won't be able to provide. Once we share the news of this plague, this illness, this end of days or whatever it is, they will begin to pray even more to a deity for a divine intervention and to be spared. That prayer will not be fruitful, leaving behind much grief and a trail of death and heartache. It happened to our fallen comrades, who were also God-fearing people. You tell me, my friend, where should I place my faith!?"

Marvin stood silent, knowing there was nothing he could say to take away the pain and sorrowful thoughts King Draven was rightfully feeling. He watched as a single tear rolled down the cheek of his friend's face. The King's kind expression drifted away and faded into a sullen look. He gazed off into blue skies that gave no hint of the horror beneath them.

"Sire, should I sound the bell to bring the villagers to the chapel?"

"Yes, there's no reason to continue to hide what's happening out there now. I just wish I knew what to tell them or how to keep the illness from our small island. If Greece was unable to fend it off, I don't know how we can. All I know is that the illness spreads very fast. It seems to start out with a stomachache and quickly turn into some form of necrosis."

"My Lord, do you think it's a form of leprosy?"

"I pondered that very thought. But it moves too quickly and kills much faster than leprosy. Besides, as far as I know, leprosy doesn't cause people to have the violent fits that whatever this is has been causing. Much less the fact that people can't be buried, simply because they turn to corpses and decay as they die. The only option is to burn what's left of them. Tell the villagers to meet at the chapel in ten minutes for a meeting."

Marvin went to the bell tower and began ringing the bell. The gong could be heard all around their tiny island. King Draven watched as his people made their way toward their church. The steeple rose majestically into the air, yet he felt sickened to look at it. The bell's noise bounced off the walls and rang in his ears like the clanking of swords on the battlefield. This, however, was not a war he could win. There will be no glory, no honor, and no freedom.

Vivid oranges came into view as the sun began to set. The ships looked almost peaceful in the distance, anchored just off shore, but he knew better. He walked down the darkened hall, lighting torches as he went. The aroma of paraffin and sage caught his nose as he turned to see the old sorceress sneaking through the corridors, mumbling under her breath.

"Nola? What are you doing? Didn't you hear the bells? I called a meeting at the chapel. I need to discuss what's happening."

"Oh, I heard the bells alright. But your meeting will help no one, not even you, my Lord."

He carefully reached out and grabbed her frail shoulders. She stopped waving her smoldering bunch of sticks and gazed up at King Draven. Her eyes had long ago clouded over with cataracts and he wondered if her mind was still there. Her hair was straggly and thinning, she was a shell of the distinguished woman he had trusted with safe guarding and caring for his family for years.

"What are you saying, Nola? Do you know what's happening here?

"Yes Sire, I do know what's going on. You have all turned away from the Gods. The old ways have been forgotten and the

Gods are angry. First Bellows fell, and then Greece. Notice we have received no such word from Egypt. They still hold to the old ways and so does most of England. You were given chances, my Lord, to go back to the old ways to bring back the Gods, and you refused. Above all others, you pushed them all out."

"Hestia is not the only God you angered, but she is why whole households succumb to this and why there is no way to live through it. Nemesis passed down her fury and this is her vengeance on the humans. I have asked, but Minerva refuses to give any mercy. I can do nothing for you."

Draven released the old woman and she scurried off through the darkened hallway, mumbling under her breath once again. He watched her, partially disgusted at her haggard appearance, and partially mad that she roamed through his house freely, with a feeble mind. He started out toward the church once again, trying to pay no more mind to the old woman, but little thoughts about his lost faith were creeping into his mind now that it had been brought up twice in one night.

By the time he made his way down the winding cobblestone path from his humble castle to the chapel, the sun was all but down, silhouetting shades of purples, dark blues, and blacks against the budding night sky. The moon smiled back at him as if taunting him to take a nighttime swim through the silvery shallows. He threw open the heavy wooden doors to the chapel, which was only dimly lit with candles and a few torches, and with his head down he took his position at the pulpit.

The eyes of his fearful citizens stared at him, ripping through him like daggers in his skin. He could feel the lump welling up in his throat. He had spoken to his people many times before in this same chapel, at this same pulpit, with good and bad news, but this was different. He was about to tell people that they might all suffer a horrible fate and die in a most excruciating manner. He was about to tell people that his very own daughter was suffering that fate now, that entire countries have already died out, and there was nothing they could do but wait.

"My people, I know you have all been hearing what's been happening. I don't know how much light I can shed on this situation, but I will share with you all that I know. Greece has fallen and so has Bellows. My beloved daughter has also been stricken and is probably dead by now. All I know is that whatever this sickness is, it kills everyone, young, old, men, women, and children. It strikes fast with little warning, and there is no cure. Nola can't help us. She informed me of that tonight."

He continued, "It seems that we, as of yet, have not had this unfortunate illness fall upon us. Maybe it is because we are a small island and not many of us leave or have too many outside visitors. Maybe it's the grace of God. That is why I have posted guards out in the water. We only have quarantine as an option. No one leaves the island, no one comes to us."

No sooner had he finished that sentence than the town's folk started to talk. Some were crying and a few stood up and began protesting. The mood in the small chapel turned from fearful to angry in an instant.

"My Lord please, if I may? My husband is far off fishing and he has our son with him. They can't possibly not be allowed home when they return."

"I am sorry, but we can't allow anyone to come onto the island right now. I will send notice to the guards to be on the lookout for our own people out fishing and tell them they must be quarantined on their own ships until we know they are not infected. If they are running out of supplies, we will send supplies to them on a small raft. It has to be this way if we want to try to survive whatever this is, and it is coming for us," he added.

He watched as the young woman sank back into her pew, her head in her hands. The others who had been standing quickly sat back down their questions seemingly answered.

"Now there is one other thing I need to address before we put a few changes in place here. There are only a few symptoms of this sickness, the first one is that it starts out with a stomachache, a very bad one. Then they began to have necrosis of the skin like leprosy, only this is very fast. The necrosis, of course, leads to bleeding and weeping wounds and a very drastic change in temper; fits of rage, violence, and death. If you start to feel sick in the stomach, please come to the prison. I know this does not sound like the place to be when you're sick, but it may be the only way to segregate the sick people for now and maybe keep your own family and children from getting this."

"If it turns out to only be a sour stomach, you're free to leave, but if it's not, you won't have much time. I also want you to be honest and raise your hands if you have left the island to visit any family or if you have, or have had, a visitor in the past two weeks. This is very important. This may be what makes the difference for our people surviving or ending up like Greece."

"Sire, the fishermen come in contact with traders on the sea constantly. They trade blubber and fish and fruits," Marvin whispered.

"I need all the town's fishermen rounded up and put in cells at the prison. But I do not want them treated like prisoners. Allow them whatever creature comforts they want and food and drink," he ordered.

"Yes, my Lord."

Marvin stepped off the stage and went to grab his list of merchant fishermen. Accompanied by the other guards, they returned to the church and began taking a few men quietly from their pews. They were carefully taken to their homes and allowed to grab clothes, a blanket, pillow, and a few books or food parcels to take with them.

They strolled through the town to the other side of the island and up to the prison. The sandstone building was dark and musty, but the air was surprisingly cooler inside than it had been on the walk or even in the church. Marvin lit the torches at the entrance and handed them to two guards to continue lighting the torches adorning the walls in the hall and lit the candles in the cells. Five men total were placed inside rooms, each alone and scared, wondering if they were infected or if they were going to see their own families again.

"You are not prisoners. You have done nothing wrong. We do not want you to feel as if you are being punished. You are here as brave fellows, making sure you do not have the infection and cannot pass it along if you do have it. You will be brought food and behind you, on the floor, you each have a large bucket of clean drinking water. Please, if you start to have symptoms of the infection, let us know. If you are not infected, it should not take long for us to find that out and send you back to your homes," Marvin told them.

He watched each man go into his cell and shut the iron gates. They left the torches lit and proceeded back to the church. Draven was already allowing people to return to their homes when they made it back.

"My Lord, the men are all in cells and as comfortable as they can be."

"That's good. But for now, all we can do is wait. I don't hold out much hope for this tactic. I think we have already been exposed, but I don't have any clue where it comes from or what causes the infection."

"What makes you think we are exposed, Sire?"

"I saw Nola in the hall and she was acting strange. Well, stranger than usual. Plus, like you said, the fishermen have contact with people not from our island all the time. They could have brought it back with them. For all we know, it's in the very water we drink or bathe in. How can I protect my people from something I can't see?"

"My Lord, you are doing all you can do. We have to put it in God's hands now."

"I think we already did and this is the hand he played."

Draven walked away, stepping off toward the sandy beach he used to watch his daughter play on when she was small. He scooped out a spot, clearly lit by the bright moonlight, and sat down in the still warm sand. The gentle waves rolled up to his feet and he slipped his shoes off. He listened to the sound of the water running ashore. In the near distance, he heard the sound of the waves breaking against the rocky outcrop of the cliffs. The ships' white sails fluttered on the breeze and he watched them glow pale against the black sky.

He slid himself down a few more inches and allowed the water to caress his feet. The white wash flooded his heels and pulled the sand from under them. The sea felt cool to the touch, but not cold, so he rolled his pants legs up above the knee and stood to wade in a bit. Seagulls flew in and out of his sight and he watched them fly back toward the cliffs, over the ship, and right back over his head.

Walking slowly, hardly picking up his feet, he waded deeper into the water, letting the waves rush past him, pushing him back little by little. His pants started to unroll and he didn't care. He stared up at the moon, studying the spots and trying to see if he could make out any voices from the ships. Another step forward and he felt something with this toes.

It was cold and hard. He picked his foot up just a little and ran his toes across the top of it, following the curvature with his foot. *A shell,* he thought? *Maybe someone threw a bowl off the ship and it was carried up by the current.* He hopped a little bit forward on the one foot still in the sand, and slid his foot completely on top of the object. He bent down, allowing the water to crash into him, as the wind picked up. The waves ran into his face and chest and he dug his fingers down into the sand and tried to pry the object from it resting place.

He reached his other hand down and pulled. The next wave threw him back, and though he was under the water, he wasn't letting go. Draven stood up, catching a quick breath, and glanced down at his hands. *A pearl? It's a huge pearl,* he thought. The ominous pure white glow cast off in the night and reflected the moonlight illuminating his face. He stood there staring at his find for a moment before walking back to shore. His pant legs began falling down as he walked and his sleeves felt as though they were melting, drooping and sticking to his skin.

King Draven carefully made his way up the steps and back down the path that led to his door. The seagulls followed him all the way up to his door, making loud caws and showering him in feathers that shed off as though being plucked handfuls at a time.

"What's wrong with you, bird, go on get out of here!" he yelled.

Then a raft coming ashore caught his attention. He walked back toward the guard pulling the raft onto the sand.

"Sire, there's something out there. The water in the shallows, there was a strange glow coming from it and some of the crew are acting very strange."

"It's probably just an algae bloom and nothing to be concerned with. You should head back to the ship with the others," he replied.

"That's not all, my Lord. There are odd things happening out there. The birds are acting weird and some of the crew are complaining about not feeling well. We thought maybe they were a little seasick, but now we really don't think that's the problem. The ships are creaking and making loud noises as if someone was trying to rip the boards off the hull. Sire, what's that? We have been pulling those strange balls up from the water all day."

"I think they're pearls. How many do you have? You have been pulling them up since you got out there? Maybe that's what you see glowing?"

"I think we might have twenty or twenty-five of them on our ship alone. I don't know about the other two ships, though. Sire, I'm not feeling so well, my stomach has been hurting since I started pulling these things up."

"Okay. I need you to go to the prison and lock yourself in a cell."

"What? Why, Sire? What have I done?"

"You have done nothing. But I think you may have the sickness that we are trying to quarantine. The prison is where we are putting people we think have it, so they don't infect others. If you're right about these strange pearls, I have a feeling that I, too, and anyone else who touched them or maybe swam in the water, will be in a cell right alongside you soon enough."

The guard headed off toward the prison and King Draven quickly took off on the raft. He mustn't allow the rest of the guards to come back to shore now. He must protect the rest of the people. He dragged the raft into the waves and started paddling out. His hands burned and his shoulders ached, but he made it to the ship.

The ladder was already down, tapping back and forth against the ship's side. He reached out for the ladder and tied the rope from the raft to it and climbed up. The voices coming from the ship told him he was right. The crew was infected. The smell of blood and puke filled his nose and he did his best to ignore it.

He looked down at the water as he reached the top of the ladder and went over the side. The water around the ship was lit from below the sand beneath them was visible, and suds circled the ship as if someone had thrown a bag of soap overboard. The seagulls flew back overhead, diving into the ships sails and plummeting to the deck below. He watched as they flopped around and took flight again, only to repeat the process.

Draven covered his nose and walked toward the door that led to the bunks. The crew was spread out from the floor to the bunks, moaning and gripping their stomachs. He avoided the puddles as he walked, but the smell was unavoidable. The yellow glow from the candles illuminated the face and arms of Arious, just enough to see a few rags they had started using as bandages.

"Arious, my friend, I'm so sorry."

"Sire, we sent Trent back to shore to warn you. He seemed to be unaffected. I think it's the pearls doing this. We dropped one on deck and it shattered. A fine powder flew up into the air and spiraled around like ashes. The liquid inside is what you smell. None of us have thrown up. The dust was sticking to us and burning our skin. We tried to wash it off, but it just foamed up. We tried to wash the deck and it spread. We have Modus shackled in the lower deck, he was trying to slash everyone with his dagger, and was yelling about things crawling on him, eating him alive."

Arious lay back on his bunk, hardly looking up at his longtime friend. The waves crashed harder against the ship, making it rock back and forth. King Draven struggled to keep his balance. The wind howled through the sails and carried the voices from the other two ships anchored just a few yards apart.

"Arious, have the other ships' crews been pulling up the pearls?"

"Yes, my Lord, we wanted them in the gardens and wanted to bring them as gifts. We didn't know, my liege. I swear it," he pled.

"I know, Arious, there is no way you could have. You mustn't leave the ship now, none of you can. I'm afraid that you would all infect the rest of the people and they would suffer the same fate."

"My King, it's in the water. The shallows are filled with these things and they are breaking with each wave. They make the seas glow and the bubbles are like acid. They are eating away at the mortar holding the ships together. The powder floats on the wind and it has caused even the birds to lose their heads. We have a great many of the wicked orbs in the bottom level, too. We couldn't bring them back up after the one we dropped started to make us ill."

"Don't worry about that now. I don't think it matters. I have to head back up to the top deck now, I need to make sure the other ships don't try to head back to shore. I've been hearing their voices since I climbed on board."

Draven turned to go back up the stairs as a large wave tossed the ship to the left. The ship lurched on its side and he struggled to regain his balance and stay on his feet, using the wall to steady himself. He could hear things rolling and clanking into each other below them. White clouds of dust started seeping up from between the floorboards. He covered his nose with his hand and ran up the stairs. Violent smaller waves continuously smashed into the small fleet, dragging the ships, anchors and all, closer to shore.

Draven looked over the right side of the vessel and the other boats were breaking apart. Stricken crew members screamed and howled as seagulls dove into them. The frothy water smelled rancid and a great cloud of white dust blew away on the wind headed toward the village. His hands were burning and his face felt like hot coals were searing through his cheeks. The frightened king made a mad dash to the ladder and threw himself over the side, climbing quickly and jumping onto what was left of the small raft. The boards were getting soggy beneath his feet and the ropes that bound them were disintegrating. He untied the tether from the ladder and shoved off.

He have to give them some warning, he thought. He paddled hard, through the pain in his hands and through stomach cramps threatening to double him over. The seawater splashed up into his face and the sores already starting to appear fizzed with foam, turning the skin around his wounds red. Loud splashes came from behind him as he turned to see his guards jumping off the ships into the water, trying to squelch the burning necrosis covering their bodies.

With each emersion, the water around them erupted into a torrent of screams and bloody drifts, calling all the flesh-eating beasts within miles. The light from the moon seemed to grow fainter as he made his way ashore. The air was filled with rot and he could hear the screams of his loyal subjects from inside their own homes. He sank to his knees, writhing in pain, and flopped over to lay on his back in the cold wet sand. The moon, once glowing bright white and calming, was now blood red.

"I told you I could not save you, no one could. I told you it was too late and you all would die."

Nola appeared, standing over him. Her face was pale in the small amount of light coming from the eclipsed moon. She was covered in her robes and white dust dotted her from head to toe, but she alone seemed immune. She shook her walking stick over him and turned toward the ocean, waving her staff and mumbling, chanting just loud enough for him to hear her. The same rhyme he thought she was saying inside and one he had heard her mumble a million times before. A rhyme she had taught his beautiful Jasmine as a young girl.

"The old moon is tarnished with the smoke of the flood. The dead leaves are varnished, the color of blood. A traitorous smile with teeth white as milk, a savage beguiler with sheathing like silk. The sea creeps to pillage and jump on her prey, a child of the village was taken today. She came up to meet him in a smooth billowing cloak, and beat him to death with one single stroke. Her bright locks were tangled; she shouted with joy. With one hand, the sea strangled a strong little boy. And now in the silence, she lingers beside him all night, and washes her fingers in the bright silvery light."

She raised both hands and the sea rose with her. Thousands of the pearls emerged from the shallow waters and burst in mid-air. A large wave rolled up, throwing the remnants of his fleet into the cliffs and causing a large section of rock to fall into the sea. Nola yelled louder and flung her arms toward the village. The sea swelled up and swallowed the cloud of powder exploding in a geyser that ascended to the heavens.

Nola turned around, facing the village, and watched as the sandstone homes collapsed and returned to the very beach they came from. All, except for two buildings and a few statues, the humble castle in which she had made her home, the church, and the last statue of Poseidon.

"My Lord, sometimes it's not okay to question the will or the path we have been given to take. Just as it is not okay to give up or turn your back on the Gods. They will hand down just as much hardship as they will blessings but when taken for granted, they will not be forgiving to us just as they did not forgive Atlantis, Bellows, or Greece."

Nola jabbed her staff into the sand and watched her king sink under the sand and the tide start to come in. She blew a quick breath on her hand and looked toward the sky as her body turned to sand and fell silently in a pile. The moons red hue began to give way slowly to shades of silvery grey. Slices of white peered through and the sea rose higher and higher with it, covering the small island and reclaiming what it had once given.

Statues in the Forest

In the dark forest of Loden, Brazil, there are stories of people that still live cut-off from all modern societies. They travel by carved-out canoes on the brown river waters, fishing for large carp and Candiru. Mark and Drew had gotten wind of the possible whereabouts of these mysterious tribes from the FUNAI and set off to see if they really exist. This would make a great documentary–video of a tribe no one has seen before. Mark and Drew had been in Brazil for three days gathering food, canteens of clean drinking water, and supplies, as well as trying to locate a guide.

That had been the tough part. It seemed like no one would go that deep into the forest. They had heard many tales of people being eaten, tortured, or sacrificed. After three long days, they had found only one person who would dare to go, his name was Cesar Romero. He spoke very little English, but agreed to take them to where everyone said the tribes were located. Drew and Mark were scheduled to leave in the morning, before the sun got too hot. They hoped to get deep enough into the forest for the canopy to keep them somewhat cool. Their packs were heavy with gear: cameras, water, and bug repellant. They tried to rent mules, but the small village stores refused to rent to them because they were going looking for the Maizmo tribe.

Mark had already packed as much as he could carry and was fast asleep. As for Drew, he couldn't sleep. Maybe it was the nearly unbearable heat. Even now, at ten o'clock, it was still 90 degrees. There was no air conditioning in the little village, no cable television, and no Internet. Maybe it was the excitement of finally embarking on their journey that kept him awake and writing in his log, rather than getting the sleep he knew he needed. He had made a list of what he wanted to pack and had packed and re-packed at least three times. He had his hunting knife and a small pocketknife, a small medicine kit, mostly for the numerous bugs and snakes they could encounter, and a few mirrors. Silly, but the villagers swore the tribe's people were terrified of mirrors and of seeing themselves in them. They said the only villager who was caught by the tribe and lived, did so because she had a small mirror. When she pulled it out of her pocket they saw themselves and took off running, leaving her to escape. This information was likely just a myth, but just in case, he had two mirrors; one to keep in the ropes on the outside of his pack and the other for his pocket. He mailed a letter back to the States, letting their families know where they were heading and when they hoped to be finished with their documentary.

If all went as well as they hoped, they would be close to the tribe in about two days on foot or one day, if Cesar was lucky enough to get a boat. They would get all the video footage they needed of the daily activities and culture and be back within a week. As aggravating as the past few days had been, Drew had a feeling things would get much better once they were on their way and out of the superstitious little village.

It was different at night there, too. In the city, they heard cars, planes, and radios blasting at all hours of the night. There, they looked out to see streetlights and maybe the moon, but here, this close to the forest, and in the middle of nowhere, there were stars everywhere. Drew looked up, to see the huge moon, hearing howler monkeys and frogs in the distance. When it goes quiet for a moment in the city, you just assume people went to bed. In the village, if it got quiet, it a survival instinct. If it got quiet, you couldn't help but wonder what animal didn't get quiet fast enough.

The alarm on Drew's watch went off at seven-thirty. It was already very hot, even with the windows open. The day had hardly begun. Covered in sweat they gathered their packs and left the small, hot hotel room to get a bite to eat before meeting up with Cesar. The entire village was quiet and there weren't many people out yet. *Perhaps it was just too early,* they thought. Mark and

121

Drew headed around the corner of their hotel building to the small restaurant. There were only two people in the restaurant that early. They ordered two pieces of melon and a cup of coffee each while they waited for Cesar.

Slowly, the sleepy little village started to come to life. People were feeding their goats and mules. Chickens were let out of their roosts and children started running around playing in whatever puddles they could find. Off in the distance, a low rumble started up and the ground shuddered a tiny bit as if a train were going by. A cloud of black ash and smoke shot up from the volcano on the horizon. The rumble stopped as abruptly as it had started. They saw Cesar walking slowly, with a large pack and a rifle strapped to his side.

"I managed to get us a boat, but it is not the best and we will have to paddle it. There is no motor, but the current is pretty swift on the river, so we should be okay. Are you ready to go?" Cesar asked.

Mark and Drew nodded their heads, swigging down the last of their coffee before they grabbed their heavy packs and followed Cesar to the boat. The bright green grass was wet with the morning dew and, by the time they had made the short walk to the river behind Cesar's small adobe house, their sneakers were soaked through. Behind Cesar's house was a small, eight-foot boat that reminded Drew more of a dingy than a boat.

"She is not pretty my friends, but she will float," Cesar told them.

They placed their packs and camera equipment carefully in the middle of the boat and climbed in. Each of them took a seat on a small wooden plank. Cesar untied the boat and they set off paddling at first, until the boat was taken by the current. Cesar sat quietly, marking paths on a map, while Drew and Mark snapped pictures of the river surroundings.

Small birds in every color flew in tiny flocks from one side of the river to the other. The sounds of the birds filled the air and somehow seemed louder than the howler monkeys from the night before. The river current was swift, but smooth. The air was still and hot, and though the water was coffee brown and muddy, they were tempted to take a swim just to cool off and get a break from the swarms of little gnats and mosquitoes. No matter how much bug spray they put on, the bugs didn't seem to mind, and the bites were slowly getting more painful as their sweat covered them. Cesar seemed to be the only person not getting bitten. Mark took notice of this, too.

"Why is it we are getting bitten all over and they aren't going near you at all?" he asked.

Cesar opened his pack, throwing a container of Tea tree oil in Mark's lap.

"They do not bite what they cannot smell," he told them. "The oil blocks your body from producing sweat, as well as throwing off the taste, so they do not bite," he explained.

Mark and Drew slathered themselves with a coating of oil and sat still. Sure enough, just as Cesar had said, the little bugs started to disappear. The Tea tree oil soothed the bites and stopped the terrible itching, but it also left them feeling dry and sticky.

The sun rose higher in the sky, by mid-morning the heat and humidity were stifling. Mark and Drew carefully splashed themselves with river water, soaking their hats before returning them to their heads, making sure not to get the gear wet. The heat seemed to even be too much for most of the animals. Except for a few alligators, most of the wildlife were hiding in their burrows until evening. The volcano they were headed towards was getting closer, inch-by-inch, as they wound their way down the river. Drew took out his log and noted everything they had seen, heard, or had taken pictures of.

Taking a few sips of warm water from his canteen, Drew spotted something out of the corner of his eye. He quickly lowered his canteen and scrambled to find the binoculars he had attached to his pack.

"Did you see that?" he asked.

"See what?" Mark replied.

Drew raised his binoculars, squinting against the bright sun reflecting from the lenses.

"I saw a person standing over there on the other bank. He was just standing there watching us."

"Are you sure? Where?" Mark asked.

"Just over there."

"I don't see anyone. What did he look like? What was he wearing?"

Drew put down his binoculars. There was a noticeable look of disappointment on his face when he answered Mark.

"He had long dark hair and not much clothing on. Actually, I don't know if he was wearing anything. I only saw him for a second and then he just vanished," Drew answered.

"I saw him, too," Cesar said. "That would be a scout," he continued. "The tribe is very territorial and protective of their land and people. They have scouts look out on the forest up to their boundaries and on the river at certain points to search for intruders," he went on. "They say that the tribe elder is over a hundred years old because they feed him the blood of any intruders they catch. You may catch a glimpse of many scouts as we start to get closer to their places and maybe even some of their warriors too, but it's just glimpses. They do not like to be seen much. Unless they want to fight, you will not see more than a couple at a time," Cesar told them.

Drew made sure he carefully wrote down everything that Cesar told them. Even if they didn't get that on camera before the end of the expedition, at least they could have that part narrated in.

"You seem to know quite a bit about a tribe that is supposed to be so mysterious," Mark said.

"I have lived here all my life, fished this river, and hunted this forest. I have seen many things, even things I wished I hadn't. You learn a few things over the years, my friend."

Mark nodded his head in the affirmative and Drew wrote down even more. Cesar grabbed a book from his pack and turned toward the front of the boat and began to read. They edged their way closer to the volcano and deeper into the forest. They were close enough to see a constant small stream of gray smoke rising from the top of the volcano now and notice the smell of sulfur and lava. The thick tree canopy hung over the river, providing a little relief from the relentless sun.

"In a short while, we will have to tie up the boat and walk into the forest," Cesar told them. "They make their home in the forest, not near the river's edge, where they could easily be seen," he added.

Mark and Drew began picking up their packs and checking their cameras, making sure to put a new, full roll of film in, so they didn't run out if they came across something interesting.

"Up ahead the river starts to curve, that's where we get out," Cesar said.

Cesar picked up the paddles and began to steer the small boat toward the riverbank. He jumped out at the shallow point, pulling the boat partially onto the bank before tying it to a tree. Drew and Mark jumped out, cameras around their necks, wearing their heavy packs. Cesar took out his map, found the point on the river where they were and marked it off.

"I am afraid my maps will no longer be useful to us when we

start going into the forest." He folded the map back up and shoved it in his back pocket. Cesar started leading them into the forest, pushing branches and vines aside as they went.

"Are you sure you know where you're going?" Mark asked.

"Oh yes, there will be signs all along the way, you will see," he replied.

There was something strange about his face this time. The smile had spread so far it gave him an ominous look. Mark felt a shiver go up his spine and goosebumps covered his arms and legs. As they walked further into the forest, the birds went silent.

"They already know we are coming, not just because the scout saw us and by now has warned the tribe, but because they listen to the animals and birds. Living off the land, they are able to use the forest to their advantage."

After a few more minutes of navigating through the thick underbrush, Cesar stopped and pointed half way up a large palm tree.

"Look there, do you see it? Do you see the painted skull on the tree?" he asked.

Mark and Drew immediately began taking pictures.

"That skull means we are heading in the right direction. It serves as a warning to other tribes and intruders."

They continued following Cesar deeper and deeper into the forest. The canopy of trees was so thick the sun was nearly blocked out completely. Small flowers and moss lined the ground and wound up tree trunks. The sound of the river was slowly fading away and the birds were just starting to get used to their presence and had begun making noise once again. There were more skulls painted on some of the trees, along with what looked like human hands tied up with vines. Mark and Drew took as many pictures as they could. All that could be heard was the sound of the shutters on the cameras going off in unison. Large chunks of volcanic rock, piled up in between two tall pines, caught Mark's eye.

"Cesar, what is that? Do you know? It must be manmade," Mark said. He walked over to the mound of rocks, so seemingly out of place, and took out his video camera. Cesar followed to explain what he thought they were.

"I believe those are grave markers. They only bury the remains of people who were not members of their own tribe under these rocks. It tells others to stay away or this could be them," he added.

He slowly reached out a hand and began to feel the rough texture of the rock.

"The porous rocks have a high salt content, that helps to preserve the bodies, and they believe that leaves a permanent gift to their gods, but also curses the intruders by not allowing their bodies to become one with the earth," he said into the camera.

Once again, Drew felt something wasn't right about Cesar when he looked at him. He couldn't help but wonder how it was that he knew specific details about the tribe. Living around the same geographical location could entitle you to see some things, but surely not this far into the forest, or to know exactly what this pile of rocks was used for.

They turned off the camera and Cesar began to lead them back onto the path. More small pieces of the volcanic rock seemed to be lining a path on the ground, circling some trees and forming small symmetrical piles at the bottom of others. There were several colors ranging from red to orange, even black and shades of brown. They took a few shots of the smaller piles; the colored ones that they thought might make a little bit of an interesting showpiece. As Cesar continued on with Mark and Drew in tow, they started to see the bottom of the volcano come into view.

Dead birds, caught in plumes of volcanic ash, littered the

ground all around it. The heat and humidity led to a dramatically rapid decomposition process, the smell wafted in and out of the trees and invited scavengers to a free feast. Mark and Drew covered their mouths and noses with their sleeves, but it seemed not to bother Cesar in the least. He looked as though he were laughing and shaking his head. They decided not to stop moving, choosing to take only a few pictures of the birds as they walked past on the path littered with bones. Streaks of sunshine pierced the canopy, lighting up small bits of the forest floor. Bits of white bone glistened back at them. Some were from animals, but there were many bones that were definitely human. Off in the distance, they started to hear strange sounds. The unmistakable smell of fire was carried on the breeze; the smell of burning flesh pierced their noses.

"We're getting close now," Cesar told them. "It's best that we remain quiet as we go through here, they look at loudness as a sign of aggression. This tribe is very leery of people and you are white. They may not know how to take to you at all. They are also not known for being very civilized," he added.

"Are we in danger?" Mark asked.

"I would say yes, we all are. If the chief elder doesn't like us, or finds us a threat, we may not make it back to the river, much less home," Cesar replied.

"Look at this!" called Drew. "I have never seen anything like it," he said. "How did they carve this, it seems almost perfect? There are no scratch marks and no tool marks of any kind. It's completely smooth."

"It's volcanic glass, it's impossible. The temperature that rock has to reach just to become magma, not to mention to somehow make a life-sized human form with no tools, well, it's just unbelievable," Mark said.

"It's impossible, yet my friend, there it stands in front of you."

When Mark and Drew finished recording and taking pictures of the statue, they stepped back and noticed a lot more of them; large and small ones, possibly children, and even a few that looked as though they were holding baskets. They walked around for what seemed like an eternity and stared at each statue, looking at the smooth features and different positions they were posed in. Most of the statues were standing in the shadows of the trees. But close to the volcano, one stood alone in the sun.

Drew noticed it first and began walking behind the rest, slowly making his way to the base of the volcano. Cesar was still standing by the first statue, just smiling. Mark followed close behind. The sun glistened brightly off the statue, sending streaks of rainbow colors in every direction, and making it nearly impossible to get a good look at it. Drew placed his hands around his eyes squinting, slowly walking forward. The closer he got, he noticed that he was able to see his reflection in the glass, almost like a dark mirror, but then something inside the glass caught his attention.

As he stood face to face with the glass statue he was able to see inside it. There was a person inside. It was as if a glob of molten glass had fallen on him and hardened instantly. He was perfectly preserved. Drew explained what he saw to Mark. Cesar seemed as unaffected by this discovery as everything else.

"It still doesn't explain how these people were covered in the glass to begin with. Not to mention how the glass became perfectly smooth and formed," Mark said.

Drew was walking around the statue, studying every inch from top to bottom.

"I know it doesn't and, as of now, I have no ideas how that would happen. There are even tufts of grass in there with him."

"Do you know what this reminds me of?" Drew asked

"No, what?"

"The crystal skulls they found a few years ago. You remember the ones with no tool marks that were supposedly from the lost city of Atlantis. It was thought that they held information, sort of like recordings, but we just don't know how to access the secrets they hold," he said.

"I see where you're going with this, and yes, there are a few similarities, but the crystal skulls didn't have people encased inside them."

"Even with the pictures and the videotape, no one back home will believe this," said Drew. His hands were still running up and down the glass, looking for a seam, a break, a bubble, anything that said that what he was seeing had more than one piece to it.

"If you think I am about to carry even a small one around, you're crazy," Mark told him.

"Oh no, my friends, you must not move the statues from their places!" Cesar snapped. His face was solid as stone, not one hint of a smile anywhere. "You cannot mess with these sacred statues. Some of them have been here for hundreds of years, maybe thousands of years and disturbing them, well, let's just say you would not make it out of this area alive. We are being watched; our every move, our words, everything we do. Many eyes are upon as right now and I think it's time we move on," Cesar added.

Mark and Drew did as they were told; leaving everything exactly the way they found it. The sun was starting to show through a little more in a bit of a clearing up ahead. There were a few mangroves growing around a small stream and a banyan tree that looked as though it were melting. Branches touched the ground at different angles, twisted and curling, and covered in moss. Large crevices in the trunk held what looked to be a basket of old rotted fruits and a completely white skull tied above it.

A few wild orchids bloomed in red and yellow, breaking up the green and brown. This spot was a particularly nice spot, shady and cool. Mark took several pictures.

"Remember, do not touch the offering basket or anything left out by the Maizmo tribe," Cesar warned.

They walked around exploring the small stream, watching a few tiny tadpoles and minnows swimming in the cool water. More large volcanic rocks lay to the right of the stream in between two trees. A few pictures of the volcano erupting and what looked like stars, were painted on the parts of their trunks that were facing the stream.

"This is an offering spot. They place food near clean water as an offering for the gods to keep them appeased," Cesar said.

Mark placed his hand on top of a handprint found on the rocks, noticing his seemed rather stubby in comparison. He stood up and stumbled, falling forward into the small stream, his hand extending out from the slick mud, causing the basket of fruit to topple over. Rotten dates, oranges, and dragon fruit rolled out, falling into the stream and were carried away. Mark slowly got up, looking at his handy work and back to Cesar.

A second later, they were surrounded by men with olive skin, long dark hair, and hazel eyes, wielding handmade spears. The tips were made of pointed volcanic glass. They were wearing some sort of animal skin loincloths and woven vines around their ankles and wrists. Mark took quick notice of the men who were wearing necklaces made of alligator teeth and wielding weapons reminiscent of a jagged-bladed knife. The men approached quickly, jabbing their spears at them, and yelling in a language Mark and Drew had never heard before. Mark was grabbed first and thrown to the muddy ground. His pack was torn off and his hands were tied with heavy green vines. The same thing happened to Drew. The men pulled both Drew and Mark to their feet, pointing at the empty basket, and then the stream, and yelling to one another.

Cesar walked up to one of the men, placing a hand on his forearm. He began to speak to them, in their language. When he turned to face Mark and Drew, he was once again smiling, and his eyes had taken on a darker, now frightening appearance. With Cesar now in the lead, the other villagers shoved and jabbed at Mark and Drew to get them moving.

"I told you, my friends, not to touch anything in the offering place," Cesar said.

He never even turned back to look at them as he spoke. The longer they walked, they began to notice that Cesar's hair was getting longer, and that his clothes seemed to be disintegrating. Every time they walked through a small patch of sunlight, there were less and less of them, until Cesar was left wearing just a loincloth, too.

"It was an accident, I didn't mean to fall, and I never would have disrespected the offering on purpose," Mark said.

"Do you really think the only reason you are here in this place, at this time, is simply because you knocked over a basket? You wanted to come here. You wanted to find this tribe. You were in that town three days and you wouldn't have stopped until you found them, found us," he said. "Oh, my friend, there is more to it than that. The full moon is almost upon us and the gods have been angered that you have discovered us. They threaten us with a drought and the volcano erupting," he said.

They walked further into the forest until it was nearly dark. They reached a small village in the middle of a clearing. It was as if they had been expecting them all along. There were fires with high flames and the villagers were all standing in lines. The men were still holding spears and the women, some holding infants, just stood there staring. They marched Mark and Drew in like circus animals. They tugged and pulled them around the entire village, giving each person a chance to see them up close.

Cesar walked around behind the parade, smiling and chatting away with some of the villagers.

"Cesar, what are you going to do with us?" asked Drew.

Cesar turned and faced Drew, but he didn't smile, even though he looked like he wanted to.

"I am going to make you a permanent gift to our gods," he told them. "They are angry that you are here. You came here to seek us out. You wanted to take away from us what has always been ours and ours alone."

Cesar pointed at them both and made a few gestures to one of his followers. Immediately, Mark and Drew were taken to the hut farthest away from the fires and tied to wooden stumps. They could barely see each other and were shaking from head to toe. Their packs had been taken away and so had the knives that they had made sure to place in them. Once it was completely dark, there were loud yells and noises coming from all around. Cesar appeared in the hut with a torch and a bowl. He placed the bowl in the middle of the hut, touched the torch to it, and instantly the hut filled with smoke.

A moment later, Mark and Drew were lying on their sides. Cesar ordered for them to be dragged out of the tent and taken to the sacred well. Over rocks, roots, and sticks they were dragged, neither one waking up. Mark and Drew were lifted up on a platform and tied at the feet. A camera was placed in Drew's hands and a notebook was placed in Mark's. They lit fires all around them and began chanting. The sky in the clearing began to move and a breeze picked up. The howler monkeys were going wild, almost singing along with the villagers.

The fires crackled, sending sparks and ashes into the evening sky. Dark purples, blues, and reds swirled around and the moon rose high in the air shining down on the volcano. The rumble started up small at first, getting louder every second. A large plume of black smoke and ash shot up from the volcanoes' summit, sending ashes flying high into the sky and then gently floating to the ground, covering Mark and Drew.

The smell of singed hair filled the air, a few hot pebbles landed on Mark, and he stirred awake. His vision blurred and he couldn't speak. Drew didn't wake at all. Mark began struggling against the vines that held him, only to have them get tighter. Cesar walked up to the largest fire and threw something into it; the fire rose, completely engulfing the bottom part of the platform that held the captives.

The volcano rumbled again and the chanting got louder, but this time both Mark and Drew were awake. When the volcano got quiet again, so did the chanting. Mark's notebook hit the ground and landed with a small cloud of ash around it. Drew's camera broke as it hit the ground and the film inside caught fire. Suddenly, the forest became clear and calm. There was no village, but when the sun rose, two new statues in volcanic glass stood as a warning; not all lost tribes should be found.

Frayed

"Hey Mr. Watkins, is Mary home?"

"Yeah, she's in her room. Go on in."

James hurried up the steps and flung the door open. He ran up the stairs and right into Mary's room.

"Mary, you gotta see this! Come with me right now," he beckoned.

"See what?"

"Look, just get your shoes on, I have to show you. I was walking up by the old tracks behind the mill and I found this rusted out swing set back there. I think there was a park or maybe a daycare center or something there when the mill was running. The air back there got really cool and I figured it was just because I was in a wooded section, so I climbed up the monkey bars. I was just hanging around enjoying the cool air and the shade when this weird wind tunnel or something started blowing hard. There was a loud noise like a train was coming down the tracks, but nothing was there."

"I know trains have not used that piece of track since the 1930s, so I don't know what that was. But I finished climbing across the bars and as I got to the end and looked down, it was like a black hole opened up. That's the best way I can describe--it looking at a black hole. There was nothing I could see in it, just empty and dark and cool air coming from it."

"Okay, James, did you by any chance get into your dad's moonshine again?"

"Come on, Mary. I'm serious. Just come with me and don't tell anyone 'til we know what this is."

Mary threw her sneakers on and grabbed her water bottle off of her dresser. She glanced out her bedroom window and gawked at the trees gently blowing over the creek in her backyard. They could follow the creek and stay in the shade all the way to the spot where the tracks started in the woods and then follow the tracks to the old mill.

They walked down the stairs, with James doing his best to stay calm until they reached the door. Mary's dad was edging the walkway from the porch to the mailbox. He was practically O.C.D. with his yard work, but Mary didn't mind since it meant he was not the nosiest dad in the world.

"Dad, I'm going for a walk with James to see if we can meet up with some friends. I'll be back later, okay?"

"Yup, that's fine with me," he replied.

Mary and James made their way around to the back of the house and down a path they had worn to the bare dirt from walking the same way day after day. The summer was unusually warm for June and they were already breaking into a sweat from the short distance to the path. The breeze from the trees, spraying a bit of creek water up, was welcomed as they made their way towards the wood line.

"Look Mary, I know this sounds crazy, but I know there is something there and that's why you have to come see it. You can hear things. Trains, voices, children, I don't know, but you don't hear it until you climb up the bars. The wind really whips around, the trees don't seem to move, but the grass sure does. It almost feels like you are getting sucked in, like it's trying to pull you off the bars," he explained.

"There was something there. I didn't feel scared at first, more curious, you know? I just wanted to get closer to see what it was. It was like something was calling me, telling me to come explore. It was only when I heard the noises get louder that I started to get a little scared. I swear I heard laughter, too. But I know I was alone."

"Well, are you sure you were alone? Maybe there were other

people there playing or walking through the woods. I mean we aren't the only people who hang out at the mill and I am sure other kids have found that swing set before you."

"Mary, in all the times we have been going there, have you ever seen kids there? I mean little kids, not teens like us. But come to think of it, besides our friends, I have never seen anyone else hang out there. People here are all caught up on old ghost stories and rumors about what happened and why the mill shut down. No one else comes here, that's why we do."

He skipped along, letting his Converse kick up small clumps of dry mud and tufts of pine needles. He grabbed a pinecone dangling from a branch and tossed it into the woods in front of him. A small squirrel scoffed at him for his efforts and ran angrily up the tree, twitching his tale and chirping. James watched the squirrel as he walked past, almost glued to it like a child seeing one for the first time. He wanted to reach out to touch it, to hold it, but he didn't know why.

Mary chimed in, breaking his fixation with the tiny squirrel. "Okay, so maybe it was a sink hole, since we are rather close to the river, or maybe it was where they dumped the old oil. I mean it could literally be a man-made catchall. It's not like they were all righteous on the environment in the industrial days."

"A dump right off the edge of a ladder for a kid's playground? Environmental concerns or not, they wouldn't dump oil or something, especially where kids play, if they were the children of the actual mill workers, which is what I think it was built for," he replied.

"Yeah, I guess you're right."

"You'll see what I mean when we get there."

They walked slowly along the path winding around trees and pieces of old track that were broken and aged. Old concrete millstones protruded from the ground and let them know they were on the right track.

"Shhh. Mary lets be quiet, I want to see if we can hear anyone or anything," James instructed.

They kept moving, but allowed their feet to hit the ground ever so gently. Small plopping noises echoed from acorns falling from the trees. The sounds of the creek trickling beside them kept the woods from falling silent.

"James, I don't hear anything," Mary whispered.

James grabbed her hand and nudged her on toward the end of the path.

"Come on, the swing set it just up here and then off to the right behind the magnolia tree."

They shoved the long grass and weeds aside and made their way over the chunks of brick and stone that had fallen from the silo years ago. The magnolia stood tall and proud, still blooming year after year in huge clouds of white fragrant flowers. Mary stared in delight, trying to count how many had bloomed already, and noting in her mind how many red seeded cones still needed to bloom. The air was cool and filled with the sweet aroma from the magnolia.

"Over here, Mary."

"Wow, I can't believe we never saw this before today," Mary said excitedly.

"But I don't see anything on the ground."

"Look it was here, but I didn't see it until I had climbed up there."

James grabbed the ladder and began pulling himself up. He heaved his body on top of the bars and crawled across them, peering through the rungs and staring at the ground. Mary took a few steps closer and grabbed the rail. She pulled herself up the ladder following James. She looked off to her right, noticing a rope hanging from a branch over the creek.

"James, look over there. Did you see that last time?"

"See what?" he asked.

"Over there. It looks like there was a rope swing on that oak tree. The rope is still there, but I can't see if the swing is still connected," Mary said.

She hopped down and ran through the overgrowth. She felt like a young child. Her excitement could hardly be contained when she noticed the board was still attached. The rope was frayed only a slight bit, having been shielded from the sun in the shade of the forest.

"Mary, wait up, I'll give you a push!" he called out.

James jumped down from the bars and stumbled a bit. He stood up, running through the underbrush, leaping over a few fallen logs and stones. Mary was already running her hands up and down the ropes, feeling the soft frayed edges between her fingers.

He stood in front of her as she placed her foot on the cloth-covered board and slowly hopped up, allowing her body weight to hang from the swing. The branch the rope was on creaked and moaned and the rope pulled tight under her weight, but the swing held. Mary threw a quick glance and a smile to James before throwing her feet off the swing, letting her hands slide down, and placing herself on the seat.

James stepped behind his friend and pulled back on the ropes. He peered upward, watching the branch sway with the swing. The creek bed dropped off sharply just behind him, but the water was only knee deep. Sharp rocks and fallen logs littered the shore line. He stepped carefully, not wanting to get knocked over. Mary pushed her feet back and forth, leaning back. She felt the wind rush by her face. For a moment, she felt so free, like she was flying.

"Mary, do you hear that? The laughing, its back. I hear little kids again."

He turned around slowly, staring at out into the woods and back toward the mill, and finally down at the creek. No one seemed to be there. The wind picked up and Mary laughed out loud. She seemed to be lost in the moment, but James was worried. The air got cooler and he could hear what sounded like the roar of a distant train. James walked down to the edge of the track and, though he knew there couldn't possibly be a train, he had to look. He had to put his hand on the exposed piece of rail and feel for a vibration he knew wasn't there.

"James, I'm going to jump!" she yelled.

She jumped and landed right next to James, grabbing his arm, together they tumbled down the embankment. Mary laughed and tugged at James' shirt.

"Oh, come on, that was fun and you know it," she said.

He smiled and shook his head.

"Look, the old mill wheel is still there and still turning," he said.

He walked a few paces, kicking a few bricks out of the way, and pulling a large broken branch out of the gear. The wheel was turning from the current of the creek, but just barely. The old wooden wheel was swollen and covered in algae. The mossy-like substance clung to the paddles and flung droplets of water into the air.

He stepped partially into the creek and grabbed the paddle, stopped the wheel, and peered in behind the gears. Cold air rushed past him and a faint rusty odor filled his nose. The cavern was wide open just beyond it. He tugged a little and the wheel moved.

"I think we could take this off and go into the hole," he said

"We should leave it alone, it's a part of the town history and we might get in trouble if we break it," Mary replied.

James pulled a little harder and the wood plank propping it in place broke off.

"No matter, we can get in here from this opening I just made."

He lowered himself down, trying not to slip on the green slime on the bottom of the riverbed. Mary poked her head in and looked around.

"Come on in, there's plenty of room," James told her.

Laughter started up just as Mary sat at the opening. The leaves on the ground began floating up and the grass was moving, but there was no one running.

Mary stared out into the woods and back toward the mill.

"Hello? Is anyone there?" she called out.

"Mary, look at this."

James held his hand out, grasping a sleeve to an old small flannel shirt in one hand, and a piece of blood-stained yellow lace in the other.

"James, do you hear that?"

"Yeah, I told you I was hearing the sounds of little kids everywhere."

"We should go. I don't feel very comfortable here now."

Mary stood up and turned to start walking back up the embankment.

"James, come on! I really want to go."

The wheel vibrated in his hand as he reached to grab the side and pull himself out.

"James!" he heard Mary scream.

He pulled himself from the hole and rushed up to see what was wrong. The dark hole was at the bottom of the monkey bars. Mary was holding a nearby tree, watching as the dark from the hole seemed to spread like nightfall over the bars and the mill. The wind howled like a train roaring down the track and small children appeared from behind the trees and dotted the area around the playground set and the hole. James reached for Mary, forgetting he was still holding the clothing he had found lodged behind the mill wheel.

It was cold. The air was thick with smoke that had begun billowing from the stack. The pale-faced children, walking at first, were suddenly running around the yard and climbing the bars. They ran in and out of the creek bed, climbing the wheel and tossing rocks into the water. A small boy tossed a grey creek stone, washed smooth with time, which landed just at the toe of James' black Converse.

The young boy smiled and stepped closer. James tugged at Mary's shirt.

"I see them," she whispered.

"No…look over here," he replied.

She stepped away from the back of the old willow she was clinging to, to look around James. The red-haired boy seemed to glide ever so lightly, kicking the leaves as he bounded closer. His blood-stained flannel shirt came into view in the dim light dotting the forest floor from the spaces between the tree branches. Mary peered at the piece of flannel in James' hand and back at the boy, who was now just in front of them.

His eyes seemed dark and so lifeless, she thought. A second later they were surrounded by children. The group stared right at them, moving closer in split second lunges. Mary and James backed up away from their tree and the ground around their feet turned black. The leaves and grass wrapped their ankles, sticking to their socks, as if trying to hold them in place.

James dropped the piece of flannel, but the lace had gotten caught around his fingers. He tried to fling his hand, hoping it would dislodge, but it wouldn't. He grabbed the cloth and tugged, falling backwards over a log partially covered in leaves, as the cloth fell to the ground.

Mary's eyes were drawn to the cloth just as the hand of the small girl reached for her. She bent down to pick up the old lace ruffle and the ghostly white child grabbed for her hair. The children followed them, forcing them back toward the creek bed and the wheel. James and Mary stayed low and close, they were freezing now, and could see their breath.

The ground seemed to disappear in front of them, the leaves were gone, and more and more faces appeared from the darkness.

James got up, grabbing Mary's arm, dragging her to her feet.

"We have to get out of here, Mary!"

They turned around to face the wheel and tried to run. The darkness was all around them and the wheel was starting to turn in the creek. The wind was whipping around and faces began to fade. They couldn't breathe. Mary fell again, sliding in the damp leaves and mud along the bank, with James struggling to stay on his feet and catch his breath.

The mill wheel turned faster and faster, the children gathered around it, and circled both sides of the creek. James fell, sliding into Mary and forcing her head first into the creek. The current grabbed her long hair as she struggled to sit up from the water and to push away from the spinning wheel. The water began to move, flowing harder and being sucked under it.

"Mary, get up! Get up now!" James screamed.

"I can't! My hair is caught or something! Help me! Please, James, hurry!"

He tried to reach her, but he was stuck. The darkness was

covering his feet and headed to the edge of the creek, now swelling as the water built up around Mary. The laughter started up again, this time that was all he could hear, the laughter. It was all around him, but now so was the darkness. Mary's cries for help were gone. He couldn't see her or the mill or anything.

He called out, but no one answered him. He could feel the ground beneath him moving, but he was not walking. He was being dragged down the embankment and could feel the water cover his feet and legs. He looked down to see the water, dark red and inching its way up his body. The laughter was gone and he could only hear the water rushing past him and through the slats in the mill wheel. The darkness was everywhere except the creek and he could see Mary's sneaker just inside the hole.

He remembered the rope swing and turned to see that it was broken. The white rope was frayed and the seat drug the ground, being forced with the swaying of the branch it was attached to. He tried to lean and reach the swing to try to pull himself from the creek, but the pale-faced children were back smiling and giggling. The redheaded boy grabbed the seat and pushed it toward James.

James looked back to the wheel, it had stopped spinning. He grabbed the wood planks and started climbing up. He got to the top and there was Mary. His heart jumped in his chest. He called out to her. But she didn't answer.

He quickly started to climb down the other side and jumped to the bank. Mary turned around, her pale skin glistening in the shadows of the trees. Her lace ruffle was still stained with blood and she smiled at James. They were kids again. The sound of children bounced around the woods and the swing was moving back and forth.

"Mary," he whispered.

She shook her head and grabbed his hand, leading him back over to the side of the mill. The monkey bars were teeming with kids. He walked quietly with Mary to the large plaque hanging on the wall.

Down the path, between the trees, a rope swing dangled in the breeze. The rope was bleached and rotted with time, but so was the willow from which it was tied. Halfway up, the rope is frayed, dirty and worn from timeless play. The wind stirred and leaves blew off. The seat was covered in faded cloth. As you approached, you heard the sound. Children laughing all around. The remains of a home not far away, a chimney stood to mark the day. You walked to the swing and looked over the edge, to the river below and a rocky ledge. Then you looked back at a board scraping the ground. A scream echoed, where no one was around. A weeping tree now grieved alone, attached to a swing and a broken rope. A heart engraved with a partial name, the only reminder when the laughter faded.

Mary ran off, back toward the swing, James followed close behind. Laughter filled his ears and he felt young again. He looked down and tried to figure out what he had done with his other shoe, his dirty flannel flapped in the breeze as he chased his friend, each waiting for their turn on the swing.

Burial Mounds

"Benji, we have to get through that big hill over there before we can make these old terraces work again."

"Oh, come on, Adam. Let's take a break. I really want to get a better look at the pile of old relics and trash we put in the cart. The historical people from the museum are making their way here today to see if we are disturbing a sacred Mayan spot. I want to make sure we don't get chased off this old land."

Benji walked over to the old cart, noticing its wooden wheels were slightly sinking into the ground, even though the ground was very dry and hard. The sparse grass they'd parked the cart on had turned yellow and brown and was clinging to the wheels.

Benji placed his hand on the side of the cart and stared at the cracked vases, water jars, bowls, and all the other remnants of pottery. There were intricate designs throughout the bunch. Some of the designs were still bright after hundreds of years of being buried and lost to the world.

A few ancient pieces of rotting cloth, quickly disintegrating in the open air, caught his attention. Benji carefully shuffled the broken bits of pottery around in the cart, trying to pull up the cloth, but the clumps of dirt attached to it made the cloth crumble and slip through his fingers with every tug.

"What are you doing?" Adam asked.

"Well, I told you I wanted to look through some of this before they got here and these pieces of cloth sort of look like clothing. Look at this," he said.

Benji held up a tattered piece of blue striped cloth and small beads fell back into the cart as it unfolded. A cloud of dust hit his face and he shook his head in an effort not to sneeze.

Adam walked away from the cart, dusting his dirty hands off on his torn brown pants. Golden dust flew from his black hair as he made his way toward open ground away from his friend. The sounds of the other workers digging and talking could be barely heard just over the sounds of the birds in the area.

He peered back over his shoulder, surveying the surroundings and the very distant moving people in the background. He carefully took the torn cloth from Benji, trying to shake as much dirt and dust off as he could without destroying the small piece.

"The patterns are definitely Mayan," he said.

But that is a given, since we are excavating old Mayan property, he thought.

"Adam, the piece you're holding was probably attached to these other small ripped bits here. I think they were a piece of a shirt for a small child," Benji told him.

Adam knelt down and moved the beads around with his index finger in the dirt. The small turquoise and quartz beads glistened brightly in the sun, making him squint.

"Well, it's quite possible you're right about it being a shirt from a child, they did have children like everyone else and they did occupy this land for over a thousand years. But I have to tell you that I don't think this piece of cloth is any more or less significant than the rest of the artifacts the villagers have been finding here," he replied.

"We knew we would be finding things from our ancestors here, that's why we have the carts to dispose of things we don't want or need, but I don't think we should spend too much time going through everything we see, unless it really pops out at us. We have to finish the terrace restoration before the end of summer or we will miss the harvest this year and our whole village is counting on this to survive," Adam reminded him.

He stowed the piece of cloth back in the cart and picked up the beads, placing them in his pocket. *My wife will like these,* he thought. Benji looked at the cart of things again and walked back over to the stone and mud terrace. He grabbed handfuls of grass and weeds and ripped them out from between the stones, roots and all. He tossed them out into a pile to use as mulch later.

The small Mayan village they lived in was quickly being demolished by new age buildings and their village couldn't afford to live the way that city people live. They had lived off the land for many years, a lot like their ancient ancestors. A meager living could be carved out of the land around them, now only to be forced off the small bit of land they had made their homes on for generations.

Every time Benji thought about this, it enraged him. The more they worked, tirelessly trying to prepare the land that had not been used for over a century, the harder it became to keep pushing on, *but we have to,* he thought.

He looked up to see Adam tossing away more grass and packing stones into the cracks in the terraces, making their way slowly toward the hill. The men were hard at work trying the restore the old terraces and tilling out the old farmland, while planting corn, wheat, rice and beans. The rest of the villager's elderly and women and children had the task of moving their worldly possessions and as much of their old small shacks as possible to the new land to rebuild.

They worked long hours as the hot sun beamed down on them. The lack of water all the way in the middle of the Peruvian terrain, made the tempers flare rather quickly. This normally peaceful village was almost always in an uproar. Benji stood up and walked a few more steps forward to repeat the process of weed pulling and filling in the cracks, while Adam, too, had his hands full.

As each two-man team finished their current spot, they moved forward to mend another spot. The carts were getting heavy with things they needed to discard. Each afternoon, as the sun was getting ready to set, they followed a small path to where they kept a few mules. The mules were hooked up to the carts and towed them to the edge of the cliff terrace land and dumped the true trash and rocks over the side.

Something was eating away at Adam about the bits of cloth. He had found many more pieces like it, all were small like this one. All of them seemed to be from small children. The thought that there may have been a sickness that swept through the land and killed a lot of the children came to mind. *Was there a reason the land here was left,* he wondered?

But there were also old superstitions that began filling his mind with wonder and fear at the same time. Was it possible that their proud ancestors left this beautiful piece of land so many years ago because it was cursed? Did they get chased off?

The sun was starting to sink a little lower in the sky. It was early evening and close to dinner. The rest of the villagers started making their way down the trails past him and Adam in their trek to get to dinner.

Dried fish and rice with beans was on the menu, with maybe some fruit for dessert. *Until we get settled in, this iss likely to be our diet pretty much every day and night,* he thought. Benji bent down again, ripping out the weeds and rubbing the raw spots on his hands that seemed to hurt more when he sat still than they did when he worked with them.

He looked over to see Adam just starting to dig into the large mound of dirt that had piled up high over the years, but was clearly placed there on purpose. The mound was placed directly on the "Y" split on the terrace and was the death of this farmland. It was placed there to stop the water and was the end of this community long ago. The question was why, he pondered?

He finished pulling up the last bit of weeds from his spot and walked over toward the mound. He grabbed another shovel from the side of the mound and began thrusting the shovel into it, cutting deep slits in the hard turf. The harder the shovel was thrown, the more his shoulder ached as he hit solid ground.

Adam was using a hoe and trying to gouge out pieces of grass and dirt. He wiped sweat from his brow, pulled out a handkerchief with his family design on it, and tied his long black hair back from his face. They moved closer together and began digging even more ferociously.

Soon they were the last two men left working on the land and the sun was very low in the sky. The beautiful oranges and pinks looked so captivating against the old stones and winding terraces etched into the mountains and plains.

Adam heaved the hoe over his head and dragged large pieces of dirt and half dead grass to his feet. With each plunge of the hoe, a large gaping tear was left in its place. The more he tried to get the side of the hill to collapse, the angrier he got at the fact that it wouldn't. There was a feeling running through his body that he had to get this hill removed. He didn't care if he worked on it all night or if he worked on it by himself

Benji continued to dig the shovel deeper into the hole they were making, throwing great globs of dirt and gravel behind him.

"Adam, come, we better start getting back down the mountain. It's getting dark and we won't be able to see the path down if we don't leave now," said Benji.

"I'm not really all that hungry, why don't you go eat and get some sleep. I'll be fine here," Adam pleaded.

"No Adam, I am not going to leave without you, you know how chilly the nights get up here, you don't have anything to keep you warm. The mosquitoes will be horrible without the fires and the lavender smoke to keep them back. Plus, man, I know you're as hungry as I am, we will be back in the early morning, you know this, so let's go."

Benji threw his shovel into the side of the hill and heard a small

150

thud as it hit. He looked at the shovel sticking out of the hill for a second, but decided not to mention the thud until they were back in the morning, when they could see what, if anything, was there.

Adam let the hoe down slowly, resting the palm of his hand on the tip of the handle. His hand hurt to sit there, as sweat dripped off his face and slowly ran down his arms. The sky was more dark red and deep purple now and the sound of crickets and locusts could be heard from everywhere.

He looked over at his lifetime friend waiting there for him and knew he would never make the long walk down to their awaiting meals alone in the darkness. Adam let the hoe drop from his grasp and used his forearm to wipe away some sweat from his head.

He shook his head, which flung dirt and dust from his hair, and gave a half smile.

"Okay, Benji, let's go eat," he said.

They walked slowly down the path, past the parts of the terraces they had already cleaned out and repaired. They seemed to be begging for the cold Peruvian waters to flow down their paths again. The sound of frogs from the distant lake at the top of the mountain made music in the air. The sounds of all the other nighttime creatures just waking up and stirring in the grass made them keep watch on their steps even closer than they usually did.

"Adam, have you noticed lately all the fighting that's been happening in our village?" Benji asked.

"Well, there has been some high tempers and a few arguments, but look at what we are dealing with. I think some arguments should be expected."

"A few over where the dirt landed or a rock getting slammed on a finger maybe. Yes, even about where they will be building their home, but the arguments seem to have no purpose…they all just seem to be angry," Benji told him.

The walk seemed to go by a little faster tonight. Maybe it was because they were hurrying and didn't realize it, or maybe it was because the topic of conversation actually took their mind off of how tired they were, how hard they had worked, and how far they were walking.

The smell of their dinners and warm fires filled their noses and soon they had all but forgotten the mound they were trying to get rid of and the topic they had been discussing. The sun was completely gone and the dark sky revealed its first of many secrets. The stars that they had used as calendars and to tell the future were out in force. No smog from the encroaching cities or dark feelings here to cloud the view.

As they reached their small campsite, they hurried over to the cooking pot and grabbed a plate, filling it with fish, rice, and beans. Their hunger took over and they sat in the cool grass eating their fill. The warm glow of the fire and the comfort of a full stomach called them for a night of sleep and, before they had washed their plates, they fell asleep under the moon.

The sun rose up early and the day began much as it had everyday over the past few weeks. They got up, grabbed water jugs, and took off up the makeshift path to the new land. The women of the village stayed behind to tend the children, clean up from the night before, and continue to gather what they could from their old homes, bringing it to their camp until the terraces were done.

They walked slowly up the path, getting a really good look at the beautiful job they had done restoring the terrace. *The ancient ancestors would be proud,* Benji thought. A smile crossed his face as they made their way around the stone walls and up the mountainside.

As they got toward the top, everyone spread out in different directions, searching for the rest of the spots they needed to clean and repair. Adam and Benji took a sharp right and headed up to the

152

hill they had started excavating the previous night. The shovel was still sticking out of the mound where Benji had thrown it and Adam's hoe was leaning against the side of the hill waiting for his return.

Adam bent down a little and grabbed the handle of the hoe. The pain in his hand was terrible as the scabs from his blisters reopened. Benji reached to the ground and grabbed a few fern leaves. He walked over to his friend who was busy staring at his hands.

"Adam, let me see your hands," said Benji.

He took the hoe from Adam and leaned the hoe up against him. Benji laid the fern leaves over Adam's blisters and wrapped them around the palm and tucked them in.

"This should help a little, at least enough to keep the blisters from getting worse," Benji told him.

"Thanks," Adam replied.

He pushed a small smile across his face before taking the hoe again.

"This part is almost done. We will be helping to build our houses here soon, you'll see my old friend, it will be all worth it soon and we will be back with our great ancestors as we should have always been," Benji said.

"Did I tell you last night I hit something with the shovel when I threw it into the hill before we left? I don't know what it was, obviously, since it was too dark to see and I wanted to get home. It may be just a rock, but who knows. Either way, I think we should have the cart moved over closer to us and maybe call a few others to help us," Benji added.

Adam's eyes lit up and he proceeded to use his hoe to pull more lose dirt from the spot Benji had taken his shovel from. The sun was already bright and the temperature was rising fast, as were tempers. Adam and Benji could hear their friends yelling and screaming, but they couldn't hear what they were saying.

Benji started digging the shovel in, throwing heaps of dirt over his shoulders, feeling tiny bits fall on him, sticking to his sweaty arms. With every shovel full of dirt, he was getting in an even worse mood and didn't know why.

"Benji! Look at this!" Adam yelled.

Benji walked over to the other side, expecting to see another vase or jar, but instead there was a small human skull.

"Oh wow! We've really found something this time, haven't we?" said Benji.

"The problem is if this discovery gets out to the museum, we won't be allowed to have this property, even if it should rightfully be ours," Adam replied.

"Well let's keep digging. If it is just this one skull, we can just re-bury it somewhere and not tell the museum anything. I mean they won't know if we don't tell them, especially if we get rid of this hill pretty fast," Benji replied.

He quickly grabbed the small skull and hid it behind a few logs next to the hill. He and Adam quickly started pulling more dirt from the hole; the more they dug, the worse it got. The rest of the tiny child's body, even the rest of the blue striped clothing that had not completely decayed started falling out.

Small beads and little dolls fell at their feet. Adam climbed on the top of the hill and started tearing into it. He began ripping large pieces from the top and throwing them beyond the logs. Benji used his hands to pull more dirt away and slowly another body started to appear. This one seemed to be a little better preserved than the last one.

"Oh Adam, there's more of them."

Adam didn't answer, he just kept digging more and more. A

moment later his hoe hit something hard. He dropped the hoe and knelt down, pulling loose dirt from the hole and noticing a large piece of sandstone like a cap. He sunk his fingers under the side and tried to pull the stone up, but couldn't.

"Benji, I need your help. I found a big rock here. I need to get it out, but it's heavy."

Benji made his way up to the top of the hill, started digging out more dirt from around the sides of the stone, and tried to stick his fingers under it. Together, he and Adam managed to pull the stone into a standing position. The large piece of sandstone was engraved underneath and there were long scratches where it looked like someone or something was trying to scratch their way through it.

"Adam, you should see this. I don't think we should have moved this stone or the bodies."

Adam crawled over to Benji's side to look at the stone. They finished dusting it off with their hands and tried to read the encryptions.

"Our land, begotten by vengeance, has torn our people. A mother over taken, as all children from her were born to evil. Let stand this tomb as a reminder to all, the land was soured by death and vengeance."

"What the hell happened here?" Adam asked.

He looked over to Benji, who was still reading and re-reading the stone. They pushed the stone over and watched it slide down the side of the hill and come to a rest, leaning against the hill and the ground.

"It's probably just some story they made up to keep intruders away from their land," Adam said.

"I'm not so sure of that. You know our ancestors believed in many gods the way we do, but they practiced human sacrifice to

155

appease these various gods. Maybe this was another place they did that. Maybe we are disturbing something we really shouldn't be disturbing."

Adam reached down and grabbed Benji's shovel and started shoveling out more dirt, tossing it just off to the side. As he shoveled a little more, he noticed what looked like hair starting to stick up from the dirt.

He knelt down halfway in the hole and used his hands to clear out scoops of dirt. A woman's body, wrapped in colorful clothing, stated to appear. Her arms were bent at the elbows, with her hands bent at the wrists, palms to the sky. Her fingernails hung from tiny strips of petrified skin. The shape of her long dead face showed she had been buried alive and had tried to claw her way out.

The dirt started to cave in around her from the weight of Benji and Adam, as they stared at their discovery in disbelief.

"Should we move her?" Adam asked.

He whispered as if she could still hear him if he spoke aloud. Adam stared down into the dark hole that had been capped by a heavy stone. That would have left this woman alone in the darkness, scared and surrounded by the bodies of her children, if the stone was right. He couldn't, no didn't, want to imagine what it must have been like for her.

"Adam, look! What's that?"

Benji pointed to a rolled-up piece of papyrus in her lap. He reached down and carefully took the scroll. He blew on it, trying to get the dirt away, and noticed some of it was skin. He pulled the tiny piece of rotting corn husk that had been used to keep the scroll closed and unrolled it. The ash ink used to write on the scroll was very well preserved being out of the sunlight.

"Well, what does it say?"

"It's a letter from her husband. It basically tells why she is being put in here, why the children are in here, that he is sorry and loved them," he told Benji.

"Well, tell me what happened to them. Now you've got me worried and curious," he responded.

"Okay. Her name is Adlorden and she is about twenty-six years old. There is more than one child buried in this mound, all of them different ages, no older than the fourth year of life. It says that basically, the tribe was being taken over by their vengeance god. He wanted a sacrifice, but when the tribe members started to rise up against sacrificing their children and wives for the gods, this woman was overtaken by the vengeance of the gods.

"The elders tried everything to get rid of the vengeance that started to possess all the tribe members. They began fighting with each other: fathers killing sons and brothers, mothers attacking the children and destroying the harvests. The new moon became known as the blood harvest moon.

"It says the ground became soured with bloodshed and violence and the drought began to crack the terraces so that water was not reaching the crops. They discovered that the Vengeance god was intent on being reborn and had chosen the woman who was saved from sacrifice to bear him.

"They didn't find out until she had given birth during the blood harvest moon, that the infant was made of pure evil. It is said that when something is pure evil, even in the most innocent form, the eyes show the windows to the soul and that her child was soulless.

"They said that the very moment the child was born to this world, the lightening gods were throwing their bolts to the ground, causing fires to run through the land scorching everything in the realm. The heat became unbearable, but the rains would not come. The days became dark and there was no difference between day and night.

"The child screamed like the howling of the mountain lions all the time. It had been born with teeth and when he tried to suckle, he would draw blood, not milk, from his mother. The elders snuck into her house in the night. When they finally got the child silenced, it was decided that they had to sacrifice it since it was not a child, but evil. They took this first child, placed it in a hole they had dug beneath a part of the terrace, and buried it while it slept.

"The father, Malidon, knew of the plan and where it was to take place. He was told he could never tell Adlorden. The next day the woman awoke, but the sky was blood red and the air was hot as fire and her child was gone. Adlorden walked all day, looking in every house, and behind the trees, but could find no sign of the child and no one would say anything about it.

"As she wept for her child and the days passed, there was no improvement in the crops, the air, the sky, the anger. She discovered she was again with child. Fearing the worst was yet to come, the elders told her she needed to get rid of the child at birth and not allow years of life trapped inside the house to be the death of their people. The Vengeance god was even angrier at the fact that they had not sacrificed her or any others.

"Adlorden would not hear of it. As she approached time to give birth, she packed a blanket with some food and water and proceeded down the mountain to the flat woods to give birth alone. The woods began to weep at the moment the child arrived. The trees wilted where they stood, the ground began to dry up, and the lightening spread over the land. The tribe knew the child had been born and feared what might come to pass.

"When Adlorden returned to her tribe, the child she had was not an infant, but a walking, talking child that was close to three years old, though they had only been away a few days. As she approached the tribe, she was surrounded by the chief and the elders who tried to pry the boy away from her. His eyes were black as coal.

"The boy raised his hand, and as he did so, the tribe elder was

158

lifted into the air, turned upside down, and held face first over the sacred fires and slowly burned to death. The boy released his mother's other hand, walked over, and began eating the elder. As blood ran down his face, dripping on the sand, it was said to be the only time he smiled.

"For a moment, Malidon was able to approach the boy whose eyes had turned green while he was feeding, and for that moment, Malidon loved his son. Adlorden walked over to him, but though she wanted so badly to have her child be pure, innocent, and loved, she knew in her heart that he was going to take revenge on and kill their people--or at least what was inside him would.

"She looked around at what was left of her tribe, all nearly starved to death, and with no water. Babies from the tribe that had numbered many, had all but died; there were only two left and they were close to death. The end of their people and their way of life was slapping her in the face.

"Adlorden looked down at her hands, her wrists adorned with the tribe's colors, and her tattered dress, with the belt of colored cloth to cinch the waist, was torn and dirty. Her long black hair was tangled and she looked old before her time. Her husband stared down at the thing devouring his mentor, tears of a father filled his eyes, but did not fall.

"The rest of the tribe stayed out of the way, as far back as they could, whispering among themselves with what was left of the elders. Once agreed, they approached Malidon and told him the plan. He asked if he could at least write a letter to send with her to the afterlife and was granted the request.

"Malidon called to the boy and asked if he would walk with his father. The boy shook his head, but his dark eyes had returned again. With each step the boy took, the ground beneath him cracked, and the heat and stench of death filled the air. The temples they passed were all but in ruins, crumbling and returning to the ground from whence they had come.

"'The elders and I have a gift. We have made you a special garment. You are destined to replace Aldare, the elder who just died,' Malidon said.

"A wretched smile crossed the face of the boy, while his father tried with all he could muster, not to show fear or that there was something about to happen.

"They approached the terrace wall in the same spot they had sealed the other child, Malidon grabbed a blue striped robe. He placed the robe, which was wet and heavy, on the boy's shoulders. There were several ties that adorned the robe and Malidon began wrapping them around the boy.

"When the boy discovered what was happening, he started to struggle, but with his arms folded at the time the cloth was placed on him, he could not exact his wrath. The remaining men gathered quickly to finish binding the boy. His howls and growls could be heard echoing off the mountainsides. They shoved a corn cob in his mouth to quiet the noise and threw him, bound, into a basket, sealing the lid shut.

"As quickly as they had placed the lid on the basket, they called for the mules, who rushed carts of dirt to them. They buried the basket in a pile of dirt, blessed and sacred from the temple. But the task was not done. In order to save what was left of the tribe, they had to sacrifice Adlorden.

"Malidon brought a wine jug to Adlorden and they drank to the harvest moon. When Adlorden fell asleep, Malidon carried her over to the hill, placed her in a basket, wrapped her in her favorite blanket, and placed the scroll he had written on her lap. They capped the hill off with the stone."

"Benji, isn't Lorena pregnant?" asked Adam.

"Yes, I told you we just found out. Why?" he replied.

"I think we just let it out," Adam told him.

160

He turned to look at Benji, his eyes were dark as coal. The water began to run in the terrace and turned red as blood. The water ran faster, washing the rest of the dirt from the hill away, and the bodies fell to the ground. Adlorden's blanket fell off, revealing her stomach large with child. They watched as the stomach slowly flattened and the sky turned dark.

Darkness in the Desert

Andy and I were called out to the centermost part of the African desert in Chad, where a series of cave systems had been uncovered after a bunch of strong sandstorms swept through the area. We decided to hire a small group of college students who would fly in to meet us at the site later in the week. Andy and I headed out to the dig site as early as we could. Our plan had been that we would get there a day or so early to set up. We wanted a little time to see what was around before everybody else's hands started getting into the middle of things.

As soon as we got to the dig site, some of the locals immediately started screaming and yelling at us. It was mostly in French, but a few others in Hausa. I guess they probably thought that we could speak either one of them. I remember telling Andy that we would set up our stuff over there, since we only have a day or two before the others arrive, and I would like to be as close to the site as possible. I could tell when I looked at Andy, that he was pretty uncomfortable with the way the locals were acting. It's not that we haven't been involved with superstitious or criticizing locals at specific sites all around the world, we have. We have been to Egypt, Brazil, and you have locals all over who can get pretty agitated with you in their ancestral sites. We have even been in a few of the big ones in the states, in New York and Texas, where our own people act the same way.

Some people are tree huggers and nature lovers, some are just plain history lovers, who can't see the importance of actually recovering these sites. Rather they would have seen them wasted to the elements, but this time, this is different. Most of the locals here still lived in tribal communities. They were nomadic for the most part and didn't stay put for long. The unrelenting heat of the desert and the sandstorms, plus the monsoon season that occasionally sweeps through, keep the tribes moving on and circling back when they can.

162

For some reason, the locals have gathered here and seem more frightened, than angry. This somehow didn't seem like a group of people just mad that outsiders are in their territory. What the locals didn't know was that both myself and Andy were fluent in French and several French dialects of the area. Some of the women were screaming louder and louder. The crowd seemed to try to get closer, as rhythmic chanting began. Andy and I could make out the words 'ame voleurs' and 'blanc mort'; in English, 'souls thieves' and 'white death'.

I tried to calm Andy down. He was getting visibly shaken-up by their words. The women fell all over themselves. The men danced around the top of the site, chanting songs in a rhythmic tune. They shook maracas made of small skulls on sticks and started throwing handfuls of sand and bones from their sheep, goats, and chickens. Andy and I did our best to ignore the locals and their silly superstitions. After all, we were very excited, and discoveries like this in Africa don't come up very often. To have the honor of going out there to uncover them, to discover their purpose, to be the first to show the world, was a lifelong dream. Not just for Andy and myself, but for any archeologist.

The officials there had the site roped off, sort of like a crime scene would be. There was yellow tape and red velvet ropes to act as a barricade. The climb down to the entrance was steep and an eerily strange cool breeze wafted out at us. The air smelled a bit musty, but the cool feel of the air was welcome against our skin. The further down the sloping pit we got, the louder the crowd seemed to get.

"Wow, Gary, I know sometimes people don't like to have their history uncovered, but this is ridiculous."

"I know, Andy. Look, let's start working and filling these buckets up and maybe they'll go away."

Andy and I grabbed a few buckets from our packs and a few brushes and brooms and began filling the buckets with sand and dumping them into the wheelbarrows at the top. As the day wore on, the crowd of younger people disbanded, leaving only the elders of the tribe looming close by. The smell of their dinners and open fires carried on the wind over our heads and wafted through our noses. The chanting and dancing around their fires and the noises of rocks smashing together, could still be heard over the noise we were making digging through layers of sand and rock.

Andy and I worked well into the evening. As we slowly uncovered the rest of the doorway into the cave system, something caught Andy's eye on the right side of the doorway.

"Gary, look at this. Are those fingers?"

I leaned in closer to get a look, they definitely looked like fingertips. I grabbed the hand broom and started brushing more sand away. Slowly layers and eons fell at our feet. More and more of the bones began to show. First, the remaining fingers and hands and further up the arms and chest. Andy worked on the top. He uncovered the skull and the neck, while I worked on the middle, stopping once in a while to fill a bucket or two with all of the sand we were brushing down.

As we exposed the skeleton on the right, I looked over and noticed small white specks glistening in the light from our lanterns. I walked a few steps to the other side, took out my pocketknife, and began gently scraping clumps of sand away; sure enough, it was another skeleton, a matching pair. This means the two skeletons were significant; they had been placed there to stand guard. This was a clear message to the outside world. Nobody enters and nobody leaves.

As the sun set a little lower over the site, the temperatures in the desert began to drop. The thing about the desert most people fail to realize is that the desert isn't always hot. Andy and I brought out a few more lanterns and continued to work. As long as we worked, we weren't cold. We didn't even bother to stop for dinner. Once the chest and legs of both the skeletons were uncovered, we could

164

see the massive wooden stakes holding them in place. White vines, still intact, held spears and daggers in their hands.

We were completely amazed at how intact the skeletons were. They seemed to almost glow in the light of our lanterns. They appeared to be covered in some sort of a resin to help keep them intact and protect them from the elements and the sandstorms. The strange thing was, as soon as we got the second skeleton uncovered, the wind started blowing, and it was blowing hard. This was no normal breeze like we had felt throughout the day. Another common misconception people have about the desert is, that unless there's a sandstorm, the air is still, hot, and stagnant all the time.

But here in the cliffs of Chad, there's always a breeze. You can hear noises as the wind pierces its way through the mountains and crevices. Sometimes it sounds like howling noises. The locals call it 'locdan', the demon in the wind.

As soon as the wind started up, the people camped out around the dig site scrambled. A lot of them were still screaming even louder, 'blanc morte'. I remember this one old woman kneeling at the steep edge yelling at us. She was begging for us to leave, until we had the police officials remove her a few yards away to her camp. I still can't get over how she seemed so terrified. Her eyes were dark, her face withered with age, her white hair telling of a hard life in the desert. I could tell by the way the people around her moved that she was a respected person amongst her tribe members. I discovered that she was their priestess. I could also tell a great deal of the tribe's members had never seen white men before either.

Although a good deal of Africa and the other countries around the Sahara Desert are modernized, there are still a great many nomadic tribes and African tribes that live by the old ways. By the time most of the elders who were left had finally scattered from our site, It was too dark, even with our lanterns, to see the edges of the doorframe, much less anything else. Andy and I had to call it a night, no matter how much we wanted to keep working. A second and third strand of energy was coursing through us, but the darkness in the desert was against us.

Andy and I rolled out our sleeping bags. As with many other nights, Andy took out his journal. By the light of the lamp, I watched as he wrote about what we found. The smile on his face had not left since we arrived, even with the criticism of the superstitious locals. But now it was my turn to be a little afraid. I started to think that maybe we should have waited for the others to arrive, maybe we should even call in some experts, or someone with cave experience. But I knew all the time that the explorer in me would never have let it go. Boy, how I wished I would've let it go, what was to follow when we opened the door still haunts my memory and my nightmares.

Even with our excitement, we slept surprisingly well, once we fell asleep that is. The long flight and drive to the site, accompanied by the amount of sand we lifted out of the dig site, made us very tired. In just sleeping bags, we were comfortable, the sand was soft under us and the air was cold in the night. There were many stars in the sky, it was quite beautiful with the silhouette of the mountains in the background. I wish I could say it was silent, or tell you we could hear birds or African wildlife, but what we heard was mixed voices of the locals and their stories of what was down there and a few faint strange creaking sounds from below us as the wind blew in and out the skeletons.

Once Andy had finished his last passage of the night, he put out the lantern and we drifted off to sleep without a word. The locals were up at sunrise and that meant we were too. Andy and I fumbled though our rucksacks, looking for our toothbrushes, water canteens, and something we could choke down quickly. We watched the locals tending to what livestock they brought with them, a few goats for milk and a few chickens. They laid out feed and water and collected a few eggs. They were quieter today than they had been yesterday and soon we found out why. Sometime during the night, the eldest woman of the tribe had passed away.

The tribe was in the beginning process of mourning. The sons of the old woman gently carried her body to the middle of their campsite, between our dig and themselves, and laid her on a mat made of hay. They covered her body with a death shroud in vibrant colors and left her face to view. The members of the tribe that were there took their turn walking around her, placing a few stones and beaded necklaces on her body. Slowly, a few more families of the tribe began to show up.

Andy and I watched, but tried to make it look as though we weren't, out of respect. Most outsiders do not get to see the burial ceremonies of these ancient tribes. The ceremonies have been passed down for generations and the new priestess, who has been selected at birth, will arrive and take the place of the old woman. She will also perform the burial ceremony, after the tribe has said goodbye and paid respects. The younger tribe members seemed to pay no attention to the old woman, but went about digging and mixing goats milk with sand and pieces of cloth.

They waited until the new priestess came to them, staff in hand, and gave them a clay pot. The youthful boys carried the pot over, along with the strips of cloth they covered in sand and milk, and began to bath the old woman in the mixture. The odor wafted our way. Honey, the pot was filled with honey. Andy and I whispered to each other, I remember him telling me he had read that some tribes still practiced mummification, and maybe that's what they were doing, but he didn't think so.

They covered the old woman completely, with the entire tribe watching and burning sage leaves around them. They even covered her hair. They stripped her body of all her garments and the new priestess proceeded to cut the head from a white rooster, walking slowly around the body, making a circle of blood surround them.

This was certainly interesting, I told Andy, who was watching everything with his jaw on the ground.

I nudged Andy in the side a little with my elbow and he slowly started messing with the tools in his hand, while still watching the events unfold. When the circle was complete, the priestess pointed the staff and directed two men toward the cliffs in the near distance. They picked up the body and carried her over toward what we thought was just a sand dune. As soon as they put her body down, the dune began to move and change shape. I squinted my eyes against the sun, while Andy was smart and took out the binoculars, zooming in against the sun.

The tribe members scattered quickly, as we watched a wave of huge ants cover the old woman, stripping the skin from the bone in seconds, like a school of piranhas. Andy looked over at me and quickly back to the binoculars, it was one of those few things where you don't want to watch, but you can't turn away.

"If she was a high-ranking member of the tribe, and this is how they bury her, I don't want to know what they do with a member who is shamed," Andy whispered.

I couldn't help but think he was right for feeling that way, even though we are not supposed to judge other cultures and we are supposed to keep an open scientific mind about us. You could actually hear the ants as they worked. They made a noise that reminded me of someone rapping their fingers against a tabletop; clearly, they were hitting bone. It didn't take more than half an hour before there was no skin or hair or anything left of the woman we saw yesterday. Once the body was cleaned, they waited as the ants retreated back into the hill, making it seem full once more. The tribe members gathered the bones and carried them back to the colorful cloth they had covered her up with earlier that day.

We once again had a clear view of the bones and they weren't white like we had expected them to be. They were a golden tan color and shiny. Whatever the ants had in their saliva produced a

168

reaction to the bones, they appeared to be sticky and looked the same as the two skeletons we had uncovered at the site. Given what we had just seen, I wondered how old or young the site really was?

So far, I had only uncovered more questions than answers. Andy grabbed his tool belt, buckets and lanterns, and started heading down the slope. I followed him, but not without looking over my shoulder and noticing the new priestess and the tribe members watching our every move as closely as we had watched theirs. The new priestess didn't look happy that we were going back down to the entrance and shot us a look of disapproval.

The desert sun was shining down bright and hot in our hole, as much as it was on every other part of the desert. We were already sweating and our clothes were drenched. If you have ever tried to work in a pair of wet pants, you know exactly how we felt, and it was not rewarding to be wet when you can't get dry and have sand blowing and sticking to you. The morning progressed and we didn't hear much from the tribe. I assumed that it was because of one of two reasons or maybe both. They were mourning the loss of the old woman, or because the new priestess saw no need to make a big deal out of Andy and I being there.

We carried on with our digging and sweeping, carrying bucket loads of dirt to the surface. Soon we had the feet of both skeletons uncovered, as well as the gorgeous framed stone doorway. We began to examine the skeletons more closely, once the stones were unearthed. We didn't want to cut the vines or remove the spears. We had to move carefully, we were afraid of stumbling and falling onto the edge of the spikes that were holding the skeletons in place, for fear that we might get impaled.

I couldn't help looking into the mouth of the skeletons, which seemed at first to be glued shut. The mouths of most skeletons will drop open, when ligaments have all gone away. It was strange that this natural process did not happen with these two skeletons. I gently pried the mouth of one skeleton open with my knife wrapped in a cloth, so I would not cut or scratch the bones. As soon as the mouth fell open, a strange leather-like pouch dropped from the mouth and landed at my feet.

"Andy, look at this, it just fell out of the mouth."

He walked over excitedly, with huge smile across his face. I started to remove the cloth from around the object and the strange carving of what looked like children, all bound in vines, fell out. The small ivory carving was very smooth to the touch, such a strange carving to find, most of the cultures we noticed cherish children. Yet for some reason, the children portrayed in this carving are not happy children.

I told Andy to go and check the other skeleton's mouth. I handed him my knife and the cloth, he walked over to the other skeleton and began carefully prying the mouth open. While he was working, I took the small carving back up to the top of the dig site. I definitely wanted to catalog this and do some research to find out exactly what it was. The one thing I knew for sure at this point, was that the small figurine could not stand for anything good.

I opened my pack and took out my catalog book and a bag with paper in it to protect the artifact. Andy and I run across carvings and figurines all the time. Usually, they are of gods or mythical beings, even kings, but not of children or children being harmed. A second later, Andy came running up the side with another pouch and I was sure it would contain a similar figurine. We cut away the wrapping, but this figure was different. It was a man with the head of a child in his hands being held by the hair. The man was holding a primitive cutting tool in the other hand that was bound in vines.

We cataloged the second strange statue and headed back down to the door. I grabbed the crowbar from the edge of the site and we slowly began prying the doors, trying to open them without breaking them. The noise from the doors creaking under our pressure caught the attention of the tribe and they surrounded us almost immediately. At first, we tried to ignore them as they threw more dirt back in on us. The priestess was shouting at us, but this time it was not in French.

I put the crowbar down and stood still, trying to figure out what they wanted and hoping that the rest of the crew or the security officers would come in and break this up, but our crew was still hours away and the security guards were nowhere in sight. Andy held his hands up, showing the tribe we were not harming anything, and we didn't want to cause trouble, but this seemed to anger them more. The priestess shook her staff at us, pointing to the skeletons whose mouths were open. A strange whistling sound that started to sound more like children's screams came from them.

Andy tried to explain that we were here only to uncover the lost relics and temples so future generations could learn from them, but they wouldn't listen. The priestess spoke to two men in the tribe and pointed at me and Andy. The next thing we knew, we were being dragged out of the site while the tribe members threw chicken heads and blood all over us. They dragged us over to their fires and tied our hands. Andy and I were unable to go anywhere and were completely terrified at what they might do.

We sat there quietly, not wanting to make them any angrier at us, and then the priestess came to us. She sat on a mat in front of us and spoke in near perfect English. She told us we should leave Chad and allow them to cover that temple and not speak of it again. She told us that it was not a temple for the gods or even for a king. There was a monster and his family buried alive down there that preyed on children of the tribes. She said that the only way to keep the people of Africa safe was to leave them sealed, if we opened the door they would still be alive, and that if they got out, in time, they would start taking the children again.

Andy and I told her we understood and that we would be careful to make sure nothing got out. We needed to make the world aware that a monster dwelled beneath us and that way it would never get out. Andy and I believed in tolerance and in other cultures, but we didn't believe in people living forever or making them live in underground tombs for eternity; if they are there, they are dead, we thought. After all, this is the 1950's and we know people can't live forever.

Andy and I were dragged back to the site and the vines were cut, but not before they gave Andy a slice to the hand and rubbed a green mixture of some sort on his wound. I watched Andy wince in pain and his eyes tear up, but he didn't dare allow a tear to fall. His hand turned bright red right away and it spread up his arm and into his neck. Like a bubble, the veins in his neck grew bigger and bigger, he fell to his knees. I watched his eyes go red and bloodshot. He looked as though he was being strangled, but he was breathing.

I was forced to climb down into the site, allowing Andy time to recover a bit. He sat looking quite dazed and confused, as though he wasn't sure who he was, much less where he was. He rocked back and forth on his knees, mumbling under his breath.

"Andy, are you alright?" I asked him. He never looked at me, just kept rocking and mumbling.

I went ahead with my plans to open the doors. I put my shoulder into the doors and pushed as hard as I could. I could feel the doors give just a little, only to bounce right back, when I prepared to rush again. The skulls on the sides of the doors rocked slightly from side to side and I could hear the teeth chatter a bit against the post sticking through the mouth.

"Andy, if you're feeling up to it, I could really use your help down here."

I stopped and waited. Andy swayed a few more times, then staggered to his feet and slowly made his way down the slope to me. I tried to get Andy to look at me, but he looked everywhere, except at me. I grabbed his face with my hands and looked into his eyes. The redness that had engulfed them started to let up and his pupils looked normal. I reached down and grabbed his hand and the cut was sealed. Not healed and gone. It was still there, but whatever they had put on his hand made a covering. It had to have been from the Dragon Tree.

Andy smiled and pulled his hand away from me. He walked toward the doors and grabbed the crowbar. I watched him using both hands to try to force the tip of the crow bar into the crack in the door. His hand didn't seem to bother him at all. He was seemingly back to Andy.

"You said you needed my help, well, let's get these doors open."

I walked the few steps toward him and together we backed up and rammed the doors hard with our shoulders. Again and again we rammed the doors, and on the fifth time they cracked open. Yes, cracked, as in we broke them. Not exactly what we wanted to happen, as we were expected to leave the site unharmed, but uncovered.

We stepped back, looking around the top of the site, wondering if any of the tribe's members had come to see what the noise was, much less had they seen that we had broken the very door that they didn't want us to open in the first place. We turned around, but no one was there. In our own minds, we were now paranoid. The wind was still blowing and we could feel even more of a breeze coming from the cracked door.

I turned around and tapped Andy on the shoulder. The rest of our crew shouldn't be much longer, but as usual we couldn't wait. I walked up to the door, with Andy steadfast to my heels. I pressed my face up to the door where the large crack was and tried to peer inside. It seemed to be lighter inside the cave than what should have been. I could see just a few feet in front of the door, the walls were painted and had beads and bones along the entrance where it began to open up.

"Andy, you have to see this!"

I moved out of the way. I was grinning from ear-to-ear, but still paranoid as to what the tribe's members were up to. Andy leaned up against the door, peering into the same opening.

"This is something else," Andy said.

He took a step back, and without saying a word, we rammed the doors with all we could muster. The door broke in half, with part of it remaining in place, while the smaller piece fell inside the cavern. I turned around again, searching for the tribe's members, the priestess, someone, but no one seemed to be watching. I looked at Andy who was staring into the door and I made a quick dash up the slope, crawling as I got toward the top. I looked over toward the campsite, but the entire tribe was gone.

I went up on my knees and looked to the side, out toward the mountain, the anthill, and behind us, but there was no sign of them. It was as if they had disappeared into the jungle regions on the north side of the desert range and had left with quickness. My heart jumped into my throat. I had a rush of fear and adrenaline run through me. On one hand, I desperately wanted to get into that cave to see what was buried in there, but the mere fact that the tribe had run away without even a sound was startling.

I slipped back down the sloping side and met Andy at the bottom. He was trying to see if he could squeeze himself into the door, without knocking more of it down. If he could fit, I could fit, and so could each member of our crew, who should be here now, I thought.

"Andy, that entire tribe is just gone. There is no fire, no people, no animals, nothing—they literally just disappeared," I told him.

"Well, that's not a bad thing, they were really just getting in the way, and we were more worried about what they might do than getting a good look inside," he said.

"Your right Andy, but don't you think it's a bit strange they went so far as to drag us over there, tell us not to get in here, and now they leave without a sound. I mean we never heard them leave, or walk by, or any of the animals, they are gone, and to be honest, I am a bit weirded out that I didn't even see tracks, now that I think about it. None, not even where they walked to leave the old woman out by the ant hill, those tracks are gone, too," I told him.

"Gary, maybe they just wanted to get away because their very superstitious about this site. Maybe it was time for them to head back to where they were from, to have more ceremonies, since they did just have to commence with the new priestess," he said.

"You're right, that's what it could be, but I just think the timing is more than a coincidence. I also am starting to get worried about the rest of the crew, they should be here by now, and with such a wide expansion of land all around, there is really nowhere for them to be out of sight. I think we should leave a note or something before we take off into the cavern."

Andy agreed and we both headed up to the top where all our gear was. We packed up our tools and water and rolled up our sleeping bags. Before heading down the slope, Andy tore out a piece of his journal and wrote a note letting the crew know we were descending into the cave and that if there was a fork, we would take the right, as we always did. We walked down the hill with our gear in our hands, pretty sure we would not fit in the door with it on. Andy stuck the note on the stake sticking out of the skeleton's mouth.

I grabbed the canteen on the side of my pack, and as I tried to take it off, the rope holding the clasps on my pack broke, and all the gear went flying. Andy bent down to start helping me gather it up.

"Don't worry about it, I can get this, I know you want to get in there, and I know where you'll be headed. Grab your lantern and go on in, I will be right behind you."

Andy leaned toward the side to fix his shoes and I saw something move in front of the door.

"What was that?"

"What was what?" Andy replied.

"I'm not sure, I could have sworn I saw something move in front of the door in there."

"Gary, don't turn strange on me now. You know there's nothing, and no way could anything or anyone be down there, especially anything alive," he said.

"I know I saw something, Andy, I don't know what it was, but…"

"Okay, Gary, then it was probably a shadow, right? I mean you have low light in there, heavy light out here, and a partially opened door. It just fits. It was just a shadow. Come on, let's go," he said.

I watched as Andy got up and walked over to the door. I was still rearranging things and shoving things into my pack. He dropped his pack just inside the door and started to squeeze his way in.

He had his right arm and leg inside the door and his head was turned sideways, looking toward the sky. I saw a dark figure behind him, coming from where there was only a stone wall when we looked inside. I stared harder, wondering if it was just a shadow from the change of light as he entered with the lantern.

Before I could concentrate on anything else, I was up and running to the door. I reached out to grab his hand, but he went all the way inside before I could do anything. I wanted to say something, but I knew he wouldn't think the way I did. Andy would have said I was paranoid.

I left the rest of my stuff on the ground and only had my water canteen and lantern, which I had attached to my pants. I started to follow Andy inside the cavern when the walls seemed to move, all the shadows and the winds followed me in. Andy was gone. It was as if he had disappeared, just as the tribes had. There were no footprints in the sand, no tracks. I walked a few feet in and heard noises like fingernails on a table.

I saw Andy's pack lying on the ground with his clothes, the same clothes he was wearing a few seconds before he had slipped in. I went a few more steps, the cavern veered off into two caves, each with a downward slope. They were pitch black, except for the glittering of white specks all over the walls. I called out for Andy, but all I heard was my own voice bouncing back and a louder clicking noise.

I chose the right path because that's where we said we would always go. I took my lantern out and lit the oil, trying to keep walking, but the sand was deep. I walked for what felt like forever, but when your terrified, every moment is an eternity. As I got down a bit further, I saw Andy, well what was left of him. We were inside the ant tunnels and Andy had become live prey inside their tunnel. I turned around and tried to walk slowly back up the tunnel and grabbed Andy's journal.

I knew I had to write about this. I had to make sure there was a record of this spot. This was not where a monster lived; this is where millions of flesh eaters—maneaters—live. This is a place of sacrifice and disposal. The ants would prey on the children and the old in this area. They were given the dead bodies as a way to appease them from going after the living.

I ran back down the tunnel as the door was being sealed shut. I could hear the tribe over top as I made my way to the door. I banged on the door, but no one seemed to hear me. I have written down my account on these pieces of paper and slid them into the darkness while I remain behind until the next archeological dig comes and finds me guarding the entrance, as we found the last one.

Small Town Vengeance

The courtroom fell silent when the jury came back so fast. They had deliberated for less than an hour. The judge sat quietly at his bench, waiting for the last juror to walk in and take her seat. They all looked tired and worn out, despite the short deliberation. They were all ages of men and women, well dressed and looking quite ominous. Mark Angler sat still, head straight forward, in his orange jumpsuit. His quiet demeanor and boyish charm throughout the trial could damn him or help him.

Mark was the leader of a small occult group, known for taking things too far in the old practices. They were said to practice anything from drinking blood to stay young, to total human and animal sacrifice. The only thing was, no one knew if they had practiced the art of human sacrifice or not. The body of nineteen-year-old Angie Jenkins was found bound and gagged in the swampland near where their compound was. They also discovered the dismembered bodies of two twin boys.

Her heart had been cut out in what looked to be the same manner as an autopsy. The entire town was buzzing with the news. This kind of thing had never happened before. In other big towns, yes, but not here in Allstead. The newspaper talked about the murder on the front page for weeks. After a while, with no leads or new information, the newspaper only printed a small article in the back about it. The whole town was aware of the cult and no one was happy about them being there so close to their children. In fact, this little tight-knit town didn't like anything that wasn't considered normal.

A few of the town's folk were convinced that the cult members were responsible for all three deaths. An anonymous call to the police was made and they were sent to pick Mark up. Mark held his innocence over his own head like a carrot in front of a horse. But he already knew no one outside his followers believed a word he said, not even his own public defender.

"I thought the days of witch hunts were long gone. This is religious persecution and nothing more."

That was all Mark would say. Those lines were even the headlines for the local newspapers. The rest of his followers protested outside the jail and courthouse to set Mark free. But everyone knew that would never happen. The judge in town loved to condemn the dregs of society and a person like Mark was just icing on the cake. The townsfolk acted like a cult in their own right, and you either fit in or you don't. Mark and his group never fit in.

The more the small group protested and brought attention to the fact that they did indeed exist; the more the town seemed to be convinced of Mark's guilt. The trial itself lasted three weeks. When the jury came back in from deliberating that soon, Mark knew the answer before they even spoke. Mark watched as they all took their seats, all except for one man. He was dressed in a black suit with a blue, green, and black tie. He held a folded piece of red paper between his fingers and ran his nails over the crease.

"Have you reached a verdict?"

"Yes, Your Honor. We find the defendant, Mark Angler, guilty on all counts."

"On the charge of murder one?"

"Guilty, Your Honor."

"On the charge of premeditated murder, how do you find?"

"Guilty."

"So, say one, so say you all?"

"Yes."

Just like that, Mark was convicted to life without parole. His followers got word of the verdict and the screaming and yelling could be heard from a mile away. The streets were clogged with people both celebrating and mourning Mark's conviction. He was led out of the courtroom in handcuffs and chains. Not a tear in his eyes, he kept his head up, never bothering to make eye contact with anyone.

They placed Mark in a white van, taking him to the small prison on the east side of town near the dump. The smell from the dump in the summertime, mixed with swamp air, was not a pleasant one. That was one reason they built the prison where it was. Mark sat in his seat, quiet and smug in his appearance. When they arrived at the jail, the yard was empty except for a few officers. Mark was led down the ramp to the yard and into a four-foot wide fenced walking path that stopped at a large metal door. Mark was thrown into a private small cell at the bottom of the basement.

The cell was damp, dark, and mold covered the walls. He was left with half a roll of toilet paper, a toothbrush he was sure was used, and a small tube of toothpaste. There was not much pressure in the sink and he had one dirty cup for water. He turned around in a small circle, surveying his new home. Disgust and anger took over his face as he knelt on the floor, speaking softly in a language no one else listening would understand.

The dim lights on the ceiling flickered on and off as jail cell doors rattled slightly as the wind began to blow. The slightest smell of swamp air forced its way in through tiny cracks in the concrete walls. He stayed there for a while, slowly rocking back and forth on his knees, before standing quickly and screaming.

"I did not kill those people!"

His eyes were black as onyx, but there was no one looking to see them. The news of who Mark was and what he was convicted of traveled quickly through the prison.

Inmates soon after began teasing and taunting Mark. They didn't tease him about the killing of a nineteen-year old girl. No, they were more intent on teasing him about his cult beliefs. Even in jail with the dregs of society, he was ostracized. Accused of starting riots and fights between inmates, he was soon placed even further down in the basement, into what could only be called a dungeon, rather than jail or even solitary confinement. There was no light in his smaller cell and the toilet didn't work at all.

Most days he wasn't even brought food. Becoming desperate and starting to go crazy, Mark spent a great deal of his time chanting spells and screaming into the darkness. But still no one heard him. His followers, once so intent on getting their leader free, had long since disbanded. The entire town had gotten back to normal in a few short weeks. Teens were once again playing at the skate park, mothers took their children on picnics, and no one spoke of Mark Angler. He simply didn't exist to anyone outside the damp walls of his prison home.

As the days passed, he began to change, to withdraw into himself. His face was changing, becoming colder and his eyes darker. He ranted over and over, calling out names of gods no one worshiped anymore, but probably should have. When the guards came in to bring him a tray of food, he was sitting on the floor covered in filth. His hair and face were dirty and oily. He didn't move or acknowledge that they had entered his cell, even with the light shining brightly in his face, his pupils never changed.

They placed his tray on a side table and grabbed a stretcher. Mark was lifted, tied to the stretcher, and placed in the shower. They sprayed him down with warm water. The guards redressed him. He was completely still.

"You'll all get what's coming to you," he whispered.

No one in the jail took anything he said to heart. They locked him back in his cell with his food. The tray sat on the edge of the sink. Mark was placed back in the middle of the floor, staring off into space. The wind began to blow outside. A whistling noise could be heard throughout the jail.

The inmates had heard the wind blow and the rain hit many times before, but not like this. The rain came cascading down, with flashes of lightening so bright they illuminated the prison through closed shutters. The thunder seemed never ending. Rumbling quietly, then crashing violently. Mark smiled, watching cockroaches on the tray in the flashes of light. The rain fell harder and harder every hour, filling the prison yard and ditches that surrounded the compound.

The roof began to leak in the upper parts of the prison. The sound of water dropping into metal cups, buckets, and anything else they could get to catch water, echoed through the halls. The temperature outside dropped and the prison became cold. Mark got up and walked to his cot, taking a seat in the only dry spot he could find. He smiled a bit bigger, before folding his arms behind his head, and lying back on his cot.

He reveled at the thought of what was coming. *The entire town will pay,* he thought. He sank once more into his mind. Pictures and memories went through his head and his breathing became slower. His eyes rolled back and he lay perfectly still. The walls shook with the crash of thunder, as a bolt of lightning struck the roof. A flash of blue light surged through the sink and seemed to bounce around the bars on the window.

The rain fell through the night and well into the next day. Mark slept for the first time since he had been sentenced. The noise of the prisoners upstairs, banging on the bars of their cells, complaining about the leaking roof, and their wet blankets, caused Mark to wake up. He sat there listening, smiling the way a child in a toy aisle smiles at a toy they really like. To this day, Mark has not had one visitor. His thoughts turned toward his followers. Not one had been arrested when he had been. Not a single one had come to see him or write him a letter. No friends or family had seemed to care. He had been thrown away like trash.

His own loyal people didn't bother to try to get him out of his new home. Rage fell across his face and lightning struck over and over. The chain link fence around the prison shook violently. Fire flashed in his eyes and he once again fell back on his cot. His teeth clamped together, grinding in his mouth. He made his hands into fists and squeezed. A small trickle of blood came from where he dug his long nails into his palms. His voice had started out quiet, in a whisper, chanting to himself. He called out for his gods to bring forth his revenge.

No food was brought to him, no shower was offered. He screamed out for the guards to come, but no one did. The rain fell harder as his anger raged on. At times, Mark could hear the television the other inmates were allowed to watch for a few hours a day. The weather was all anyone seemed to worry about. The rivers in the town were already at flood stage and the lakes could only take so much overflow. The sewers in some parts of town had already begun to back up, toilets started overflowing into the cells, and gravity brought the nasty sludge trickling down the walls through cracks and into the basement cells where Mark was kept.

Mark laughed at the news reports, thinking it was only going to get worse. The rain continued into the evening and on into the next morning, still no one came to Mark's cell. The reports now told of retirement homes being evacuated away from the river areas now cresting. Lake front properties were already a total loss for a good majority of the owners and there didn't seem to be an end to the storm that they could predict.

Mark was very hungry and there was no one coming to provide him with food. He was, in every sense of the word, trapped like an animal. The tray of grotesque food from a few days ago still sat on the sink where he had left it. Only now, he was considering actually eating it. Bugs flew around the top of the crusted potatoes and meat.

His cramped dark cell started to slowly fill up with water. He placed his feet on the floor; he stood up to his ankles in filthy water. The water had been tainted, not just from runoff from the towns dump close by, but also from the backed-up sewer system, including his own toilet. Mark walked a few steps with his hands extended out in front of him to find the sink. He reached carefully for his tray of food and sloshed his way back to his cot.

He was so hungry he didn't care anymore about what was on his food. He couldn't see it and couldn't smell it over the foul stench permanently etched into his nose. He wolfed down his food, barely bothering to try to chew it. He tossed the tray into the water and walked over to the door of his cell. He peered out into a dark hall, looking for signs that someone was there.

He would have been happy to see a door out of the hall at this point, but he could see nothing. Mark began yelling at the top of lungs, calling for the guards, for anyone. *I know they can hear me. If I can make out the weather station reports, they can hear me.*

"You can't leave me down here! I'm not an animal! I know you can hear me!"

He grabbed the metal handle on the door and shook it violently, as hard as he could. The entire door rattled, but did not open or give at all.

He let go of the handle and flew into a fit of rage, pounding on the door with his fists, and ramming into it with his body. His shoulder quickly became sore and throbbed. The bottom of the cot was only inches from being covered by the rising waters.

Mark had been thinking more about how he was abandoned by his followers. *Where were they all at? Why did they just totally forget about me?* he wondered. *No matter, I will find them when I get out,* he thought.

There was a loud commotion up above and he could hear people scrambling around, the sounds of metal doors sliding open and closed and thuds as people fell to the floor. Pieces of the ceiling in his cell, wet all the way through, fell out, landing in the water and causing tiny splashes to reach his legs. Mark smiled, as he couldn't help but think this was all his doing, too. He was causing chaos to the people responsible for ruining his life.

He stood there listening closely, trying to figure out what was happening. Inmates were yelling and screaming. He could hear the buckets used to collect water being kicked over and drug along the metal floors.

"The vans are here, get a move on!"

Mark listened, ear pressed against the opening in the door.

"Take only your clothes!"

They are evacuating the jail, he thought. The water was rising in his cell at the bottom of the basement, so it only made sense.

They'll be down to get me soon, he told himself.

Mark waited there at his door, listening to the footsteps get lighter and lighter, until he heard none at all. It hadn't been too long before the entire jail was silent and yet, there he was, still alone in his cell. He turned back and walked the few short steps to his cot. Water was now touching the bottom of the bed liner and he was getting wet.

The cell was going to fill up with water and he would have nowhere to go to escape it as it flooded in. Although the prospect of drowning in the jail had not immediately crossed his mind, he told himself it might be better than spending a life sentence in the dungeon for a crime he did not commit.

Mark thought for a moment about trying to stop the storm he had created, but he knew ultimately it had to run itself out. He figured they would have definitely evacuated the jail, but thought he would have been evacuated, too, not left behind. He had planned it out in his mind, they would have to take him with them, and he would make his move, under the cover of chaos, to get away.

Then everybody would have been safe, left with a huge mess to clean up, but he would be free and he would wait to collect his payback. The wind outside howled and whistled, water streamed in faster as the cracks in the walls began to get bigger. Mark could barely see, with the emergency lights in the hall finally coming on, but it was better still than the total darkness he had been subjected to.

Water dripped from spots all over the ceiling and small rivers cascaded from each corner. A constant trickling and dripping sound echoed through the small cell. It was almost deafening. Mark sat there looking around his dark room, trying to come up with any way possible to escape. There were no windows and his cell door was steel with a small window obscured with bars. Even if he managed to take the bars out somehow, he was too big to squeeze through them.

In the middle of all the rumbling thunder and crashes of light, faint voices could be heard. Mark stepped forward again, listening at the window of his cell door. He was unsure if he actually heard the voices or if he wanted so badly to hear them that his mind was creating them. The voices got slightly louder and splashing could be heard. They were coming his way, someone was coming for him.

Mark started yelling, "I'm here, down here!"

The more he yelled the closer the voices got. They didn't reply to Mark and it infuriated him.

The splashing was louder still and Mark could see water getting flung onto the walls in the dim lights of the hall. A shadow loomed closer and then a second one. Against the grey walls of the hall, the shadows got bigger and bigger as they approached. Water dripped, making the shadows hands appear to have huge claws. Mark began to feel a bit scared. He carefully began stepping back slowly, not lifting his feet too high, trying not to splash. He crouched down behind the end of his cot, waiting to see if they would stop at his cell.

"He's down here, I heard his voice."

Mark listened quietly as the voices became clear. That voice sounded so familiar, he told himself.

"Come on, hurry up, we've got to get Mark out of here before the whole place fills up or collapses on us, Joe."

"I'm going as fast as I can. This water is nasty and I would rather not fall face first. In case you haven't noticed, there is raw sewage and who knows what seeping in from the dump," Joe replied.

Mark jumped up from his hiding spot, recognizing the voices as two of his closest friends and followers. He walked to the door so fast he nearly fell from the force of the water pushing him back.

"Hey guys, over here!"

"Mark, we've got to get you out of here and fast," Joe told him.

To Mark's surprise, Joe had a set of keys. He watched as Joe went through his keys one by one, calling out, "house key, truck key, boat key."

Allen stayed quiet behind Joe, looking scared and paranoid.

"We would have been here sooner, but we had to wait for Kyle's wife to become a guard to get the key," Allen told him.

"Why is it that not one of you from the group came to visit or even write letters? Did anyone try?" Mark asked.

"We can talk about all that once we are out of here. This whole place is about to go under," Joe told him.

Joe grabbed a slender black key and clumsily fumbled around to get it into the lock. The clanking sounds as the lock opened echoed through the hall. They pushed hard against the water pressure to open the heavy metal door.

Mark stepped out, happy to be out of his cell, but not too sure yet how he felt about his two would-be rescuers.

"We have a boat waiting outside, tied to what little of the fence is still above water. We have to keep moving, the water is rising fast."

They walked fast, holding an arm out to the wall to keep themselves steady. The further they got from Mark's cell, the brighter the hallway seemed to get.

As they walked, bits of paper, combs, and trash floated down the hall. A steady gushing torrent of dirty water flowed from the staircase on the left.

"Mark, the water gets pretty hard to walk through on the stairs, so keep a good grip on the rail," Joe said.

Mark didn't reply, but did as he was told. Allen stayed behind Mark just in case and Mark followed Joe up the narrow staircase to the main hall of cells. It was dimly lit from the emergency lights and the hall was a steady river.

The ceiling was crumbling from the relentless amount of rain and poor drainage. Cracks poured water and dripped small chunks of paint and ceiling tiles as it fell. The odor was not quite as bad as the basement where Mark had been housed, but the unmistakable smell of backed-up toilets and garbage was still present.

The walls once light gray, were now stained with dark brown lines and pieces of trash clung to them. Mark followed his companion, taking in all the surrounding cells as he went. The cells were all empty, but pictures, magazines, and newspapers littered the area. The emergency lights flickered on and off, casting eerie shadows on their path. Lightning flashed through the bars on the cell windows, making the rain outside appear to be one thick sheet.

As they made their way toward the end of the main hall, the entrance door they had hoped would stay open from the force of the water, was being pushed slowly shut by the wind. There were a few stairs that led down to the door. They were completely covered by water and it created the illusion that the water outside was only thigh deep, like the water they were navigating through in the hall. They reached the stairs and stepped down, the water was neck deep. Surprisingly, the water was colder than what it had felt like inside and darker, as well. They could not see their feet and probably didn't want to see what was floating beneath them.

They reached the door and squeezed their way through it. The three men grabbed the fence and made their way toward the boat. Joe was the first to reach the boat and climb in. The rope was taut and the head of the boat was starting to point down from the rise in the water. The wind pushed the rain in great sheets, making it nearly impossible to see. Waves chopped against the side of the small motorboat. Mark reached the boat next, grabbing the edge of the side, and trying to pull himself in.

The boat swayed and tilted against his weight, Joe reached over, grabbed the waistband of Mark's orange jumpsuit, and hauled him into the boat. The rain had already begun to fill the bottom of the boat in the short period of time they had spent inside the jail. Allen was the last one to get in the boat. Mark and Joe leaned to the other side to keep the boat from tipping over.

As soon as Allen got in the boat, Joe pulled the string, and started the engine. The engine smoked and sputtered, but at least it started. Allen reached over, untied the rope from the boat, and they began to slowly turn around.

"Okay," said Mark, "we're out, so start talking. I want to know everything. I was in there for over a month, no letters, no phone calls, no visits. No one tried to appeal the conviction or investigate, you all just left me there!"

"Mark, man, that's not what happened at all. After you were sentenced, we all protested," Joe began. "We marched up and down in front of the courthouse. We held up signs, we rallied in front of the police station. We wrote letters to the governor and the congressmen, but no one listened or cared."

"Yeah Mark, we did all we could think of, short of digging a tunnel. We were denied visitation rights to see you. We would try and get told you were no longer allowed to see people, you were causing problems, and had been moved to maximum security in solitary," Allen replied.

His eyes were dark and slightly sunken in against his pale skin. He looked more like a rat than a person. The small bit of facial hair he had in patches, that he considered a goatee, only made the rat-like appearance stand out more.

"We called the newspapers here in town and the few towns over from us. We even called the television stations and radios, too. We told them there was an innocent man in prison, but no one wanted anything to do with us. We were ignored, no matter what we did," Joe explained.

"They stopped printing anything in the papers at all about you or the murder. All the letters we wrote would get returned to sender. The governor opened the letters we sent to him and even replied. All he would say is the justice system works and evidence don't lie. The right man was in prison for a horrible crime. The compound was burned to the ground and not one newspaper reported it," he added.

Mark sat in his seat, quietly listening. The thunder began to rumble, matching the fury he felt inside.

"Mark, we tried. We knew you had gotten a raw deal and we wanted everyone else to know it, too," said Allen. "One day I was looking at the newspaper with Kyle, and there was an ad in the paper for a guard. Well, since Kim was a guard in Ohio before her and Kyle were married, we asked her to apply for the job. Kim did and was lucky to get the position."

"She never saw you the whole time she was there and said that it was only once in a while when someone would say something about you. She was provided keys to the cells and one key, she was told, was for the bottom cells that were not in use except for storage. We knew that's where you were."

"Once the rain started up and the flooding began, we made the plan. We could, of course, only hope that the flood would get bad enough to evacuate the jail, and even then, we wouldn't know 'til they had evacuated, whether or not you were in there or had been evacuated, too. But we went on a hunch that you would be left behind."

"We waited. Kim let us know when they had finished evacuating that she didn't see you and they had said all were accounted for. Kim had agreed to leave the key with us today so we could get you out. She told us your name was never even put on the prison roster. For all intents and purposes to the jail, you did not exist," he told Mark.

"Where is everybody now?" Mark asked.

"Well," said Joe, "like we told you, we were run completely out of town. We had no place to live and, even before they burnt down the compound and the woods around it, we were harassed day and night. People would throw bottles all around the compound. Broken glass was everywhere. The kids could hardly play outside at all. We would be stared at if we went to get food and the kids all had to be kept out of school."

"We were all asleep when Kyle heard a crashing noise. In a few seconds, we looked out the window and saw a few police cars and townsfolk leaving, and then the porch was on fire. We managed to get everyone out who had come down for the summer solstice, but after that, we all pretty much had to leave town. Kyle and Kim are still here, they bought that little cabin a few years back and that's where they have been staying," he continued.

"Then of course, you got me and Allen," said Joe. "Everyone

else just left us addresses where they would be, but we are spread out all over the place now."

Joe smiled at Mark, who was clearly a little happier to have the information and be out of his dungeon.

"Joe and I got a small apartment in Holten, you can stay with us so we can get everyone back together and build a new compound," Allen said.

The smoke from the small outboard motor dissipated fast in the rain and wind. Even though Mark was free and damage that would take weeks to clean up was already done, the rain continued. The sky stayed a constant shade of grey, with occasional dark black clouds. Mark was happy just to see the sky, regardless of the color.

"Mark, there's more. Something else you need to know about," Joe said.

"Okay," Mark replied.

For a moment, Joe was quiet, as if he was debating on whether or not he really wanted to tell Mark what was in his head. Allen pursed his lips together and looked down, as his feet were being covered by water in the bottom of the boat. Mark stared intently at his friend waiting, looking back and forth between his friend and the trees and rooftops they passed along the lake's edge.

"Mark, you know how when they found that girl, the newspapers reported that her heart had apparently been cut out?"

"Oh yes, I remember," Mark replied.

"They stated that it looked almost like it was done in the same manner as an autopsy would have been done. Well, after doing a little digging, we found out that she had not died when they said she died, but the reason for the strange way the heart had been cut out, was because she was already autopsied.

"What!?" Mark yelled. "What do you mean!? How do you know that?" he asked.

"I had Allen go to the funeral service for her, and that's where he overheard the father talking to one of the police officers, who he was obviously friends with. The girl had died from a drug overdose. They had arranged for her body to be found near our compound," Joe told him. "It was the same cop who found her body, that was talking to the father at the service that day," he added.

"Are you sure? Are you completely sure about that?" Mark asked.

"Yes, unfortunately we are. That's part of the reason why we couldn't see you or call you, this thing is bigger than what we thought it was," Allen told him.

"Not really," Mark said. "I suspected the whole time I was in there that it was something like this. From the time I was arrested, to the trial, to my sentence. There was no evidence other than the body being found near our grounds.

"I was ignored and starved and moved into that dungeon and forgotten about. I knew it was a way to get rid of us and our group."

They reached the first bit of town above water and Joe turned off the boat. They coasted onto the land and one by one climbed out. Allen's blue Ford Explorer was waiting for them. They pulled the boat up and around the truck to the gate. Allen jumped inside the back and Mark and Joe lifted and handed the tip of the boat up to Allen.

Allen pulled and walked back slowly as Mark and Joe pushed from the bottom, loading the boat onto the truck bed. Once it was completely on, Allen grabbed a dark blue tarp from the corner of the bed and began to toss it up, spreading it over the boat. Mark and Joe each grabbed a corner and proceeded to tie them down, while Allen secured the boat to the inside of the truck.

Jumping off the side of the truck, he walked to the door and unlocked them. They were all dripping wet and cold, from the top of their heads to the bottom of their shoes. Allen started the truck and turned on the heat as they began their long drive out of town.

Mark sat quietly, watching out the passenger side window, feeling the warm air on his cold skin. The rain continued to fall and the streets were full of standing water the ditches could no longer hold. The further away from the lake they got, the lower the water level was, but water still pooled everywhere.

The wind pushed the truck back and forth on the road and the trees bent to the will of the wind. A few times, the sun tried to peek out just behind a cloud, only to be covered again as fast as it had appeared. Allen reached over and turned on the radio. The weather was on every channel and all said the same thing: rain, rain, and more rain was on the way. Coastal flooding in the lake regions had forced evacuations from the retirement homes to the jail, and has now been blamed for several deaths in the area.

Allen reached out to turn off the radio, but was stopped by Mark, who placed a calm hand on top of his and shook his head no. Joe looked at Mark for a moment, but returned to gazing out the windshield without saying a word. Mark listened as the radio announcer began telling of how the storm had caused the deaths.

Three people had been found dead from the flooding. One man, a well-known prosecuting attorney for the state, was found dead in his car. The coroner's report stated the car was swept into rising water and that Mr. Averal drowned in his vehicle. Mark, Joe, and Allen all looked at each other with eyes the size of baseballs. That was the prosecuting attorney who convicted Mark.

Officer Pavis was found dead in his home yesterday morning by his wife. She had found her husband slumped over the kitchen table. The coroner report stated Officer Pavis died of heart failure. He was 35 years old. We have one more death to report. 41-year-old Derrick Jenkins was found dead last night at his lake front home. He was apparently trying to move more of his belongings, that he thought would have been salvageable, and was caught by the current. The coroner's report showed he died of drowning. This, only a short time after his daughter, Angela, had been found dead.

Mark sat back in his seat a little more and looked out his window at the rain that had now started to slow down. They continued their drive into Holten's city limits, where the water was now only a few inches deep on the road, and the sun was starting to come out. Allen looked over to Joe, who couldn't help but smile back at him, before glancing at a smiling Mark Angler. Mark looked over at his companions and said one word, only one before falling asleep, "Karma".

Lost Pages

Journal entry 9-16-2010

The ancient Mayans aren't dead and gone. They went underground. These aren't the descendants, but the entire population that was left after the invasion by the Spanish. They must really have discovered the fountain of youth, or some very powerful ancient magic is at work here. So many explorers throughout the centuries have searched for a fountain of youth or some way to live forever, and I found it. It's more than just a spring or well. It's an entire lost world. A whole civilization of forgotten people right under our feet. The sun shines, there are birds, trees, and flowers. Water runs through a river, feeds waterfalls, and they irrigate crops. There are fish and animals in this place we long thought to be extinct. It is as if the world opened up, swallowed a part of itself, and let evolution and time stand still here, while it kept moving forward everywhere else. I have to get close to these people. I need to talk to them to find out about how they have survived, thrived, and how they managed to stay hidden for so many centuries.

Journal entry 9-17-2010

I have stayed back a few days trying to watch from a respectful distance. I have seen the children run and play a non-lethal version of the adult's deadly ball game. The children seem to play fight with sticks, as if they are training for battle, but with whom? At least with the children's games, no one was getting their heads cut off for losing. I have seen the hunters come back with great large cats and wolf-like creatures to eat. How big is this place that animals of that size can roam and be sustained? The fishermen come back with nets full of fish, including the largest piranha I have ever seen. They know I'm here. They have sent a few warriors to see me, and they have brought me food and sat with me to check me out. I have been asked to come see the chief today.

Now I am getting nervous. These people have great advances in technology and culture, but are still known for human sacrifice and harsh punishments for perceived wrongs. When the sun is about to set, I will be brought down to meet the chief at the temple.

Second entry 9-17-2010

The chief was surprisingly kind. He had many questions about me, where I came from, the outside world, and my reasons for finding them. He seemed very preoccupied with asking about me being here alone. I don't know that I have been accepted, but I have been given a hut to sleep in, and a basket of food to take with me. I am now in the center of the village and it is more spectacular than I could have thought. The colors are so vivid and bright. The grass in their stadium is a brighter green than I have ever seen. And they have made walking paths out of limestone, like small streets that wind through the place. There are clouds and the trees extend high into the air. I don't understand this, but it's amazing. I would love to take pictures, but they believe that it will capture their souls. There is opium and marijuana growing wild everywhere and they smoke them as part of their rituals. They all walk around with a pouch of some sort tied around their waists. They drink out of this, but I only see the teens and older people with them, the young children don't seem to need them. I have to know what's in their pouches.

Journal entry 9-18-2010

This could mean several things or it could mean nothing, but, today I woke up and all my stuff was missing. Everything, except for my journal and pen. And that's because I sleep with them on me. I imagine some of the children may have taken off with my pack, which had my clothes, camera, and cell phone, just out of curiosity. After all, I am a stranger in their village. I know I look out of place and maybe a bit scary to them. They may not understand seeing someone that looks like me. I wear jeans and hiking boots, they wear loin clothes and walk barefoot. I Have light skin and blonde hair, they are all darker-skinned with black hair. I think I might be able to look for my stuff, but the chances are I won't get it back. However, if I do, my cell gets no reception and my camera is probably broken by now. The strange thing is they gave me a basket of fruit and I only ate one avocado and one orange, but the rest was completely shriveled and covered with mold this morning. I have never seen fruits go bad this fast before. The basket is even starting to decay as if it had been sitting here for weeks with the acid from the fruits eating away at it.

I have seen them watering the trees and their crops with irrigation water running through the terraces. The water is a slight green color, but so is the river. I want to say it's just algae from the humidity but I wonder if that's not all there is to it. Do they have to have special powers to keep this place growing and green? Do the crops get treated with whatever they have to keep themselves immortal? When they are removed from the water source, do the plants die? Do they die? This place just keeps me wanting to know more and more. So many scientific breakthroughs could be held in this place. Cures for diseases and aging could be right at my fingertips. But I know I need to stay on their good side, if I want to get any real information, but also if I want to leave here with my head still on my body.

9-25-2010

This week had been so amazing. But I think I need to get out of here soon. The people and chief have been acting a bit strange the past day or so. They keep talking about the festival and a storm that's supposed to come. A storm underground, can it be? There are hundreds of human-shaped dolls being hung everywhere, made from ears of corn and sticks. They are placing spears and weapons on small altars all around the temple and the stadium. The men in the village have given me a loincloth to wear and a small headdress with leaves and a few small bones. You know what they say--when in Rome. I found my camera today, it was smashed and the film was missing.

My clothes were torn to pieces and are being used to tie the dolls together. I have felt the ground shake, like small earthquakes have been happening. Every time one of them occurs, the people start chanting and everyone looks at me. When I go to lie down in the hut at night, they have meetings I am not supposed to attend. These are for the tribe's men only, and yet I hear them mention my name. I have been able to find my pack. It was hanging on a banana tree near the pool where the river lets out. It was empty, as I knew it would be. I have managed to collect a few seeds from some of the trees and a small sample of water. I think I have worn out my welcome. They have been sacrificing animals to their gods, trying to stop the earthquakes. And they have been harvesting loads of fruits and corn and giving them as offerings. Although I know earthquakes are not signs from gods, they don't.

The entire village seems to be changing. I caught a glimpse of the men walking to the temple for their meeting with the chief and they were different. They had some sort of dye or paint on them, making their bodies glow orange in the night, and they carried their spears and weapons with them as if they were about to go off to war. This morning, when I woke up, there were body parts, as shriveled as the fruits, on stakes sticking out of the ground next to the dolls. The temple was suddenly off limits to me and they had two large armed warriors standing guard at the doorway. The stadium was being prepared for something big to happen. The offering table was set up with all their offerings and water bowls. There were several men and one woman adorned with tribal ritualistic clothes that were tied to the bottom of the altar. They weren't asking to be released or crying, they seemed to not care that they were there. I could see pillars of smoke circling their heads; maybe they were drugged.

I am pretty sure I don't want to be part of what's about to happen. Somehow, though, I feel like they have every intention of me being part of whatever it is they are trying to do. If I have ever felt like something bad was about to happen to me, it's now. I think I have figured out what the cavern was that I got into. It was at the bottom of that shield volcano. That's where all the heat is coming from. It could also explain the trembling, telltale signs of an eruption. Either way, I need to leave tonight during their big game, while everyone is focused on the players.

"Aaron, Chief Monochan requests that you come sit with him during the festival games tonight. There will be much feasting and stories. We will take you to meet with him at sundown."

"I really need to be on my way to get back to my home tonight. I have been gone for a long while now and my family is sure to be missing me. I was hoping to leave soon, while the sun is still up," Aaron replied.

"The chief will be most displeased to hear that you are not going to attend the festival. It is being held in your honor. You are a very important part of tonight's festival. It is best that you attend the festival. I will tell the chief you will be ready shortly."

As Imon left the hut, Aaron sat down, looking out the door and watching the people walk around. Two guards stayed behind to make sure he didn't try to escape. Aaron stuck his head out the door just slightly and was greeted by the two guards staring down and crossing their spears in an x pattern, to make sure he didn't get out. They smiled down at him and forced his head back inside the hut. As the shadows got longer and longer, Aaron could tell the sun was fading fast and his chance to try to get back to his own world was passing him by.

A moment later, Imon was back at the hut.

"Aaron, the chief requests your presence now."

Aaron crawled out of the hut and stood up. He followed Imon down the path, with the two guards and their spears following close behind. He had left his pack in the hut. *I'll either be able to get my pack later and be on my way, or I will not need it ever again,* he thought.

There was music playing that got louder as they went down the path. The sounds of drums and pan flutes filled his ears. People chanted and danced around and he could smell the food, wild boar and duck were on the menu tonight, along with corn and other vegetables. But there was also something eerie and more sinister. He rounded the corner of the stadium, walking up the limestone steps. The smell of marijuana filled his nose and he could feel himself getting a bit lightheaded. The guards must have been used to the smell and the effects, they seemed to be undaunted in their task. As Aaron walked, he was greeted by children running around him and stabbing him with mock daggers and spears, then laughing and running away.

He was getting more scared and more paranoid with each step. They walked down a narrow corridor that led to the top of the stadium where the chief and his wife were seated along with the medicine man. There was food laid out before them in large amounts. There were several kinds of meat and fish, two wines, and sweet breads. They were grabbing handfuls of food, eating and laughing.

The chief raised his hands and the guards backed away slowly, standing against the wall.

"Aaron, have something to eat. The feast and festival are all for you. It is not often we have guests from outside our village; not in many years, actually."

"Thank you, Chief Monochan, but at the moment, I am not hungry," Aaron replied.

He tried to pass off a smile, but inside he was twisted up and scared to death. His hair was standing on end and he had goosebumps, even though it must have been 80 degrees.

"Ah, very well then. At least have some blanche wine with me.

It may help to bring back your hunger and help you to enjoy the festival," the chief said.

Aaron was handed a wooden bowl filled with blanche. He sipped it gingerly, trying not to offend the chief or his medicine man. The taste was bitter and it dried out his mouth, making it hard to swallow the next sip. Aaron started to feel drowsy within just a few sips. He tried to focus on the dancers on the field. They were now wielding torches. They swallowed fire and tossed the torches around in a show of light. He could see trails behind the moving torches and was being hypnotized by the performers.

Aaron reached out, grabbed a chunk of wild boar, and began tearing away at it. But he could no longer keep himself from slowly falling forward as sleep washed over him. As Aaron lay passed out, the dancers continued, unaware that Aaron was ready. The chief raised his hands, the guards rushed to collect Aaron and drag him down to the field at once. They brought him down to the middle of the field and moved a small wall of carved stakes from in front of the offering table.

They placed Aaron on top of the offering table and placed his pack on top of the wooden wall. The medicine man came down from the stadium walls and began sprinkling Aaron with sulfur dust and orchid petals. Pieces of cedar wood were shaved and placed on his chest and all around his body on the table. The chief reached down, grabbing pieces of Aaron's ripped clothing, and began tying his hands and feet together.

The music played louder and louder while the dancers chanted in unison. Aaron began to stir just as the earthquake started again. This was still a relatively small earthquake, but the villagers were frightened nonetheless. The chief and medicine man were left thinking about how to move the festivities along faster, to appease the gods and the villagers at the same time. The chief bent down, grabbing a bowl filled with a mixture of opium and marijuana and began swirling the bowl around Aaron's head. Small circles of smoke rounded his face and disappeared in his nose.

The ties were pulled tight. To demonstrate that Aaron could not move freely and would not feel any pain, the chief used his knife to slice off one of Aaron's fingers. Aaron stirred just a bit and opened his eyes to see the chief standing over him. His eyes closed again and he fell back into a trance-like state. The chief raised his hands and ordered the musicians to be silent. The entire village, gathered in their seats around the stadium, fell silent, waiting and watching the chief and medicine man.

He walked over to the wooden wall and grabbed Aaron's pack. He placed it on a small fire pit and emptied a bit of his pouch onto it. The flames shot up green and left embers floating around the dark sky and landing on the ground and on Aaron's chest. The ground rumbled again and the villagers began to chatter and screech. The medicine man looked over to the chief and smiled. He slowly lowered a jagged knife into the underside of each of Aaron's arms and sliced them from elbow to wrist. Aaron moved his head slightly back and forth, but never opened his eyes. At the sight of the blood running down the table, the villagers cheered and the warriors clanked the ends of their spears on the ground.

Blood ran down both sides of the table and began collecting in small pots under the corners. The chief grabbed a bowl and poured a small amount of blood in it, then painted three lines across his forehead, and then did the same to the medicine man. Aaron opened his eyes for a moment and could see only blurry figures walking around him. He tried to move, but could not feel his body. The smell of blood filled his nose and in his head, he knew it was his. There would be no glory, no immortality, and no legacy of finding a lost civilization.

The medicine man then thrust the knife into the middle of Aaron's belly, slicing down to the pubic bone. He began taking out Aaron's organs one by one. Each organ was placed into the fire, as the chief prayed and begged his gods to accept the offering. Bits of cedar and flower petals were tossed into the flames, turning the smoke to a grey smoldering puff. The ground shook again, more violently than it had before, and the stadium walls began to crack and crumble under the pressure. The villagers scrambled down to the middle of the field. The ground they walked on started to open up, revealing trenches of the immense lava flow they had relied on to keep them warm and safe for centuries.

People slammed into one another, trying to find a place where hot steam, smoke, and lava were not spewing out. The ground shook again, taking the offering table down into a huge crevasse, the medicine man along with it. The chief ran out to the edge of the field, trying to get his people to stop, but no one would listen. Rocks and boulders started to fall from the sky, carving large holes into the ground and cracking the riverbed. The green waters began draining slowly, escaping into the endless caverns and volcanic caves below them. At once, the trees and grasses began to wither and decay. The walls aged and turned grey and the paved walking paths crumbled into ruin.

The baskets and clothing began to turn to dust. The people sat down in place and watched as their entire world returned to the earth in which they had lived for centuries. A rushing wind came racing through the cavern. Ashes filled the air and made a thick cover, choking out the rest of the light. The remaining people clinging to life, began to slowly suffocate. The grass huts went up in flames, quickly turning into piles of ash. The once great civilization would remain lost forever, covered by a layer of ash and hidden beneath the volcano.

"The earthquakes have really wreaked havoc on this area. We have been searching for Aaron for days and, after today, I think it's time to call off the search," Captain Holden said.

The rest of the team carefully walked around, stepping over stones and lava pillars, looking for any signs of Aaron. They discovered bits of his tent and camping gear that had been caught in the path of lava and shoved down from the volcano, but no real sign that Aaron was alive.

"At this point guys, I think we have to assume he was caught in the path and couldn't make it out of here. There would have been no way for him to know what was happening until it was too late. He didn't carry a radio and there is no way his phone would have had reception way out here," the Captain told the rescuers.

"Wait Captain, I found something you should see. Maybe we should keep looking for him. I think I found his journal. Well, I found parts of it at least. Look at the dates of the entries. The last one was the day of the eruption, but it's more than that. I think Aaron found something, something important," Mila explained.

"What is it, Mila?" he asked.

"It looks like he found people and he thinks they are Mayans."

"That could be. The Mayans did live in this area of Mexico, but that was centuries ago. They do have descendants, but they would not be living in regular tribal units and are more modern now. Here, let me see that, but don't alert the rest of the rescuers yet. I want to finish out today's search."

He took the pages from Mila and started reading them. His eyes squinted against the sun piercing through the ash still floating around. Sweat dripped from his brow in the humid heat of the tropical forest and greed began sweeping through him.

Could it be? Could he really have found a lost civilization? he wondered. "To bring back a discovery like that would let me go down in history." He read on while Mila continued searching the ash and rubble along the sloping side of the volcano.

"Sir! Come look at this!" Mila called out.

Captain Holden walked over to Mila, who was trying to remove thick ash from her feet.

"It's a hand," Mila pointed out.

"It has to be Aaron" Captain Holden replied.

"I'm not so sure. Look, there's something in the hand," she said.

Mila swept more ash away and tried to take the small leather pouch from the hand. The fragile leather tore open and green water poured out. The grey, withered, burnt hand clenched into a fist and extended the fingers. Mila and Captain Holden jumped away, staring at the hand for a moment as the tan color began to stand out and the fingers grew plump. The ground around the hand started to turn green and grass spread quickly around the hand and their feet. Mila bent back down, trying to dig the hand out.

"Hold on, we're here," she said.

As soon as she touched the hand, it was sucked back down. The ground began to quake and move. This time the volcano had nothing to do with it. The ground beneath their feet opened up and Mila and Captain Holden fell into the chasm.

"Whoa. What is this place? This has to be what Aaron was talking about," Mila said.

As they looked around at the scorched ground and fallen rocks, they noticed one small Mayan boy. He was standing by a small green puddle in the middle of the debris. He was splashing himself with the water, and splashing the ground around him. Each bone he sprinkled began to pull together and reform. The grass began growing, and trees were sprouting up.

The boy walked over to Mila and Captain Holden, and held out a small bowl of water. Captain Holden was the first to take the water, drinking it quickly and watching the world around him change. His hair grew darker, his eyes turned brown, and his skin darkened. Mila backed away from Captain Holden, now holding a spear and looking as much like a Mayan as any other. She walked slowly over to the crumbled wall, and tried to climb up. The young man walked over to the water hole, which was getting bigger moment by moment, and refilled his pouch and bowl. He slowly poured water along the ground, and sprinkled the limestone that began to regenerate. The walls began to reform, and the clouds returned, making the place glow orange, as if it had its own sun.

The small water hole had grown into a stream by now, flowing and returning the plains and trees to full size. The volcanic ash washed away, and the remains of withered people began to move and come to life. Mila fell backwards, slipping off the smooth limestone, once again adorned with the gold shields and symbols that bounced the light around. Captain Holden walked over to Mila and poured the water over her. Her scratches healed and she grew thirsty. She grabbed the bowl, taking a large gulp from the green water. Her change was minimal, as she already possessed the mocha skin and deep brown eyes. Her dark hair grew longer and she was able to speak in a tongue she could never speak before.

As they stood there, the stream grew back into a rushing river. The fish came back to life and the sounds of frogs and other amphibious life returned to the air. The crops of corn and melons sprouted up like shoots of bamboo. Mila walked over to the river and looked down at herself. She wasn't getting out of there, just as she now knew that Aaron didn't get out.

"My people, we have appeased the gods. We are here and our world has survived," Mila Heard.

She turned around to see a whole tribe of people gathering around what once was Captain Holden.

"We needed to sacrifice the one who would seek to conquer us and we have done so. His blood allowed us to be able to return. We have also brought one of our lost daughters to us. Mila, who was descended from the great King Tumilian, has now returned. With her blood, we shall have a strength and purity we have not had in many centuries. Her children will live on and help us to become more powerful," he told them.

He pointed to Mila, who was standing behind the crowd, watching as they stared back at her. The villagers knelt, lowering their heads, and holding their hands out to the one woman who has been promised to bring their kingdom back to glory, and out of the underworld. Mila grabbed the pages from Aaron's journal. She glanced down at the pages, crumpled in her hand and tossed them into the river. Along with the written words that would never see the light of day now, went the memory of Aaron, who was searching for immortality and youth. She held her hand out and took hold of Captain Holden, now calling himself Chief Monochan.

The villagers moved aside, allowing her to walk through them with ease. She stared back at Chief Monochan before casting a sheepish grin. The world above was quickly fading from her mind and with that, the chasm they fell through disappeared in a haze of clouds and a covering of leaves. Mila and her Chief walked back to the stadium and took their places in their seats, watching the villagers rebuild their huts now that the forest was restored. The medicine man joined them, painting three lines in blood on Mila's face before having her sprinkled with orchid petals. The petals stuck to her face from Aaron's blood and she smiled as the pleasant smell from the flowers filled her nose. She took her place among her people.

Grey Areas

The door opens and a gurney is slowly wheeled into a large white room. The curtains in here stay drawn all the time. The walls are washed with white paint and steel instruments line the tables. Along the ceiling above them, two long, bright fluorescent lights flicker. The young doctor slowly walks in behind the gurney, pushing it into the center of the room.

Wearing a blue scrub uniform, right down to his protective foot covering, he reaches for a lamp switch. A small white bulb forces a stream of bright light down on the foot of the gurney. The bottom edge of the light green blanket sways against the wheels. There is silence in the room, except for the occasional humming noise from the fan in the corner.

The doctor pulls a mask out of a box on the counter and dons a pair of gloves. He pulls the top corner of the light green blanket down, revealing the pale face and dark hair of a woman in her early thirties. Her skin is still soft to the touch and her grey-clouded eyes stare blankly off into nothingness.

He pulls the blanket down to the edge of the bed and uncovers a smaller table. An array of small knives, scalpels, and other tools, are laid out waiting for his hands to guide them. He reaches over her, grabbing a showerhead attached to a water tank. By pressing a small button on the top of the sprayer, he starts to wet down her hair and begin the process of getting her ready for burial.

Her eyes were open and she could barely see, but the image was there. She was cold and could not move at all. Her chest was screaming for breath, but she could not inhale or exhale. She could feel her eyes, wanting, begging to water, to blink, to do something, but they would do nothing except burn.

Her body was naked. She could tell she was wearing no clothes, even though she couldn't see herself. She was so cold, but there was no goosebumps and no shivers. She could feel the warm water flowing through her hair as the doctor washed her off. He dragged his fingers through small knots in her hair and tugged out what he could; she could feel every single pull of her hair. Each piece that was ripped out from the root sent a spike of pain.

Where am I? she wondered. *Why can't I move or talk? What happened to me? Why am I here?*

She tried to wiggle a toe, a finger, anything at all. She listened closely, trying to talk, to make her eyes blink, to scream, but no sounds would come out. The doctor moved down from her head slowly, washing her face. Soap and water ran in her eyes and down her cheeks, even dripping into her nose.

She desperately wanted to yell that her eyes were burning and she felt as though she was drowning. Terror swept through her body and still she couldn't move. Slowly, the water ran down her neck and chest. The doctor carefully washed her arms and fingers.

What's wrong with me? Who are you? she said, but he could not hear her.

The doctor moved slowly down her torso, washing her legs, and turning her on her side to wash her back. Once the doctor turned her on her side, for that brief moment she was able to see the instruments on the table. The wall on that side of the room came into view and the mirror allowed her to get a look at herself, as well as the sign above the door… 'Morgue'.

She could see her pale grey skin and lifeless eyes staring back at her. The doctor carefully laid her back down on the wet cold gurney, leaving her hair to hang off the back and dry out. He replaced the sprayer and turned off the water. He walked a few steps away from her, pulling down his mask and taking off his gloves. The metal lid on the trashcan clanked as he stepped on the lever with his foot and tossed his wet pair of gloves in. The clank happened again as he let the lever go and began to walk over toward the gurney.

He grabbed the light green blanket and pulled it up over her chest, letting it rest at the base of her neck. She watched, scared and cold, as he turned the only source of warmth off, the small bright light at her feet. The doctor walked toward the door and she could hear him reaching in his pocket for keys. The lights went off and he left her alone and cold in the dark.

She laid still in the darkness, listening to the sounds of his footsteps fading away as he went further down the hallway.

The alarm went off at seven thirty as it always does. I remember getting up and putting on makeup and getting dressed. I walked downstairs and watched the weather report. It was raining. I grabbed a banana and my purse and I remember running to the car.

What else did I do? I remember, I stopped at the corner and grabbed a newspaper. I went to the Dunkin Donuts like always and grabbed my iced coffee. I even made it to work this morning, she thought. *I know I walked into work and clocked in. I even remember speaking to Michelle at the break table before going upstairs to my desk,* she told herself.

It was pitch black in the room she was in, but Natalie could see just one spot on the ceiling that was illuminated by the smallest bit of light peering in from the window in the door. Her vision had begun to blur ever so slightly since she had been wheeled in. The burning in her eyes was still there, but that too had begun to lessen a bit.

Every muscle in her body was tight and she ached all over. Occasionally, she would twitch in her feet and hands, she hoped that was a sign she wasn't paralyzed. But something wasn't right. She wasn't willing the movements. She was not making the twitches happen.

People who are paralyzed aren't left alone, naked in the dark. They would still have an IV or a monitor and be getting checked on, at least, she thought.

Where's my mom, my dad, someone would surely want to be with me, she told herself. *My friends from work. No one would leave me all alone the whole time.*

Natalie listened, concentrating, trying to hear if anyone was in the hall. She tried to talk, but still nothing would move. Her mouth, her throat, nothing. Her mouth and throat felt so dry, she could feel everything sticking together. The hall was silent, there was no sound, not even the fan was running. In the silence, there was a slight ticking. It seemed to get a little louder, then faded back in the distance, as her hearing went in and out. It was a clock, but she didn't know where it was.

She tried to focus on the clock's ticking for a while, at least it was something. But it was short-lived. Her hearing went out again and it felt as if her ears were going numb. There was no ringing, just a numbness and a clogged feeling, as if she were wearing ear plugs.

What else did I do today? she thought. *I had lunch and I clocked out after lunch today. I was supposed to meet my parents for their anniversary party. I don't remember the party. I know I left the building and I am pretty sure I called them on my phone to let them know I was on my way.*

Where's my purse? Where are my clothes? she asked herself.

The more she tried to remember the events of her day, the more upset she got. Her chest felt heavy, she was angry and scared, and there was no one there. She couldn't call out, she couldn't cry. The ticking of the clock, that she had hoped would be a comfort to her, had slowly faded away. Total silence filled the air around her.

The night passed by slowly for Natalie as she waited for someone, anyone, to come back for her.

Maybe my parents don't know I'm here, she thought. *Surely, if I was missing they would be looking for by now, and a hospital would be one of the first places they would look.*

A few seconds later, she could hear the muffled sound of footsteps in the hall, coming her way. The darkness she was left in was cast away by the lights above when the doctor walked in.

The doctor walked back toward the gurney, turning on the small light, and pulling the smaller table closer to him. Natalie could no longer make out the details of his face. Her eyes had turned blurry through the night. Shadows of light and dark passed over her eyes and she could feel the breeze generated by the doctor as he walked around her.

The doctor looked down at Natalie's face and gently placed his hand on her forehead, running it down over eyes, closing them for her. Once again, she was cast into total darkness and left only with the slightest sounds.

The doctor was walking around the room and she could hear things being moved about. Natalie tried to open her eyes, but just as she could not close them, she couldn't open them. Now even her mind was starting to get foggy. She could hardly remember what happened yesterday and could not remember anything before that.

What's happening to me? she wondered.

Natalie concentrated as hard as she could to recall what happened after she left work.

I know it was still raining and I ran with the newspaper over my head to the car. I got in and waited for the windows to defog before trying to leave the driveway.

I was on Route 1 heading north into Amherst station. I was on top of the hill coming into town. There were a few road construction signs out and a flashing sawhorse in the right lane. I was stopped behind a car and could barely see the taillights. All I can remember now is getting wet. Rain was falling on me, I was in the middle of the street. I could smell gas and my chest was hurting.

While she was busy trying to remember how she got to the hospital and what had happened to get her there, the doctor was brushing her hair out. He tied it back and began to cover her face in makeup. She could hardly feel what was happening to her. Her chest was no longer screaming for air and her muscles ached no longer.

There was a man, he was yelling and screaming, but I don't know what he was saying. He was pushing on my chest. I saw the ambulance, I saw paramedics. My car, I saw my car, she thought. *It was upside down. There was a semi behind it.*

The doctor continued to cover up her bruises, stitch up cuts, and even get her dressed. She could no longer hear what was going on around her. The doctor pulled her onto a clean gurney and started to push her out into the hallway.

The hall was considerably warmer than the room they were just in, but Natalie could not tell the difference. Her parents were waiting in the hall. Natalie's mother touched her arm and kissed her head, signaling the doctor that it was her daughter.

Natalie could feel her mother's touch, but only as a slight brush. Now she could barely tell that it was her mother whispering in her ear. She was now lost inside herself. They wheeled her farther down the hall into another room. Natalie's parents walked away. They would see their daughter only one more time at the funeral, but Natalie would not see them.

I was in a car accident. That's why I'm in the hospital. The doctor—I remember the doctors talking. "We're losing her."

Natalie noticed that she could not even hear her own heartbeat now.

Where's the white light? Where's the Pearly Gates and St. Peter? Where's the lake of fire? Am I in Limbo? she wondered.

I know I have always said that when you die and they bury you, when they dig you up you're still there. But I never thought that this was what death was like. Where are the angels and the people you have lost before you that you are supposed to be reunited with? she asked. *Where's the euphoric feeling of calm splendor? All I feel is scared, cold, alone, and angry.*

The longer time passed, the fewer thoughts Natalie had. There were no more questions, no more wondering. There was only silence.

No one knows what really happens to you when you die. Scientists have said that they have been able to catch the last electrical impulses, these impulses are said to be your essence, your spirit leaving your body. It is thought this process can happen very quickly for some, while for others this process can take weeks to dissipate.

If in fact it takes weeks to dissipate, then how long do we feel this alone and terrified? Do we feel what is happening to our bodies as they change and decay? Do we here our own funerals and grieving companions? Do we figure out what has happened to us long before we wake up in heaven or hell?

But who knows what really happens. For the few people who died and came back, they came back because their brains never fully stopped working, though undetectable as it was. What if everyone around you says you're dead, but you're not gone yet? What if there was some awareness, something of you still there?

What if you could hear, see, and feel what was happening around you, up until the day you were buried, or even after you were buried? What if until the very last bit of energy your body gives off is totally gone you, were still aware in some way?

These are things we may never know. Is it possible that there is nothingness after you die, or is it true that everything is perpetual energy; even in death there is life? What if between life and death there is a grey area, just as there is between good and evil?

A Stone's Throw

"Mommy, Mommy, look. It's the pond we saw in that old picture at the town hall," Ceara said.

The wide-eyed little girl tore her hand away from her mother's and ran steadily toward the still pond. Silver shimmers from the sunlight pierced between the new cypress leaves and danced around like fairy dust, calling for the girl to take a dip.

"Ceara! Wait! Don't you go in that water!! You wait for me. We don't know what's in there, or if it's safe to swim!" her mother yelled back.

Ceara stopped just at the water's edge, watching the small ripples caress the gravel bank. Her white sandals allowed the water to gently bathe her toes; she wanted to go in with all that her heart could muster. She stared down towards the middle of the pond, waiting to see if there were any fish, frogs, or mermaids, to play with. She let her mind wander as the breeze picked up and lifted her long blonde hair.

Her mother appeared at her side, peering into the clear water, and smelling the sweet spring air. There were no signs, no picnic tables, nothing to suggest that this was a place used for recreation at all. But the beauty and serene look of the tall green grasses and yellow flowers almost made her want to sit and stay right where they were.

"We can come back tomorrow, sweetie. Now that we know where this is and it's just up the trail behind our house, we can come back anytime. But listen Ceara, you must promise me to never come here without me. Do you promise?" she asked.

"Yes, Mom. I promise."

"Good. Look baby, I know you can swim, but if something were to happen to you, I just don't know what I would do."

216

"I know, Mom. I won't come without you," Ceara replied.

"Mom, can I take my shoes off and stand in the water, just up to my knees? I won't get my dress wet. I just want to see the stones a bit better."

"What stones? The whole shore is made up of stones, the same kind we saw on the trail up here."

"No Mom, look there in the middle. Don't you see them? The stones are blue, and purple, and silver, like in a fish tank, but these are bigger," Ceara told her.

She kicked her sandals off and left them on the shore as she waded out slowly, pointing towards the middle of the pond. Her mother's eyes were fixed on her the whole time. The water was cold after such a hard freeze over the winter, the goosebumps swept over Ceara's body. Shivers made her teeth chatter as she tried to reach a stone with her feet.

The water was so clear that the stones looked close, but they were down very deep. Mazes of seaweed stretched upward as if they were extending a long green arm to wrap the girl in and pull her down for a closer look. The silver stones glistened back with the streams of light and Ceara squinted, stepping out just a bit further.

She held her dress up away from the water and bent down. She kept her eyes focused on the stones, as one large dark spot seemed to poke through the barrage of color.

"Ceara, that's far enough until we come back with our swimsuits."

The girl squinted a little more, trying to make out what the dark spot was. She heard her mom's voice, but it sounded so far away. She bent down even closer, until the tip of her nose was nearly under the surface.

"Ceara, did you hear me?" she asked.

The girl's long hair, now drenched from dangling in the water, stuck to her face in the breeze. She reached her hand up, pulling her hair out of her face and mouth, and tossed it onto her back. Her shadow clouded her view as the stones seemed to move just a little.

The seaweed swayed back and forth, straining to reach her, when a small frog protruded from the bottom of the pond. Large green eyes stared back at Ceara and, for a moment, she could have sworn it waved at her and smiled with a nearly human-looking face. She smiled back and leaned in until her face was in the water. She blew bubbles out of her mouth and dropped her hands, letting her dress and hair fall in. She was weightless. She was happy. She desperately wanted one of those stones and to swim with that creature.

A second later, she was on shore, sitting on the damp bank with her soaking wet dress and hair clinging to her. The wind blew again and she could hear the rustle of the leaves and her mother's voice.

"Ceara, are you okay? What happened? Didn't you hear me calling you? Didn't you hear me tell you to stop?"

She grabbed Ceara's face with her warm hands, snapping her back into reality. She pushed her daughter's long hair back behind her ears and rubbed her arms, which were covered in goosebumps and cold as ice.

"Mom, didn't you see him?" she asked.

"See what? All I saw was you nearly drowning yourself. You just put your face in the water and wouldn't come up. It was like you fell asleep or something. Are you sure you're okay, Ceara?"

"There was a frog or a mermaid, Mom. I saw him, he waved at me and smiled. He has a face like a human, but he looked like a frog. He was down there where that dark place is in the middle of the stones. I think it's a tiny cave or something. Mom, we have to come back tomorrow. Can we? Please."

"Well, I guess so. It seems nice and quiet here and I don't start work for another week. You have your room all unpacked now, right?"

"Yes, I finished that this morning before we went for ice cream," she replied

"Well good, let's go home and get some dry clothes on. It's getting late and we have to walk back down the trail. I would like to get back before it gets dark."

Leanne stood up and held her hands down for Ceara. She smiled gently as she stared into the face of her little girl. She was seven-years-old, but she still sees a toddler waddling down the hall with wobbly legs and a toothless grin. Unicorns and fairies adorn her bedroom walls and she draws pictures of mermaids and butterflies. The very limits of her child's imagination were open and spread out for the world to see. Pure innocence and curiosity stared back at her from her big blue eyes.

Ceara grabbed her mom's warm hand and stood up. She slipped her sandals back on and gazed absentmindedly into the pond. The center swirled and rippled as tiny little frogs swam around a small patch of duckweed. The sun starting to set made the colorful stones look like an underwater kingdom and she wanted to be a part of it. *Tomorrow,* she thought, *I will swim down and get a few of the rocks to add to my collection.*

She turned around, walking slowly next to her mom, looking back over her shoulder, and noticing a set of eyes popping up from the surface. A cat's eye-like glow shown back at her and a Cheshire grin. She waved and smiled and the creature waved back, looking more and more human, as it rose higher from the water.

Leanne turned around, looking around the bank and down a portion of the trail, and into the pond.

"Who are you waving at, Ceara?"

"The man in the pond, Mom, don't you see him? He's waving at us."

They got to the bend in the trail and quickly lost sight of the pond. The sun set lower in the sky behind the trees and her house came slowly into view. Ceara ran across the field towards her back porch and into the kitchen. She peered out the window, watching her mom walk up the steps.

"Go change for dinner, Ceara."

Ceara turned towards the doorway leading though the living room and scampered off. It was getting dark fast and, even though she loved mystery and fairy tales, she was still nervous about the dark, and in their new home that was even more of a reason to have a night-light. She flipped on her starlight and kicked her sandals off into the closet. They hit the wall and landed with a slight thud on the hardwood floor.

Her nightgown was still folded on her bed, where she had left it this morning, she quickly threw it on and slid her slippers in place. She was warm and comfy. Her slippers felt soft and velvety around her wrinkled feet.

Ceara could hear her mom getting the dishes down and making supper. She looked up at her ceiling, watching her fairy stickers glisten in the light, while her mobiles cast shadows of fairy wings fluttering through the room. There was a slight tap on the window. Ceara turned to see the glowing cat's eye and big frog-like grin peering in her window. He placed a hand on the pane of glass. Suction cup fingers pressed and fanned out, leaving streaks against the glass.

"It's you. I knew I saw you in the pond today," Ceara said. "Can you hear me?"

He smiled and shook his head yes.

"I can do more than hear you, my dear. I can talk to you, dance with you, swim with you," he replied.

220

"Are you a mermaid?"

"If you want me to be, then yes, I am a mermaid."

"What's your name?" she asked.

"I have been given a lot of names by people over the years, but my favorite is the one I was given at creation. Alastra Frodnar. You can call me Alastra. Why don't you come outside and down to the pond with me? We can sit and talk under the moonlight."

"I can't, my mom won't let me outside after dark. Plus, I'm scared of the dark."

"You wouldn't need to be scared with me, and the pond is always bright from the moonlight. It shines off my collection of stones. I saw you admiring my collection today. You liked them, didn't you?"

"Oh, yes, very much. I collect rocks. See here in that jar on the shelf. It's a rock from every place I have been, like parks, beaches, ponds, and everywhere else you can think of. I would love to have one of each color for my collection. Would that be okay?" she asked.

"Well, I don't know. I have never given away any of my stones. I, like you, like to add to my collection. I get them from different people I meet. I don't like giving them away."

"Hey, I got it. How about we trade? I will bring you three stones out of my rock collection tomorrow when my mom brings me down for a swim, and you can let me have three of yours. That way you didn't give them away. You won't be missing three," Ceara added.

"I shall have to think about that. I can only come out of the pond at night and, without my help, the pond is much too deep for you to swim down to my house. But you said your mom will bring you tomorrow. I will see you tomorrow. Maybe you will be able to see the moon over the pond soon. It's very pretty. If you decide you want to come see me, you know where the trail is and I am only a stone's throw away," he replied.

"Ceara, dinner's ready!" her mom called out.

Ceara looked out the door for a second and back to the window, but Alastra was gone, leaving only four suction cup marks on her window. She made her way back towards the kitchen and sat down at the table. Her mother had ended the day with scrambled eggs and maple sausage for dinner. Ceara's favorite meal. She wolfed down her meal, looking around at each window in her line of sight, but Alastra was nowhere to be seen.

"Mom, I met the mermaid. He came out of the pond and followed us home. He said his name is Alastra Frodnar. He lives in the pond and he can only come out at night. He collects rocks like me."

Her mom stared back and smiled.

"Well that's nice, dear," she replied.

Leanne cleared the plates and began washing the dishes. Ceara headed straight back to her room. She grabbed the glass jar off of her shelf, dumped it on the purple rug at the foot of her bed, and began going through them. She had several pieces of white quartz, red lava rocks, and petrified wood. She pulled one of each aside to take to Alastra in the morning.

She put the rest of the rocks back inside the container and put it back on the shelf. The moonlight was bright tonight. She ran back towards her window, placing the three rocks on her windowsill, and gazed out into the yard to see if he was out there. She could see the trees and grass swaying in the breeze and a few birds flew between tree branches. *Just a few small dark figures bouncing between the spaces in the night sky, but no mermaids,* she thought.

She walked towards her bookshelf and grabbed a book with fairytales and myths. Ceara turned the pages until she reached the tale of mermaids. It's funny, but Alastra doesn't look like these at all. I didn't see a tail, but if he can come out on land he must not have a tail. The mermaids in the book look so pretty and human, but he really looked more like a big frog with a human face. She pondered this a bit more before closing the book and climbing into bed. She left the star light on and tried to drift off to sleep.

"I must get the stones ready, she will come tomorrow. I don't want to give up my stones, but I will get another one to add to my collection."

Alastra was busy moving the stones away from his doorway. He piled the stones up all around the entrance and created a small path at the very front. The white moonlight bounced off the silver stones and he peered into one, watching the tiny human creature inside pound on the wall of the stone. He picked the rock up and held it close to his face, the withered old woman silently begged for him to release her. But he wouldn't, he couldn't.

He laid the silver stone on the top of the pile where he could see her face from his doorway and went about turning the blue and purple stones in the same direction. Faces and bodies came into view in the moonlight, he could see them all crying, screaming, and frozen inside their soundproof bowls.

He laughed and swam around, singing and making quick work of his hasty cleanup job.

"Purple and blue for the children are new, and silver, not gold, for the new who are old."

He grabbed a blue stone, peering inside. The small boy, who had gone missing twenty years ago, was still sitting there. He looked at Alastra and smiled. He had no concept of time or how long he had been gone. Alastra rubbed his hand over the surface of the stone, it changed to silver, and the boy was now old, wrinkled, and feeble. He threw the stone on the pile of silver and his brown spots and warts were gone. He was still greenish-grey and still had his suction cups and frog-like body, but he would be younger and full for weeks. That would have to do, since he had to ration his collection. Over the years, people have stopped coming to his pond so often. But each time a person bought the home, he had a chance to obtain new souls for his collection.

Sometimes he had adults to turn into his collection, rather than just children. The adults gave him just a full feeling and no real change to his age or appearance, but he kept them anyway. They were dark grey and buried under the rest. They didn't attract the children the way the shiny or colorful stones did.

When the person inside the stone died, the stone would become solid and no longer reflect the person inside in the light of the moon. But he still had the stones to see. He finished his piles and went inside to anxiously await morning, which would be arriving soon. He knew he probably wouldn't get to add Ceara to his collection yet, but it wouldn't take long, her very innocence and trusting nature would see to that.

Ceara was up bright and early and dressed for the day trip to the pond before her mother had even had her first cup of coffee. The sun was shining bright and the thermometer on the back porch read 72 and it was only 9 am. It would be a great day to spend the day at the pond, maybe have a picnic lunch, and maybe she could convince her mom to bring a flashlight and stay to watch the sun set over the water.

She ran out of her room, grabbed two towels from the bathroom closet, and ran to the kitchen. Her mom had coffee brewing and cereal waiting on the table for her.

"Mom, let's bring the picnic basket today and a flashlight. I would love to stay and watch the sunset, maybe draw it for my room."

"Hmm, well why not. We don't have anything else today and I wouldn't mind getting some sun. We could make a whole day out of it and just relax. Go ahead, grab the basket from the pantry, and throw the chips in it and a few apples, too. I will make us a couple of sandwiches and get a few sodas."

Leanne finished her coffee while Ceara ran to collect the items her mother requested. They filled the basket and grabbed a flashlight from the drawer. As they opened the door, a waft of hot air slammed into them, and hastened their walk towards the pond. The sun bounced back up from the ground, nearly blinding them with the bright light.

The trail seemed to be slightly cooler than the yard and much cooler than the wooden deck of her home had been. They could smell the water in the air and the sweet dandelion fragrance drew them ever closer. Ceara ran up ahead of her mother once again, eager to get to the pond and jump in. The rocks she hoped to trade were tucked inside the basket. She kicked her shoes off as soon as the crisp cool water came into view. She ripped her long beach shirt off over her head, tossing it on the gravel, and ran right in.

The cold water hit her and she gasped for a breath, only for a second, before plunging under the water's surface completely and opening her eyes. She swam out a bit farther, came up for a quick breath of air, and dove down. The stone called to her and she smiled, but didn't see Alastra. Ceara kicked and paddled back to the surface.

"Mom, toss me the three rocks in the basket!" she called.

Leanne placed the basket on the beach and dug through it. She tossed each one, one at a time, into the shallows where Ceara could grab them.

"Why did you bring the rocks? I thought you wanted to collect them."

"I do, Mom, but I made a deal with the mermaid that I would bring him three of my special rocks, if he could trade me three of his. Look, Mom, there are purple, blue, and silver rocks in here."

Ceara grabbed the three rocks, swam back out toward the

middle of the pond, and put her face under the water. The seaweed once again seemed to stretch upwards, not just reaching for the sunlight, but reaching for her. She watched them move and sway beneath her body as she floated above the opening of his lair and the piles of rocks.

She left her ears above the water. She could hear the leaves rustle in the breeze and the noise the bamboo beach mat made as her mother flapped it in the air, allowing it to unroll and come to rest on the gravel beach. She took out her sunglasses, put her earbuds in, and laid down on the mat, facing the grass and feeling the warm sun on her back.

Ceara took another deep breath and retuned her face to the water, waiting for Alastra to appear to her. She felt a tug on her foot and turned around quickly, nearly swallowing water.

"Alastra, you scared me," she said.

"Did I? Well, I never meant to frighten you. I'm sorry about that."

"Where were you? I was looking for you and I didn't see you?"

"I was here. I wanted to make sure I had the rocks all in order for you. I piled them back up. I went in my house to make sure I had them all when you arrived."

"I brought three pretty rocks for you, but when you startled me, I dropped them," she told him.

"That's okay. They were going to be brought down there to begin with, right?"

"Yes, that's right."

"Well Ceara, would you like to come see my home? We can gather up the rocks you brought for me and you can pick the rocks you like best out of my collection."

"I would love to, but I can't hold my breath that long, and I can't swim as well as you can."

"That's quite alright. Do you remember that last night I told you I could help you?"

"Yes, I remember."

"Well, I can give you a little bit of magic and you will be able to stay down all you want. You will never need to breathe air when you are in the water. Would you like that?"

"You mean you could turn me into a mermaid?" she asked excitedly.

Her face lit up with a smile from ear-to-ear. He could feel her innocence and energy. His eyes turned yellow and got narrow, he placed his hands on her head, and ran them down her face and neck. The breeze picked up slightly and Ceara shivered for a moment. Her mother turned around and smiled at Ceara, not able to see Alastra.

"Mom, look, this is Alastra. He is going to make me a mermaid, so I can swim like he does."

"That's great, Ceara. Have fun. But don't forget to come out of the water and warm up once in a while. Okay?"

"Okay, Mom!"

"Alastra, why can't she see you?"

"If she were still young, like you, and her mind still open, she would see me. She will not see me until she believes I am here. Once she believes I am here, she will see me, and she will want to come with you to see my collection. Are you ready?" he asked.

"Yes."

"Okay, follow me," he replied.

Alastra dove down, looking back, making sure that Ceara was following him. It was deep and cold and the seaweed tried to grab at Ceara. He flung his hand toward them, a flash of light shot from his fingers, and they were still. She kicked her feet faster, trying to keep up with him as he disappeared into his cave. He stopped just at the entrance and looked back, holding his hand out for her.

She was tired when she reached the entrance and looked up at the surface. From the bottom, it looked so deep. The water churned in front of her eyes. She slid into the cave and looked back out at the blurred water on the floor of the pond. After taking a few more steps, the cave rose slightly and there was no water. There was a collection of toys, balls, towels, and even beach furniture.

"Wow, how did you get all this stuff down here?" she asked, as she picked up a purple and pink beach ball.

"I have managed to collect a great many things that got left behind."

She bounced the ball on the floor of the cave and stared at the holes carved into the walls. Jars, and even the three rocks she brought, were now inside a hole, displayed for him to see.

"Come, let's have you pick the three rocks you would like to have. Now I do have to warn you, choose carefully. The first one you actually touch, will be the closest to your heart."

"Okay," Ceara replied.

She put the ball down and walked back towards the mouth of the cave. The water seemed to be clearing back up and she could see the surface. She stepped out, looking closely at the three large piles, which looked more like a wall around the cave than piles when you were up close.

One of the purple rocks caught her attention.

"Is there something in that rock? I thought I saw something move inside it."

"It was probably just a shadow from the surface. Pay no mind to it. Is that the color you like best?" he asked.

"I like the purple one. It's so pretty. What's that noise?"

"Ceara!" Oh, my god! Ceara!"

Her mother was shouting for her and though it was muffled, she could still hear her. She could make out every word she said.

"Pick your rocks, my dear, before it's too late." he said with a slightly agitated tone.

"My mom's looking for me. I should go up. She probably thinks I drowned. Maybe I can get her to come down here and let her see you. You can make her a mermaid too, right?"

Ceara could hear splashing, her mother was in the water, she was swimming into the middle of the pond, and she was searching for Ceara. Her mother was right over the top of her. She looked up and waved and her mom began trying to swim down to meet her. Her mom paddled and kicked, she was struggling to get to the bottom.

The seaweed began to move again, reaching out for Leanne, but she kept swimming. Alastra poked his head out of the cave and looked up.

"Pick a color, she is trying to reach you, and she will not make it unless you pick a color. She still doesn't see me, only you."

Ceara reached out, grabbing a purple stone and holding it close to her chest. She watched as the seaweed grabbed at her mom's feet. Alastra held his hands out and a flash of light came and stopped the seaweed, but Leanne was still as well. He swam up, grabbed Leanne by the hands, and dragged her down into the deep. He placed her on the floor by the pile of stones and put his hands on her head and face. He grabbed a purple ball from below her feet and put it in her hand, holding it up in front of her.

Ceara pounded on the sides of the stone and screamed in silence. Her mother's calm face stared blankly back at her and she saw her own reflection in her mother's eyes.

Then Alastra began singing again. "Purple and blue for the children are new, and silver not gold for the new who are old."

A silver and purple stone fell to the floor. Alastra picked them up, swam back into the mouth of the cave, and placed them in the hole next to the very rocks from Ceara's own collection. He smiled at them and turned the stones so that Ceara and Leanne could see each other. Leanne sat up, looking at her daughter. She thought she was going to drown. The seaweed had tangled up around her legs. She banged on the sides of the stone and rolled back and forth just bit.

A shadow came back into view and she stopped, waiting to see what it was. Alastra appeared, holding her picnic basket and blanket.

Armed with Death

"General Logsted, sir, we have secured the upper hand here, but we lost many soldiers. Our men are gathering the bodies as you asked and they are being placed in the cooler. When should we send the notifications to their families?"

"We don't, Greg. We have plans for those men. They are not technically dead to us yet."

"Excuse me, sir? I don't follow you."

General Logsted pursed his lips together and stared out the top of the command post. He could still hear gunshots in the distance and screams from the injured men that had not yet succumbed to their injuries. The air around them was heavy with the scent gunpowder and blood. *Yet, through tragedy, we will push on,* he thought.

"Greg, come sit with me," the general said.

He pointed to two chairs facing the rear of the compound. Greg walked slowly toward the chairs and sat quietly waiting for the General, his long-time friend, to start talking.

"Greg, how long have we known each other now?"

"Sir, practically all my life."

"That's correct. Cut the 'Sir' crap, for now. For right now, you are my friend's son, the man I have watched grow up and become my best confidant and friend, since your father passed. I am speaking to you as two friends and not as your commanding officer. That stated though, this conversation never took place, you can't tell anyone about this or anything I am about to tell you. Please understand there would be grave consequences I could not protect you from, if this gets out. Now with this knowledge, I will give you a choice to leave this room and have this go no further, or we can continue and I will let you know some information that goes far beyond classified."

"Okay, Carl, I'm all yours," he said.

Greg took his hat off and placed it on his lap, grasping the brim with both hands and pulling it around, feeling the edge slip between his fingers. He was nervous, but not just because he knew there were more than a dozen young men waiting to die from their wounds, not just because there were more men already dead waiting for a proper burial that they may not be getting, but also because he was sure he didn't want to know what he was about to know, but he still had to know.

The general grabbed his metal chair by the back, turned it around so he was facing Greg, and took a seat. He sat staring at the pale face of his friend. A million thoughts ran through his head. This was a conversation he never wanted to have when it was his turn to learn what they were going to be asked to do. Now he was turning the tables on his friend.

"Greg, last year when I was at that month-long meeting in the caverns with the other generals and the president, I told you they were briefing us on some new technology that was bound to help us have less casualties and win the war."

"Yes, I remember."

"Well, they had been doing research and experimentation to see how they could create soldiers that could be immune to disease, to injuries, and even death."

"Okay, I can understand the being immune to disease, since we come in contact with people who are not immunized, not sanitary, and infected with all kinds of things. I can understand wanting our men and woman to fight through injuries, we already do that to a certain degree. But no one can beat death," Greg replied.

Carl smiled, but it was not a smile that felt comforting to Greg. It was the smirk that gave it away; there was something more he really didn't want to hear, but he would hear it anyway.

232

"Greg, I may be a general, but that doesn't give me all the information and inner workings of our government. I was thrown into a position and asked to be a part of something that I don't agree with. Quite frankly, it scared the hell out of me and still does. To be honest, one of the reasons I am telling you about this, is because of the inherent dangers and the unprecedented rate this could get out of control."

"Sir, you have my attention and with all due respect, you are starting to scare me and I still have no clue what you're trying to tell me yet."

"I know, look there is no way to say this that will not sound crazy. All I am going to tell you is, regardless of whether or not you believe me now; I will be showing all the proof you need soon enough."

"They have developed a formula, so to speak, that when ingested or given like a vaccine, can keep a person with broken bones walking, running, and able to resist all pain or disease, and continue on their mission. But that's not all it does. That vaccine doesn't heal or make the injuries go away, they just don't realize they are injured, and push through 'til they die."

"They have also made a separate version of this that is supposed to be placed in the medic's kit. This drug is to be given in a syringe when they know a person is going to die; when they have used that soldier's body past the point of help, but still want them to be all they can be for their country. This not only would be the normal painkiller that is given to ease the pain of death, but also alters the brain's metabolic state. The person would still technically die or be dead, but would not know it and still be walking around."

"General, you lost me. I don't think I understand what you mean by they would technically be dead, but would still be walking around. Do you mean zombies? Like 'Night of the Living Dead' or voodoo, Santeria-type curses on people?" Greg asked.

"Well, for lack of a better term, yes. I guess a better way to describe it is to think about a turtle. You can cut off a turtle's head and it will still try to breathe, it will try to bite, and this will last for hours and hours. You can even think about it like a snake. A snake can be beheaded and cut into a few pieces and it will still curl up and coil and move around."

"The impulses and nerves still seem to make a connection and, for the turtle, the brain still functions and maybe the body, if left intact. The turtle is dead, but it doesn't know that it's dead yet. Even a chicken, with its head cut off, can run around for a while. We have seen this kind of thing happen in the natural world, but we have found a way to harness it to make it happen for a longer period of time and to use the habits ingrained in the soldiers for our benefits."

"The soldiers would still be able to walk and kill, but since they are already dead, the body will decay to the point where they can no longer move. But until the brain was completely gone or severed from the body, they would still be able to kill."

"Sir, that's playing God."

"Well, we have been doing it for years. We clone people, we kill people, and innocent people are just casualties of war. We have cures for diseases we do not distribute, so we do not end up like China. This is just one more thing. The problem is, Greg, that just like anything else, once in the body, especially the ones who were given the vaccine before death, it's in the body like a flu or H.I.V. It's transmittable."

"It's not airborne yet, but if you get bitten and break the skin, like a rabid dog, you get it. If you eat the flesh, like E.coli, you get it. This basically eats away at your brain, changing you from the inside out. You do die. But it's the brain that keeps you going. You are a walking corpse and you eat, you seek out warm bodies, and you do not discern the difference between human and animal, you just kill."

"For weapon purposes, it's a great tool. You can use the same men in life and death, send one death certificate to the family after they die the second time, and lose less soldiers. That's how they see it, but it's not that simple. These things are not thinking humans anymore. They do not see the difference between enemies or friendlies. They do not see civilians and soldiers. They only see flesh. When we release these things onto the battlefield, everyone is a moving target and we cannot control the spread. If you get bit and get sent home, you will have your brain eaten by this, you will turn, and you will spread it. They have no way to cure this since the brain cannot repair missing, rotten pieces. You just have to destroy the brain."

"They can't do that, sir. What about the Geneva Convention and not killing people when we don't have to, what about the C.D.C? Surely, they won't allow this to take place. I mean if this is true, this will be worse than a plague or AIDs, this could annihilate the human race if there is no way to contain it."

"I know it. That's why I made the choice to tell you. I care about you and Donna and the kids, as much as I care about my own family. I don't want them in harm's way. I can't tell the rest of the men or I risk way more than just losing my rank and career. But you have to understand that the government thinks this will stop the war, the casualties will be less, and the balance of power will stay in favor of our country. Come with me, Greg, I feel you have to see what we are about to unleash."

Carl stood up and waited for Greg at the door. He looked at his friend's face, staring blankly back at him. Terror and disappointment washed over him as he pushed the door open and walked into the hall. Daylight pierced through the cracks under the doors and around the halls, but it was as dark as it could be in his mind. The images of men lying tied to gurneys with grey skin, receding gums, and the smell of decay, overran his rational thinking. They groaned and moaned, not because they were trying to speak, but because they were filling with gasses from the decaying process that was somehow slowed by the vaccine.

The gasses were expelled from the lungs and made the noises. He had nightmares almost every night after he saw them. He wanted to spare his friend from this, but he knew he had to show him. These would be on the battlefield soon enough and he would be right there with them. They took a right, headed toward the medic's area and the cooler. Men were crying, screaming, and growling. They had heard this noise before, pain is pain, but somehow this wasn't all it meant.

Carl pushed the door open and held his hand up for Greg to remain where he was. He wasn't supposed to let anyone know what was going on, so bringing Greg down to the quarantine area was a mission he had to do with great secrecy. He left Greg standing in the hall and nervously proceeded down the corridor and peered into the small plastic window in the quarantine room. For the moment, the medics were not there. They were probably at lunch, but that would not give him much time for a tour.

He hurried back to Greg and signaled for him to follow closely and quickly. They entered the room and Carl stepped aside, allowing Greg to see, for the first time, what they were up against.

"Carl, is that Private Jettings? I was at his bedside when he died, I still have his tags. I saw him die—he had too many pieces of shrapnel in his chest."

Laying in the gurney was Pvt. Jettings. He was dark grey in spots and his eyes were clouded over. Blood clots clung to his arms from trying to tear away at the straps. His stomach was bloated, yet there he was struggling to get up, to get at the very officer who was there to comfort him as he passed. Greg took a step closer, trying to study the facial features. *Could this be real? Maybe he wasn't dead when I left,* he thought.

General Logsted grabbed a hold of Greg's arm and gave a sharp tug.

"You don't want to get to close there. He was Private Jettings. He isn't anymore. He moves around and he wants to get up, but not to shake your hands and have a cup of coffee, he wants to eat you, me, or anything else he can. What's there is a shell of a man. Not even that. There is no humanity in there, no reasoning, no feelings. He doesn't feel pain or fear. He doesn't feel compassion. He rots as we stand here looking at him and he doesn't know that. It only wants to eat. Feeding is a basic primal need for everything on the planet. If he could get to us right now, we would be on the menu."

"This is something straight out of a horror classic, Carl, and there has to be some sort of law against this. It's unnatural."

"I know it, you know it, and of course a handful of others who helped create and test this. But that's as far as it goes. You can't have a direct law against something that no one thinks is possible. That's exactly why this is a weapon. No one will suspect this. Our enemies will shoot, but the targets will not die, unless you hit them in the head. They will keep coming. They will never sleep, never change clothes, never need a gun. They are the weapons. Come on, we have to go before I get caught with you down here."

They turned to walk away and what was left of Jettings began to struggle harder against the straps that held it to the bed. He moaned and groaned and his bloated skin tore in places where the bindings sunk in. The straps held firm.

"General, how long will someone exist like that if not killed?"

"Typically, four to six months, depending on the size and fat content in the body. A person who is turned is not embalmed. They are subject to the elements, heat and humidity play a role as well. Just like any other decaying process, the heat and more exposure to the elements can accelerate the decomposition process, but in

237

climates like this one, where the temperatures are mild and cool with dry spells, they can last longer."

"Okay, have they released anyone like that yet?" Greg asked.

"Not here, they are planning that tonight after lights out. There is a whole cooler full of soldiers ready to go. That is another reason why I wanted to tell you today."

Carl opened the door to his office and he and Greg sat back down in the chairs.

"I know you have a lot of questions and, trust me, so do I, Greg, but we have no other answers. I don't know how they plan to keep this from spreading. In fact, I am sure it is going to go out of control as soon as it is unleashed. It is transmitted in blood and saliva. It isn't airborne yet that I know of, but keep in mind they have had a year to practice this, to test it on prisoners."

"General, we have to do something! We can't allow this to happen, we are talking about a potential to kill everyone indiscriminately."

"Believe me, I wish we could. But by the time I was informed and shown the way I just showed you, it was too late. These wheels have been set in motion for a long time and we are just along for the ride, I'm afraid. You better get back to your post, it will be dark soon, and we don't want to be out after that. They plan to put us on lockdown and let the dozen or so men we have go. They have already done this very same thing in other camps, but I have not heard about the progress of them. Just keep your eyes peeled, someone staggering or bleeding or looking like Jettings, is probably infected. Remember who was on the death list and watch for them."

Greg got up and left the office, he was scared to death of what he had seen and been told. This was more than playing God. He retrieved his wallet from his back pocket and picked out a photo of himself with his wife and twin girls. They all smiled and looked so happy with the lake in the background. He tried to get the image of Jettings out of his head, but with his dog tags still in his thigh pocket, knowing he couldn't send the family a notice of a burial, and he couldn't tell anyone he was still there strapped to a metal bed, the image was stuck. He pushed the door open and walked out into the field. Gunshots had faded for the moment and the sun was low, but not quite setting.

He could smell the food from the mess hall--turkey and mashed potatoes was for supper tonight. It was one of the only meals he ever thought was better than an M.R.E., but he was no longer looking forward to it. He walked quickly toward the tower and opened the door, taking the steps two at a time. The door at the top was opened slightly and he could see Sgt. Davis sitting in his chair playing with his M16, watching out the window overlooking the field and the surrounding woods and buildings.

"Hey Davis, it's almost time to go eat," Greg said.

"I know, sir, I was waiting for you to come back before I left. I wasn't sure if I should lock up or if you were coming back. I have the keys."

"Good call, I needed my gun, so I am glad you chose to stay," he replied.

Sgt. Davis stood up, handed the keys to Greg and made his way down the stairs and toward the mess hall. They would all be filing in to eat by now, yet he didn't feel like eating. His stomach had dropped as soon as he laid eyes on Private Jettings.

He stood there staring off into the distance, watching the sun set behind the trees. The temperatures here at night tend to drop down and get pretty cool. The mornings are cooler and since it's early fall, the temperatures will only keep dropping as we go. The very thought of these things wandering around at night in the cold air and stumbling out during the day, making snacks out of the locals, sent chills up his spine. *What have we done,* he thought.

He gave a quick glance around and there was nothing else he needed, but he decided to leave the door unlocked. With his gun in hand, he made his way out of the tower and headed off toward his barracks. The rest of the men would be eating and he wanted to have a few minutes to gather his thoughts, to think of what he was going to do, to make sure he could get every small weapon he could, close by. Sgt. Davis was standing outside the medic's tent, instead of eating, when Greg rounded the corner. The sun was down and the lights around the camp had come on. Not quite lights out yet, but it was slowly getting closer.

"Did you eat yet, Davis?" Greg asked.

"Nah, I wasn't all that hungry and I have a few M.R.E's left in my trunk. It's nice out, thought I would go visit Clark in the medic's tent. He got hit pretty hard and I am not sure if he is going to make it, but I know I wouldn't want to be left all alone if I was hurt," he said.

"I heard they were maybe going to call an early lights-out, so stay close to the barracks, and watch the time," Greg replied.

Davis walked into the tent and Greg's heart sank deep in his chest. Should I have told him? Should I have said something? Slowly he walked on past the tent and toward his barracks. The medic's tent was on the backside of the cooler. He is so close to where they are. A dozen or more men like that, just waiting for the door to be unlocked. He shook his head and took his cap off before opening the door to the barracks.

Ten beds were lined up on the left and ten more on the right. No closets, but plenty of trunk space. He walked to bed number three and placed his gun on his pillow before opening his trunk. He took out his dagger and placed it in his bootstrap and his pistol went in his waistband. He shut the lid and stood up, the lights were all on, but it was still dark and so he took a seat on his bed. If they called lockdown, they would all be sent to the main building, which was more secure, but he was going to be prepared.

Sirens went off, he looked down at his watch, it was 9 pm, lights out should have been called an hour ago, but no one was in the barracks. *Did I fall asleep? I must have,* he thought. He grabbed his gun and started running out of the barracks, there were people scattering everywhere, but no one was screaming. The lights were being turned off, but the moonlight was bright enough for him to see. He got to the main building and banged on the doors. No one was answering. He banged harder.

"It's me, Sgt. Piller, let me in!" he yelled.

Still no one answered. The sirens stopped and he waited at the door, gun in hand. Suddenly, he could hear again. Screams filled his ears, all coming from the main building, behind the very door he was trying to get in. He banged on the door again.

"Hello! Let me in!" he screamed.

Greg stopped and listened again, there were still screams, he could hear footsteps, and people falling into things and banging on the doors. They were locked and he didn't have the key to get in, only the general has the keys during lockdown. He turned around to make his way to the generals' office; as he made it to the other side of the building, there was the general. He had his gun in one hand and in the other his pack.

"Greg, we have to go, we have to get out of here now," he whispered. "I told you I didn't have all the answers and knew this was going to get out of control as soon as it was unleashed. We have to get to a cart now. Jettings bit the medic who was there to release him, the medic ran to get help from one of the others. He was bleeding from his wrist badly and he didn't restrain Jettings. Jettings had free reign in the mess hall. As they dealt with Jettings, the medic infected the other doctors and someone opened cooler," he said

They ran toward the covered shelter that housed their cars, looking back to see the doors to the mess hall open and people begin flooding the field. Blood filled the air and carried on the cool breeze. People were bleeding from bites, cuts, and even gun shots and were scattering for help from medics.

"Carl, you have the keys during lockdown and you were supposed to release those things tonight. You left all our guys in there to die and I was supposed to be in there, too. You were going to let me die as one of those things?"

"No, that's why I never called for the lockdown. Once you told Davis about the early lights-out, I let the rumor spread that anyone not in the main hall by 8 pm would be locked out and punished. They all went from the mess hall to the main building, all except you."

The general pulled the tarp off the first jeep and threw his pack in the back, while Greg ran to the other side. He put his gun in the front and looked up to see Jettings grab Carl and bite down on his neck. Greg grabbed his gun and aimed. Blood spewed from around his mouth and Carl sank slowly to his knees, grasping Jettings by the hair.

Greg ran, trying not to draw attention to himself, holding his gun in front of him. The motion lights were on and staying on. He could see the cooler door wide open and the bodies he had seen being dragged back in, were walking around the compound. He headed for the tower he knew he had left unlocked, made his way to the lower level, and started running up the stairs. There was a radio, food, and water in there. He could hide out there, closed in until help arrives. Help would come. The government would not allow this, he would get help.

He made it to the top of the stairs, Davis was standing in front of the chair staring out the window, watching them all scatter into the woods and inside tents and buildings.

"Davis, oh thank God, it's you," he said.

Davis turned around, his left cheek was dangling from his face, and his eye was missing. Blood covered his face, neck, and shirt, there where large bite marks on his arms. He held a pistol in his right hand.

"Oh man, Davis, I'm so sorry," Greg said.

Sgt. Davis took a small step forward, his pale skin was almost shining in the stream of moonlight. He inched closer again. Greg aimed his gun and fired a shot to the chest. The kickback from the gun made him move more than the bullet made Davis move. He walked closer again, no new blood ran from the bullet hole, and Greg shot again, aiming for the head.

Davis fell forward, landing in the doorway. Greg threw his gun on the floor and stepped into the stairwell, pulling on Davis' arms, trying to get him away from the door. He was trying to be as quiet as possible, but with every step Davis' feet hit the floor, clanking and echoing off the walls. He could hear boots stepping on the ground outside, someone was just outside the door, he waited for a moment, hoping they would pass. He could hear scraping sounds against the outer wall. He turned around to see Jettings and the General. He tugged Davis one last time, getting just far enough to be able to close the door. His hand was burning. He pushed the door shut and latched it, sitting on the ground behind the door.

Greg stayed still, with his ear to the door he could hear them at the door scratching it, bumping it. He hoped he could remain quiet and they would be drawn back downstairs, where the rest of the noise and screams were coming from. His hand was throbbing now, he inched his way forward toward where they kept the medic kit, and he peered down at his hand. His blisters had opened up again, he reached for a bottle of alcohol and the band aids; he was covered in blood from pulling Davis down the stairs.

He looked at his hand again; *it's transmitted through blood and saliva,* he thought. Greg looked at the medic kit and pushed it aside. He thought about using the radio to ask them to send more help, but what good would it do. He took out his wallet and pictures again and sat down in the chair, staring at the moon behind the trees. His pistol called to him and he raised the gun to his chin.

"I gave my life for this, but I won't give my death."

www.ingramcontent.com/pod-product-compliance
Lightning Source LLC
Chambersburg PA
CBHW070556130626
46556CB00001B/181